Good music filled the room. Shelly kissed Pharoah on the cheek.

"You know what I want?" she asked softly.

Her high, full breasts came free, pink nipples hard with excitement. She took both her hands and squeezed her breasts together around his hard organ and stroked back and forth. Her hands moved to his hard shaft and began gently stroking it as she lightly kissed his balls. She held it up from the base with both hands and licked it like a lollipop. He leaned forward and reached under her chest to find her hard nipples. He kneaded her breasts and tugged on her pink nipples. She groaned and took more of him into her mouth. She took a little more of him into her throat and gasped for air. Slowly Pharoah stroked her cheeks, feeling his organ fill her mouth. He gathered her hair in both hands and twisted it for a firmer grip. Shelly began to buck as he forced himself the rest of the way, pushing her chin down to his full balls and her nose into his pubic hair. She could feel his organ tense and throb as he neared orgasm and bobbed her head faster.

Suddenly Pharoah's whole body tensed and he locked his arm over Shelly's head. He let out a loud groan as he came in her throat. When he released her, she fell back against the coffee table, lips swollen and puckered, a trickle of cum running down her chin. She caught the dribble with a finger and licked it. Pharoah collapsed back onto the couch. Shelly crawled over and climbed on top of him. They rested for a few minutes before either of them spoke.

COCAINE FEVER

COCAINE FEVER

by Mark Windsor

based on the screenplay
by Roland S. Jefferson
from the original story
by Demetris Johnson, John Poole, IV,
and Roland S. Jefferson
Based on a concept
by Demetris Johnson

HOLLOWAY HOUSE PUBLISHING COMPANY
LOS ANGELES, CALIFORNIA

Published by
HOLLOWAY HOUSE PUBLISHING COMPANY
8060 Melrose Avenue, Los Angeles, CA 90046
All rights reserved. No part of this book may be reproduced or transmitted in any form or by any means, electronic or mechanical, including photocopying, recording or by any information storage and retrieval system, without permission in writing from the Publisher.
Copyright © 1982 by Mark Windsor. Any similarity to persons living or dead is purely coincidental.
International Standard Book Number 0-87067-726-8
Printed in the United States of America
Cover illustration by Jeffery
Cover design by Kim Smock

For My Wife

COCAINE FEVER

1

Five thousand feet above Los Angeles International Airport, the pilots of the Pan Am 747 were preparing for their final approach. The pilot and co-pilot both put on white cotton gloves to absorb the sweat from their palms. It was a typical landing, but very few pilots ever got used to the fact that once the plane slows down for landing and the nose comes up, they can't see a thing except for blue sky.

In the first class section it sounded like a party was going on. Marcellus, a very successful promoter of music concerts and beauty contests, was returning from another triumph in Europe with his twelve lovely women. While the women chattered excitedly, Marcellus gazed out the window at the city of Los Angeles. He felt like he owned the city. In just a few years he had become the largest cocaine dealer on the West Coast. The concerts and beauty pageants made enough money to make several men rich, but the cocaine business was fast making Marcellus richer than the damn oil companies. He looked around the cabin and considered buying a private jet. It would save a lot of time at the terminals, however customs always went over private jets with a fine tooth comb. No, it was better to travel with the regular public and blend in with the crowd. Marcellus already had everything a man could want anyway, includng the huge mansion and more luxury cars than he needed. His thoughts were interrupted by Juggler, his bodyguard, as he passed him a last glass of champagne.

A few rows ahead of Marcellus, Natasha sat with her gold jewelry sparkling against her dark skin and Shelly in her designer dress, her skin pale white. Shelly was one of the few white girls that Marcellus had working for him. Like all his other models, she had left an exclusive modeling agency and a great career to work for him. The girls all liked the fact that Marcellus treated them so well and, of course, paid them much more than they could make through a legitimate modeling agency.

Shelly talked with Natasha about how anxious she was to see her boyfriend, Pharoah. Natasha teased her about what she'd been missing while they were travelling in Europe. Geneva, another model, was sitting across the aisle from them playing her cassette deck and rocking to the funky beat. Geneva's long, shapely legs were crossed, and the high heel shoe that dangled loosely on her right foot swayed in time with the music.

The stewardess for the first class section came into the cabin and checked to be sure everyone had their seat belts on. Everyone but Geneva watched as the plane sank from the bright sunshine into the smog layer over the city. The 747 jet landed smoothly and started its taxi toward the terminal at the other side of the runway.

Inside the international terminal, a group of inspectors ascended an escalator and headed toward the observation room on the second floor. A senior guard named Conner was lecturing the new recruits about the drug smuggling business.

"I don't care what you read in the paper or see on television. Ninety percent all narcotics smuggled into the country come in on international flights," Conner told them as they reached the top of the escalator.

The group started walking down the brightly lit corridor, listening with slight disbelief to the older officer's words.

"Our job is to stop as much of it as possible," Conner continued.

"But how?" a young recruit asked. "We can't detain everyone who comes through customs, not without cause!"

The poor recruit was considering the impossibility of their assignment. Many thousands of people flooded through the international terminal every day. The odds against finding all the narcotics were great. Especially since the guards only caught the more obvious smugglers and this kept them busy all day. The sophisticated ones, the professionals, hardly ever got busted. It was usually the poor slob amateurs looking to make some big money from a business they knew nothing about that were caught and arrested. This still added up to some impressive figures every year and the airport brass could convince the public and the news media that they were successfully combatting the drug problem. If the public and media knew that what the customs officers managed to catch was only about one percent of the total drug traffic through the airport, it might be a different story.

The group reached the door marked private and Connors unlocked it to let them in. The observation room was special in that the wall that faced the passenger arrival room below was a one-way mirror. The hundreds of people going through customs in the crush on the floor could only see large sections of mirror over their heads. The room was equipped with chairs, a coffee machine and a few other amenities.

"You'll see how we do it. I want you all to look carefully at the passengers coming in," Connors told them.

Down below, in the crowded room, people had their suitcases open for inspection on the long tables while the customs inspectors quickly searched their belongings.

"People try every trick in the book," Connors continued, resting his right hand on the gun at his belt. "They hide dope in aftershave and perfume bottles, cameras, even behind the lining of their suitcases." Connor went on to detail one of his favorite stories about a man who had swallowed the drugs in large metal capsules and gotten caught in the walk-through metal detector.

Down on the floor, a customs agent was rapidly checking out a man's suitcase and pushing it on. The man's girl friend was next. The agent noticed what fine luggage it was. These people must be pretty successful, he thought. He got to the girl's vanity case and the girl's hands visibly tightened on her pocketbook. The agent flipped open the case and saw the rows of nail polish. Nothing there. He lifted off the top section. and found several bottles of perfume in the bottom. The bottles were still in the boxes they had come in. One of the boxes was for men's cologne. The agent puzzled over it and took it out. Strange, he thought, wonder why she'd be carrying this.

"It's a present for my brother, sir. We claimed it in the form and paid the tax. It wasn't much over the limit. We got it in Paris, cheap," the attractive girl blurted nervously.

The agent looked at their form and it was listed. "Yeah, it's right here, lady. You don't mind if I look do you?" he said, watching her face.

"No, no, of course not. Please be careful though. It is a present." The girl was acting pretty nervous now and the agent opened the box. He held it up to the light, but the glass was too dark to see through. He set the bottle on the table and the girl audibly drew a breath when he started to unscrew the top.

"Could you hurry it up, please?" a fat man in a Hawaiian shirt called from behind.

Everybody on line got impatient; their trips were over and they wanted to get home, or their trips were beginning and they were in a mad rush for the sights. The agent ignored the man and pulled on the bottle top. There was a string attached to the cap, which the agent pulled out of the bottle. He'd seen this before and calmly pressed a button underneath the table for assistance as he pulled a small white pouch out of the bottle.

"I'm sorry, but you'll have to go with the gentlemen," he stated without emotion. The girl, who was sobbing softly, was led away with her boyfriend by two armed guards. The agent went on to the next suitcase.

At another table an agent was finished with a man's luggage and was asking to have a look at the two cameras that hung around the man's neck.

"I have fresh film in both of these cameras," the man protested. "I work for a travel magazine."

"Sorry, sir, you can wind up the film and remove it if you wish," the agent said. The man rolled his eyes and acted exasperated.

"But, I'm in a real hurry. I've got a deadline to meet," the man tried again.

It was no use and he handed the cameras to the customs agent, staring grimly into space. When the agent opened the back of the cameras, little white packets fell onto the table.

"I can explain," the man said.

"You can explain it to the officers, sir," the agent said mechanically and moved on to the next passenger.

At still another inspection table, an entire family was passing down the table. The agent was routinely feeling through the five large pieces of luggage, while the three children ran back and forth on the other side of the table.

"We just got back from a great vacation in South America," the father of this noisy brood said. "I'm a teacher out here. Boy, you poor guys must really go nuts doing this all day."

"Right you are, sir," the agent said as he continued to check the luggage. The smiling teacher and his wife kept chatting at him, when they weren't restraining their kids from climbing up onto the inspection table. The agent wondered if they had everything they owned with them, there were so many large pieces of luggage. Probably some straight jackets for the brats, he thought.

The third piece of luggage didn't seem quite right. He had felt around the neat stacks of children's clothes and hadn't found anything. It was the bottom. It was an inch higher than the inspection table it was resting on. The agent pulled out the stacks of clothing rapidly and piled them beside the suitcase.

"Would you like this?" the teacher said, grinning like a nervous fool and holding out a straw hat. The agent shook his head no and then noticed the 100 dollar bill folded into the band at the crown of the hat. He looked hard at the man and placed the hat on a shelf under the table, pressing the aid button as he did so. He knew this suitcase was it and felt around the bottom edge. There was no ribbon or string to pull the bottom up with, so the agent took out his pocket knife.

"C'mon, fella. We've been nice to you," the teacher said, his eyes were pleading. The agent didn't say a word and dug his knife into a corner of the suitcase. The bottom came up with a tug, revealing about forty small plastic bags, all filled with white powder.

"I told you, Harry," the wife yelled as they were led away by the guards. "I knew it wouldn't work, but would you listen? Oh no, not Mr. Smarter-Than-The-Cops Harry Green."

"Shut up, Agnes," the teacher snapped. The customs agent smiled to himself when he heard this and moved on to the next passenger.

Up in the observation room, Connors had made himself comfortable in a chair and was still lecturing the recruits. He had explained how each part of the security system worked with the other and how every agent had to develop an eye for smugglers.

"People give themselves away a lot of the time just by the way they act," Conners said. He then told the new agents to look over the lines of waiting passengers to see if they noticed anything suspicious. After a couple of them fingered a man in a black cape that turned out to be a nun, Connors pointed to the line at table number six.

"For example, see that guy down there? The one in the purple shirt?" Connors asked. "Something about him bothers me." He reached over and picked up the red security phone that connected him with agents downstairs.

"Yeah, Ben, it's the booth. The guy sporting all the cameras with the purple shirt at six. Bring one of the guard dogs in close, will you?"

On the main floor stood a forty-year-old man with three cameras hung on his neck and wearing a purple shirt. He was looking nervously around the customs area. He seemed very worried about something as he waited for the line to move forward. He tried to squeeze in close to the other passengers when he saw one of the guards moving toward him with a German Sheperd on a leash. The man couldn't control himself any longer when the dog stopped at his feet and began snarling. He turned to run, but the dog was much faster and sank his sharp teeth in his ankle, pulling him down to the floor.

"Bastard! Pull him off me," the man screamed as he stood up and prepared to assault the guard. Suddenly he found himself restrained by three other guards and pinned to the floor. The guy was still yelling as they carried him away.

In the observation booth, the new recruits were very impressed and Connors was enjoying it.

"But how did you know?" one of the recruits asked.

"Experience. Aren't many who can fool me!" Connors said proudly. Connors was good but only good at the obvious.

"Wow, look at those broads!" one of the new agents exclaimed, seeing Marcellus' girls enter the customs area.

"Jesus, they look good enough to eat. Looks like they won a load of prizes," said another. Connors explained that the well-dressed man near them was Mr. Armstrong, a very rich business man.

Downstairs Marcellus and his entourage approached the inspection tables. Marcellus was cool and confident, a model of sophistication. He placed his suitcase on the table before an agent and watched his girls, seemingly unconcerned about the customs check.

The girls were all carrying the large gold trophies they'd won at the beauty contest in Paris, along with a variety of designer bags. They definitely had an electric effect on the room. All that sex appeal in one place made it nearly impossible for anyone to do anything but stare. Geneva still had her tape machine playing when she set it on the inspection table. The customs agent was frozen at the vision before him, watching Geneva's breasts sway under her red silk blouse. She just laughed and pushed the stop button on the tape. He blushed and resumed his work.

Marcellus' stocky bodyguard, Juggler, had his three steel balls out and approached a familiar guard, while he juggled.

"We're back again," Juggler announced.

"I noticed the trophies," the guard responded, grabbing the balls from Juggler. An impatient scowl passed over Juggler's face, then he smiled as with a child one had to be patient with.

"I've been practicing while you were gone. Look," the guard said proudly. Juggler folded his massive arms across his chest and raised an eyebrow in mock suspicion. The guard started with two balls to warm up. This was a final exam for him. Nervously, he tossed the third ball into the air. Somehow it collided with the other two in mid-air and sent the balls in three directions.

"Hang on, I can really do it," the guard said as he scrambled across the floor to gather up the balls. Juggler rolled his eyes and smiled. He'd been going through

19

this every time he and Marcellus came through the airport for the last five years and this poor clown still couldn't juggle. 'Course this guard didn't have the background.

Juggler had been with a small circus in the southwest for a couple of years. He learned to juggle out of boredom. His regular job was boxing all comers who had ten dollars burning a hole in their pockets as "The Great Jungle Killer." Juggler's stage name was more accurate than any of his hick challengers knew. He'd been a recon man in Nam and was one of the best. He had to be to live through it.

The guard had gathered up the steel balls and was preparing to try again. He stood with feet apart and knees bent, making small circular motions with the balls clutched in his hands. His tongue snaked out a corner of his mouth. This model of cool concentration was ready. The balls went up. The poor guard did an impressive spastic dance as he lunged to catch the falling balls. All three of them landed on the floor at his feet. Juggler shook his head and bent to pick them up.

"Keep at it. In a couple of years maybe you'll be ready," Juggler offered. The guard was perplexed, scratching his head.

"Don't know how you do it," he said.

"Sort of comes natural, I guess," Juggler answered, as he turned to check on Marcellus and the girls. He figured that he'd spent enough time keeping the guard's mind on juggling and off smuggling.

Marcellus was casually watching the customs agent go through his last suitcase. The agent finished, finding nothing, and Marcellus thanked him for being so fast and efficient.

"You're welcome, sir. Glad you had a nice trip," the agent said, smiling. "See you next time."

Marcellus' handsome head gave a slight nod toward the agent, as he handed his bags to Juggler. Marcellus' expensive sunglasses hid the relief that flickered over his eyes.

Natasha and Shelly were the only girls left at the inspection table. All the others were waiting on the other side of the barrier. The two of them had three agents going over their things. Marcellus couldn't blame the agents for taking their time. Those two were beautiful enough to be movie stars. He made a mental note to tell Natasha not to wear a dress that was so revealing next time. These guards would take three hours if they could just to have have her stand there. One of the agents took Shelly's trophy and looked it over. He started reading the inscription aloud. Finally one of the supervisors walked over to the three agents.

"You guys having fun? We've only got forty people waiting," the supervisor exclaimed. "Goodbye ladies." Natasha and Shelly laughed sweetly and gathered up their trophies and walked out to join the others. The agents watched them walk away, shapely hips rocking on top of long legs.

"C'mon guys," the supervisor yelled. Shelly and Natasha looked back and giggled. They were well aware of the effect they had on men and enjoyed it immensely. It gave them a lot of power and influence wherever they went.

Beyond the customs check doors, in the noisy crowd of friends and relatives, awaited their loved ones. Grandmothers hugged their grandchildren with tears in their eyes and lovers embraced in long tender kisses, while porters rushed about taking luggage to the sidewalk outside the terminal.

In the midst of the noisy throng stood a flashily dressed young man with a bouquet of flowers; Pharoah.

Shelly's handsome boyfriend had come to pick her up. He looked successful in his expensive clothes, but there were a few too many gold chains and bracelets. He was clearly still in the process of making it with his various enterprises. Pharoah still tried too hard for the big impression. His drug dealing operation made him enough scratch for a small house and the Cadillac, but he was nowhere compared to Marcellus and he knew it. Knowing Marcellus had it so together was a never ending source of pain to Pharoah. He had hopes though. Maybe if he got to know him, Marcellus would cut him in on some of his action. There sure was enough of it to spread around.

The large double doors to the arrival area swung open and Marcellus strode in with Juggler and the girls behind him. As soon as they were in the room there were shrill screams of recognition and delight. This dude sure gets the star treatment, thought Pharoah. He noticed Shelly standing in a group and made his way through the crowd, waving at her.

A semi-circle of television lights now illuminated Marcellus and the girls. Juggler stood slightly away from the blinding lights and camera to check the crowd out for potential threats to his boss. The steel balls never lost a beat as he scanned the people waiting for passengers. He looked sharply at the man thrusting the microphone closer to Marcellus and the cameraman. Juggler held up one hand and they backed off a foot and nodded respectfully. They didn't want to cross him, they just wanted their story for the local news stations. A few radio and newspaper reporters were edging in now and Juggler took a step toward them.

"Four feet, that's close enough. Thank you," he announced firmly, the steel balls always in motion. Marcellus looked over at Juggler and nodded graciously.

"Congratulations, Mr. Armstrong. Seven firsts, three seconds and two third place winners is quite a record. How do you feel?" asked the first reporter.

"Like planning for next year," Marcellus answered confidently.

"Of course, but will you sponsor twelve girls again? That has to be quite expensive," the reporter said, trying to draw Marcellus out. The television lights were drawing people like moths. It was getting jammed as people tried to get a brief glimpse of the person getting all this attention.

"Twelve. Maybe more—" Marcellus answered and looked over at Juggler. Neither of them was comfortable with so many people around them. It would be too easy for some hard case to slip in close with a gun.

"Then you are saying that money is no object?" the reporter tried putting words in Marcellus' mouth this time. He really wanted a quote, even if he had to say the words. Marcellus sighed and raised a hand.

"I'm saying I'm very tired. Excuse me," Marcellus answered smoothly and motioned for Juggler to part the crowd of reporters and onlookers before him.

The girls were well trained. They stayed behind Marcellus and Juggler, refusing to give interviews. Marcellus couldn't stop the press from taking pictures, but he could stop the girls from yakking with reporters. They only gave rehearsed interviews that he approved personally for the pageants. It was his rule that if the girls didn't talk, then they couldn't say anything that they would all regret.

Shelly noticed Pharoah and waved to him. She was all smiles, working her way through the crowd toward him. She loved Pharoah. He was her protector in a rough world. He was considerate too, she thought, seeing the pretty bouquet of flowers.

23

She had been with Marcellus a few times before Pharoah came along and liked the difference. Marcellus was like ice, never getting too close and changing women whenever it suited him. Pharoah was all hot tempered passion. He was very direct about what he expected, while Marcellus was a cool sophisticate, just a honey bee sampling the flowers.

Shelly and Pharoah made their way around the luggage cart and embraced. She smiled up at him and they kissed deeply.

"Oh baby, I missed you. You just don't know," Shelly said softly, running her hands across his chest.

"Two months is a long time," he replied, giving her shapely ass a loving squeeze.

"Just wait till we get home. You'll see what two months away from you does to me," she grinned girlishly, touching his belt buckle.

"Show me!" Pharoah chuckled and pulled her close. Shelly smiled seductively and wet her lips. They kissed.

"Baby, your Shelly is gonna do just that!" Shelly giggled. Pharoah noticed that Marcellus was working his way toward the exit near them and released Shelly. He thought that this might be a good opportunity to get acquainted with the super dealer of the West Coast and stepped over to him.

"Congratulations, man! Looks like you copped another one," Pharoah said with a broad smile. Pharoah held his hand out to shake with Marcellus. Marcellus just kept staring straight ahead as if Pharoah didn't exist and passed him by. Pharoah's jaw tightened with anger and humiliation. His smile became a snarl.

"Well, screw you too! You black son of a bitch!" Pharoah hissed in a low voice. It was bad enough that Marcellus had freaked with Shelly before, but embarassing him in front of her was too much. Pharoah turned quickly to Shelly and grabbed her arm. "Just 'cause the nigger's got money he figure he's too good to speak?" Phaorah said, watching Marcellus exit. "Shit! I'd like to kick his narrow black ass one day." Shelly slid in front of him to prevent an ugly scene. She didn't want him to assault Marcellus and then have to watch Juggler go into action.

"Don't take it personally, Pharoah. Marcellus is like that with everyone. He ain't bad once you get to know him," Shelly said sweetly. Pharoah was still angry and pulled Shelly toward the exit. A luggage porter got in his way near the door. He brushed the man out of the way, spilling the suitcases and nearly knocking the man to the floor.

Marcellus had noticed Pharoah and his outstretched hand. The point was he didn't trust him. He didn't even want to get close enough to be polite. He recognized something in Pharoah's eyes. It was the same hunger that made Marcellus the biggest dealer of cocaine in the West. The hunger that made people do anything they had to, to satisfy it. Marcellus had enough problems without adding a nigger crazy with greed. He saw a younger, less educated version of himself in Pharoah and it was poison. They could have come from the same womb.

In front of the terminal, Marcellus Armstrong's black stretch limousine was waiting for him. Hector, his driver, was standing on the passenger side to open the car door for him. Marcellus walked to the car and greeted Hector, motioning for him to help Juggler collect the trophies from the girls.

Pharoah stood at a distance while Shelly approached Marcellus to hand over her trophy. She kissed him lightly on the cheek as he took the trophy. He passed the trophy to Hector, who was placing all the prizes neatly inside the limousine.

"Party at my place Saturday night. Everyone who's anyone," Marcellus said, noting the worry on Shelly's face. "Try and make it, okay?" Shelly smiled and looked over her shoulder at Pharoah.

"You don't really believe I'd miss it, do you?" Shelly asked, trying to sound gay.

"You're a winner, Shelly," Marcellus said, as he watched her run back to where Pharoah stood glaring at both of them.

Marcellus climbed into the limousine, followed by Natasha, Geneva and Juggler. Hector closed the door and trotted around to the driver's side. Slowly the limo pulled out into the flow of noisy airport traffic.

In the back of the car, Juggler began to manipulate one of the steel balls with a twisting motion. Gradually it started to unscrew into two halves. The hollow ball was tightly packed with bags of cocaine. Juggler took the little bags out and set them on the bar's custom mirror top. He set about opening the other two balls, grinning to himself. He was thinking about that silly airport guard. The guy had been playing with enough cocaine to pay his salary for two years.

Marcellus leaned over and picked up one of the trophies. He took a pen knife from his pocket and began to jab around the bottom edge. Natasha watched intently as Marcellus pried the bottom away from the trophy base. Marcellus held the trophy away from himself and let a pound of sand spill out onto the carpet. He shook the last grains of sand out and set the trophy on his lap. This was his favorite part. He reached into the base and withdrew a large plastic bag, filled with cocaine. He tossed the bag up and down, feeling the weight.

"Keep one kilo for the party. Fatten the rest with lactose, some amphetamines and a little procaine. When it's cut to twelve percent, put it on the market," he said to Juggler. The girls were excited, seeing all this cocaine at once and wanted to party. Geneva popped a cassette into the limousine's tape machine and soon funky music filled the car.

"I'm ready for toot right now," she spoke, like a little child asking for candy.

"I wanna freebase, myself," Natasha added, stroking Marcellus' neck with her long painted fingernails.

She loved being with Marcellus. It was like a never ending party for her. They gave each other what they needed. She got to share the good life and live like a queen. He got one of the most beautiful and freakiest women alive he could trust. Once in a while she felt the chill of not really knowing him, but not often.

Marcellus looked at Natasha and Geneva, chuckling.

"We'll do it all, ladies. We'll do it all," he said as he went to work on another trophy.

The sleek black limousine was guided onto the freeway by Hector and sped toward Beverly Hills. Marcellus had indeed pulled off another coup. A greater one than the television reporter could ever suspect. He'd just brought in twenty million dollars worth of cocaine. This trip would add nicely to his private account in Switzerland and allow Henry, his white lawyer, to make a nice profit.

Marcellus liked the system he had developed because there were very few people who knew he was moving cocaine. This meant that he was less exposed to the legal risk and made the cocaine cheaper since he didn't have to pay off as many middle men. It was a lot safer than using couriers, like some dealers did on the East Coast. Those guys were crazy.

One of the dealers had a South American ambassador bringing the stuff for a while. The ambassador would fly right into Kennedy International Airport in New York. His diplomatic pouches would be locked, sealed and filled to the brim with cocaine. Unfortunately, the ambassador got greedy and wanted much more money for his trouble. The dealer got upset and told his best friend about the situation. Next thing you know, the dealer ate a car bomb and his best friend took over the connection.

At least Marcellus didn't have to worry about that problem, but he still had to stay aloof from everyone. The less people knew, the better. If they didn't know anything about him they were a lot less likely to find his weak spots and hurt him, or maybe finish him. Marcellus was lucky in that his friends didn't want to see anything happen to him. The rich and influential people he dealt with would be ruined if he was. Everybody sort of looked after everybody else.

Marcellus sat back into the soft leather seat and relaxed. This party he was throwing at his mansion to celebrate his winning girls was going to be great for business.

Back at an airport parking lot, Shelly and Pharoah were laughing as they tossed her bags into the trunk of the new grey Eldorado. Pharoah stepped around to the passenger side and opened the door for Shelly. After Pharoah got in the other side, he reached out and pulled Shelly to him. They kissed passionately. He ran a hand along her calf and up her thigh. Shelly squirmed as his hand continued upward. A strong shudder passed through her entire body when he drew a finger across her mound. Abruptly he pulled his hand away and looked at her.

"You bring me some coke, girl?" he asked seriously. Shelly smiled seductively and unbuttoned her blouse. Reaching into her bra, she proudly withdrew a neatly folded hundred dollar bill.

"In here," she said. Pharoah looked at the bill incredulously. He couldn't belive his eyes and he slapped the bill from her hand onto the floor.

"That's all you've got to show for your time?" he asked. "Shit! I could've got more than that from the niggers in Watts and they can't afford to smell it, let alone buy it." He slammed a fist on the steering wheel and watched the line of cars leaving the parking lot. Shelly moved closer to him, her blouse still open to the waist and flicked her tongue into his ear. Pharoah pushed her back to the passenger's side.

"Take it easy baby! It's not easy to get that stuff through customs. Marcellus has it hidden in the trophies. Besides you'll get some at the party Saturday. Don't worry," Shelly said, hoping his anger would subside. Pharoah just stared at her hard for a moment and opened the armrest on the front seat. He pulled out a free base pipe, along with a small silver box. The box contained severa pellets of base, but he took out only one and dropped it into the pipe's bowl. Lighting the pellet, he took a deep puff and exhaled a cloud of base smoke. He glanced at her, anger still in his eyes as she buttoned up her blouse. He wasn't really mad at her, it was Marcellus. That nigger had it all.

Pharoah put the pipe away and started the Eldorado. He put an arm around Shelly as he drove from the airport. Shelly was content. On the way to Pharoah's house, she told him all about the trip and actually had him laughing. The pair were lovers again.

2

Pharoah's Eldorado turned onto the shady, tree-lined street where his house sat in a row of other neat, moderate income houses. It was a pleasant neighborhood of working class men and women and their children. These people all took pride in owning their own homes and kept them well painted and the small yards mowed. Even the flower beds were immaculate, with bright red geraniums and pretty roses lining the picket fenced yards. Most of the houses were one story, but Pharoah had managed a good deal on a two story brick house with a small yard. He had a couple of high school kids take care of the lawn and gardens for him and they did a good job, although they got a bit carried away with the flowers. When the yard was in bloom, it looked like a Rose Parade float.

Pharoah pulled into his driveway and parked in front of the garage. Helping Shelly with her bags, they went inside. Just over the threshhold, Pharoah dropped the bags and turned to Shelly. She gave him a little smile and held her arms up, reaching for his neck. He put his arms around her and kicked the door closed in one motion, his lips meeting hers. She whimpered as Pharoah crushed her to him. Pharoah's tongue darted into her mouth, feeling her tongue, tasting her. They both began to breathe more heavily. Pharoah leaned her against the framed mirror in the hallway and deftly unbuttoned her blouse. He pulled it free of her skirt, exposing her firm breasts in the black lace bra that held them. He cupped one and then the other, kissing and licking them. Shelly shuddered and bit his strong neck. She was glad that she was leaning against the mirror, as she was getting too hot to stand. She could see their reflection in the mirror on the opposite wall as Pharoah fondled her, her pale white skin pressed and squeezed by his powerful dark hands. Pharoah moved up to kiss her full on the mouth again and his hands searched for the zipper on the back of her skirt. He stood back as she wriggled out of the skirt and tossed it aside, looking at her lovely body. Pharoah loved her long, sexy legs and curve of her hips, and the fact that she was his.

She stood, legs slightly apart, wearing only her black lace bra, bikini panties and matching garter belt holding up her silk stockings. She still had on her designer high heel shoes. Pharoah moved close and put one arm around her waist, the other hand found its way into her panties and stroked her. She let out a moan as her body quivered with her first orgasm. Her head shook her long brown hair back and forth. Her legs finally buckled and spread apart, her hips thrusting against Pharoah's hand. He had a firm grip around her waist and held her up refusing to let her collapse on the floor. He kissed her, rotating it as he went deeper.

"Oh, baby. Your touch," Shelly sighed, her head falling back. Her breathing was short gasps for air now and low moans. Pharoah kissed her neck and pulled his finger out just as she was on the verge of another orgasm. He slid his hand around, underneath her already soaked panties and massaged her firm ass.

"Please, please," Shelly cried, her pelvis grinding against his wrist. Pharoah smiled down at her, feeling the power of sexual domination. She gasped as he stuck another finger deep into her to moisten it, then withdrew it again. One of her garters had come undone, rubbing his thigh, and the silk stocking was collapsed around her ankle.

Suddenly Pharoah moved his hand away from her,

ripping the panties completely off. She was still helplessly cradled in his arms, now fully exposed. He stroked her again, this time with a second finger pressing her tight rear entry. Her arms moved up and pushed at him in a weak effort at resistance.

"Easy girl," Pharoah whispered into her ear as he nibbled at it. On the next hungry thrust of her hips, he penetrated both of her holes at once. She shrieked and went into a frenzy while Pharoah pumped her fast and hard, almost lifting her feet off the thick carpet. Shelly felt her body filled with high voltage electricity and convulsed with one orgasm after another. Pharoah kept working her till she seemed incapable of another. Her cries gradually became quiet and her body went limp. Pharoah took his hand away and, grabbing her under her arms, leaned her against the mirror and looked into her half-closed eyes.

"Welcome home, baby," he said tenderly. She smiled and sighed.

"I love you," she whispered. "More than I could ever tell you."

Pharoah picked her up in his arms and carried her into the living room. After sitting her down on the couch, he walked over to the bar and poured himself a drink of Scotch. He filled a glass with ice and made Shelly a Scotch on the rocks.

"How 'bout some music?" he asked, as he set her drink down in front of her on the oak coffee table. Shelly propped herself up on one arm and took a sip of her drink.

"Mmmm, sounds good. Hey this drink is strong. You wouldn't try to get a poor country girl from Seattle drunk and seduce her would you?" Shelly giggled. Pharoah laughed.

"No, ma'am. This Bible Camp is strictly on the up and up," he snorted. "You can put that in your letter home to the folks." A pained expression passed over Shelly's face.

Her parents really were Bible thumping missionaries for Christ in a small church in Seattle. They had planned a very different life for her than the one that she led. They were violently opposed to everything she'd done since high school. Her parents couldn't understand her desire to start a career in modeling. Her father thought it was evil for her to pose for men and have her photograph in fashion magazines. She'd never been able to talk with them anyway, unless it was about the ministry. Her father used to beat her whenever he felt that she had strayed from the straight and narrow and by the time she was graduating from high school, this was about once a week. She finally decided to run away and become a model, first in New York City and then Los Angeles. She wanted to prove to her parents that she could do as she pleased and be happy and successful.

She took a big swallow of scotch and shook the thought away as Pharoah joined her on the couch. Rolling over onto her back, she took her shoes off and removed her stockings. The sounds of good music filled the room, relaxing them both. Pharoah stroked her soft hair and listened to the music.

Shelly sat up on her knees next to Pharoah and kissed him on the cheek. She ran a small hand down his chest to his belt and smiled.

"You know what I want?" she asked softly, licking her lips. Pharoah gave her a knowing look and relaxed back on the couch while Shelly stroked his hardening member through his pants. Pharoah stretched one arm out along the back of the couch and rubbed her back with his other hand, tracing her spine down into her buttocks. Shelly laughed giddily and got up from the couch.

She picked up Pharoah's legs and placed them on the coffee table, first one, then the other and removed his shoes and socks. Stepping between his legs, she bent over his waist and undid the belt and pulled the zipper down. Shelly then slipped her thin fingers into his pants and tried to tug them down over his hips.

"Come on, girl. I know you're stronger than that," Pharoah laughed. Shelly stepped to the other side of the coffee table and pulled on his pants by the cuffs. Pharoah lifted his hips and the pants came free. Shelly threw them across the room.

"Now it's your turn, mister," she said, stepping between his legs. Shelly knelt down and began kissing and nipping her way up his thighs. She kissed near his balls and thick shaft, careful to avoid touching them. Pharoah leaned forard and unsnapped her bra, helping her out of it. Her high, full breasts came free, pink nipples hard with excitement. He sat back while Shelly moved up to kiss and lick his stomach, rubbing her breasts over his shaft. She took both her hands and squeezed her breasts together around his hard organ and stroked back and forth. Pharoah sighed and let his head rest on the back of the couch, arms at his sides. Shelly released her breasts and raked his thighs with her long nails making him shiver. Her hands moved to his hard shaft and began gently stroking it as she lightly kissed his balls. She held it up from the base with both hands and licked it like a lollipop. She swirled her tongue around the top and flicked at the sensitive head. The veins along his shaft were throbbing with blood as she took the head into her soft, warm mouth. Pharoah raised his head and watched her twisting like a hooked fish. He leaned forward again and kneaded her breasts and tugged on her pink nipples. She groaned and took more of him into her mouth, her head moving up and down. He watched her back arching like a cat's and releasing, her head rolling over his aching shaft. Her muffled groans filled the room. Pharoah let go of her nipples and slid his hands down her back, thrusting his hips at the same time. Shelly took a little more of him into her throat and gasped for air. Slowly Pharoah stroked her cheeks, feeling his organ fill her mouth. He gathered her hair in both hands and twisted it for a firmer grip. Shelly began to buck as he forced himself the rest of the way, pushing her chin down to his full balls and her nose into his pubic hair. She could feel his organ tense and throb as he neared orgasm and bobbed her head faster.

Suddenly Pharoah's whole body tensed and he let out a loud groan as he came in her throat. When he released her, she fell back against the coffee table, lips swollen and puckered, a trickle of cum runing down her chin. She caught the dribble with a finger and licked it. Pharoah collapsed back onto the couch, swinging his legs up so he could stretch out. Shelly crawled over and climbed on top of him. They rested here for a few minutes before either of them spoke.

"I'm going up to take a shower and take a nap, sugar," Shelly said. "I'll make you a good dinner later, okay?"

"You go ahead. I've got a little business to take care of now," Pharoah answered, helping her up. Shelly gathered up her things in the living room and hallway before padding weakly up the stairs.

Pharoah walked over to the bar and picked up the telephone. First he called his supplier, the man with all the pills from the pharmaceutical company, then he called a couple of his big buyers.

"Jimmy, I've got a delivery for you this evening," he told the pimp who kept his hookers downed out with pills. They agreed to a time and a meeting place. Pharoah hung up and put on his clothes.

"I'm going out for a while, baby. Behave yourself," he called up to Shelly.

"Too tired to do anything else, daddy," she laughed, peeking out from behind the bathroom door. Pharoah finished his drink in one gulp and went out the front door.

A couple of hours later, Shelly came downstairs yawning, wearing her red Japanese robe and headed for the kitchen to cook dinner. She passed the small table where she and Pharoah always put the mail and stopped to sleepily thumb through it. There were a few postcards from girlfriends who also modeled. One was in Burma for a suntan lotion company promotion. Another was in Rome to model the collection of some hot new designer name Gianini or something. The front of the card was a heavily retouched photo of the Colliseum. The sky shone dayglow blue over the ancient stone. A piece of junk mail warned her in bold red letters that she could lose a million dollars if she didn't reply. All the usual stuff. She leafed past a couple of bills from her credit cards and came to a letter with no return address. Shelly's stomach knotted when she deciphered the blur of ink in the upper right hand corner as a Seattle postmark. The letter had been forwarded from an old address in New York by a friend. Some friend, she thought. She shifted her weight and bit a finger, staring at the letter. The handwriting looked like her mother's. The knot in her stomach tightened. She tossed the envel-

36

ope back as if it were burning and continued to the kitchen.

Across town, Watts was turning into a dangerous hunting ground as the sun set behind the run-down apartment houses and abandoned factories. The iron bars and metal grates over the store fronts and apartment windows gave it the depressing feel of the world's largest prison. Street gangs and hustlers cruised the night, fighting for their turf, their piece of the action.

Pharoah's Eldorado was parked in an alley behind a burned out factory. There were no street lights near and the shadow of the factory was midnight dark. Pharoah was inside. He stood on the second floor, watching the street in front of the building, a carton of boosted hospital drugs at his feet. Pharoah leaned on a pillar and smoked a cigarette. He like doing business here, in the ghetto, where he grew up. It was one of the most dangerous places in Los Angeles, but he knew the layout perfectly. The old buildings and alleys had saved his life more than once when he was younger. It did make him nervous because he knew what was here. The kids, hungry like he was for a way out no matter what it took. The good thing was that Watts made his customers even more nervous than it made him. They were reluctant to pull anything in this war zone he thought, fingering the pistol in his coat pocket.

A green metalflake Rolls came down the street and parked in front of the factory. A fat man with a shaved head, wearing a white suit heaved himself out of the driver's seat. Pharoah checked his watch and saw that Jimmy the Pimp was right on schedule. The fat man looked up at the darkened window where Pharoah stood. Pharoah lit a match, then blew it out quickly. Jimmy kept looking and sort of nodded before walking to the side door. God, thought Pharoah, this chump is lucky he's out of here. He's about as sneaky as a brass band at a funeral.

Pharoah watched Jimmy disappear into the building and glanced up the street where some street punks were tuning a car and playing loud music. He heard Jimmy's footsteps on the concrete stairs and kicked the box of drugs to the middle of the floor.

Jimmy was puffing when he walked into the room.

"Pharoah?" he asked in a muffled voice. "That you?"

"It had better be, friend," Pharoah answered in a normal voice. "There's your stuff. Where's my money?" Jimmy went over to the box and pulled back the cover. There were eight large bottles of pharmaceutical grade downs. Pharoah clicked off the safety on his revolver as Jimmy stood up.

"Looks okay. How much you want?" Jimmy asked. Even though they'd already agreed to a price, Jimmy couldn't resist the urge to cut a cheaper deal.

"Does this look like the fuckin' fruit market, chump?" Pharoah answered tensely. "Just give me my due." Jimmy couldn't help but notice that one of Pharoah's hands was in his coat pocket and there seemed to be a finger pointing at him beneath the material.

"Okay, okay. Here's the bread," Jimmy said fearfully, pulling a roll of bills in a rubber band out of his pocket. He held out the money to Pharoah.

"Take off the rubber band, Jimmy," Pharoah said, easing up at the sight of the roll. It looked fat enough but he wasn't about to take his hand off his piece to count it. His brother had died being over anxious to hold his deal money in his hands, not far from the place they were standing. The amount was fifty bucks. His brother had been fourteen years old.

"All right," Pharoah said, taking the bills in his free

hand and fanning them to check the count. He was an adding machine after all the years of practice. It was all there. Thirty one-hundred dollar bills.

"You're my favorite customer, Jimmy," Pharoah smiled. "You'd better leave before some kid field strips your wheels." Jimmy waddled over to the window to check his car and looked back at Pharoah.

"Next month, Pharoah," he said, going to pick up the carton. He drew a heavy breath and started for the door.

"I'll tell you where, Jimmy," Pharoah told him as he left. Pharoah listened to his steps recede down the stairs and watched him as he emerged from the building. Jimmy didn't even bother to put the stuff in the trunk he was so anxious to get out of there. He just threw the carton on the front seat and roared off into the night. Pharoah saw the gaudy Rolls Royce go down the street past the car where the kids had been. He noticed for the first time that the music had stopped and the kids were nowhere in sight. The car was still there.

"Shit," he hissed under his breath, wondering how many minutes had passed since the music had stopped. There were footsteps again, this time underneath him on the first floor.

Pharoah quietly stepped to the door and listened for another sound. There were voices whispering. It sounded like maybe four or five people were combing the first floor. He heard hushed laughter. Suddenly a bottle shattered against a wall downstairs. They were arguing.

"What he gonna do? Call the damn police?" a voice shouted.

"Yoo-hoo. We know you're in here," a second voice called out. "You a dead motherfucker, Sam," followed by much laughter.

Pharoah figured they were making enough noise to

39

cover his steps and bolted into the hallway and up the stairs. He reached the fifth floor and tried the door to the roof. The handle came off in his hand and went clanging down the steps. The door was rusted shut. The sound of footsteps running up the steps intensified. Pharoah dashed into a cavernous cutting room. The factory had cut metal patterns. The huge machines stood around the room like dinosaurs, long ago abandoned by their masters. Pharoah felt his way across the room, being careful not to step in any of the holes that the fire had burned in the thick oak floor.

Below him, he could hear the floor boards creak. They had obviously divided up and were searching the floors carefully. He knew it was just a matter of time until they got to the fifth floor. He had to find a way out. His heart pounded in his ears as he crept to the grimey window and peered through a shattered pane down to the dark alley where he had left his car. Straining his eyes, he could just make out a dark mass perched on the hood. These punks weren't that high, he told himself. They had left a guard with the car. Pharoah tried to think. A fire escape! If he could beat these sons of bitches down the fire escape, he would only have to overpower the one with the car. He didn't want to kill anybody tonight, especially crazed children from the ghetto. The cops did a great job of that already and the gangs took the leftovers. He started creeping toward the back of the cutting room. It was a likely spot for the fire escape since the stairs to the roof were at the front.

Suddenly the door to the cutting room crashed open behind him. Turning, he saw the sillouette of a large figure carrying a crow bar.

"I know you're in here, asshole," the figure said loudly, slamming the crow bar down on one of the cutting machines. The sound echoed through the building. Pharoah kept an eye on the figure as it moved about the room and backed toward the door he hoped led to the fire escape. The figure was moving from machine to machine, smashing the heavy crowbar against each one he passed. Pharoah was only thirty feet from his escape and the crazed punk had covered about half the room. Pharoah decided to run for the fire escape.

He took three strides and fell against a chair that was hidden in the shadows. He went sprawling to the charred floor.

"He's up here!" the large youth shouted. "All right, motherfucker, you're a dead nigger." The punk ran toward Pharoah, the steel crowbar raised over his head to crush Pharoah's skull. Pharoah struggled to his feet and drew his revolver. He heard the footsteps of the other gang members as they raced up the stairs. He hesitated pulling the trigger. He didn't want to kill this kid. In the darkness, he hadn't seen the punk whip the crowbar at him. It struck him on the shoulder, knocking the gun from his hand onto the floor. The coat had cushioned the blow, but the pain was temporarily blinding. Pharoah staggered a couple of feet and saw the punk rush him just in time. The kid had pulled a knife and thrust it at his stomach. Pharoah automatically grabbed his arm and jerked him in close. He brought his knee up into the punk's groin and smashed his fist into his face. The kid fell back onto the cutting table of the machine behind him.

Pharoah glanced quickly around the floor for his gun. The other members of the hunting party had arrived. They were running to help their fallen comrade and finish Pharoah.

He saw the gun. It was in the dust by the fire escape

door. They must have kicked it there during the scuffle, he thought. Pharoah darted past another cutting machine toward the gun. Suddenly, the first punk recovered and jumped at him with the knife from behind the machine. Pharoah pushed his knife arm aside and smashed the punk in the stomach with his foot. The kid doubled over and leaned on the cutting table for support as Pharoah dashed to his gun. He clutched at the weapon and spun around to see the night predators closing in from all directions. Pharoah pointed his gun in the air and fired three shots. All of them dove behind machines for cover. Pharoah put a hand on the fire escape door and pushed. The rusting hinges squealed open, letting a cool blast of night air into the dusty ruins. As he backed out onto the fire escape, he could see shadows moving toward him and fired two more rounds into the room before dashing down the rickety fire escape.

One of the shots struck the kid with the broken ribs in the leg. He screamed out in pain. His friends helped him onto the cutting table and then rushed to the fire escape door.

Pharoah was already down to the third floor and flying toward the second. One of the punks threw a large metal file which went clanging down after him. Two followed after Pharoah and the other two ran back for the stairs, yelling down to the guard at the car.

The wounded kid tried to sit up at the table, but he was already dizzy from loss of blood. There was a torn, fleshy mass that sprouted from his thigh. Blood soaked the pant leg. He noticed a handle on a rope above his head and reached for it. He wanted to see his buddies tear that nigger to bits. His hand closed on the handle and he tried to pull himself up. On top of the old machine, a bit of dust fell from the iron cog that released the huge cutting blade..He tugged on the rope again and suddenly the weight of the blade was free. In an instant the blade fell two feet toward the table and stopped, prevented by a rusty patch from continuing its journey. The kid gasped and fell back down on the table, afraid to move. His waist was stretched right across the blade's path. More bits of dust fell on his t-shirt as the hundreds of pounds of iron weighting the blade pushed it down a quarter of an inch.

Pharoah had hit the alley at a dead run for his car. His gun was ready and had one shot left, if he needed it. The two punks on the fire escape were still clattering down by the second floor.

"Move it!" Pharoah shouted at the kid standing on the hood of the Eldorado. The kid stood his ground and pulled a chain from his waist. The two punks inside were just reaching the first floor and bolting out the front. Pharoah aimed to wound the kid and fired. The shot missed completely and the kid jumped off the car to assault Pharoah. Pharoah didn't miss a beat. As the punk drew back the chain to strike, Pharoah ran straight into him and grabbed his head. He twisted the punk's neck and smashed his face onto the windshield a few times. He let the kid fall to the asphalt and jumped in the car. The two from the fire escape were charging after the car when it shot back out of the alley and into the street. Pharoah passed the other two, screeching around a corner toward the freeway. He realized that he had blood all over the driver's side of the windshield and flickered on the washer and wipers. The blood streamed down the windshield. Pharoah found the on-ramp and gunned the Eldorado for home.

When the five punks went back up to the fifth floor, they were surprised that their friend didn't answer their greetings. None of them had heard the heavy blade flash down onto the cutting table. Three of them stopped to throw up as they ran from the factory.

3

Shelly had set the table in the dining room for a romantic supper for two. There was a pretty little vase with flowers as the center piece and crystal wine goblets sparkling beside each table setting. The two goblets were the only crystal they had, but Shelly loved to use them whenever she could. On her way to the kitchen to check the roast and vegetables, she heard Pharoah's car pull into the driveway. Quickly, she took two new candles out of a kitchen drawer and hurried to set them on the table. She wanted everything to be perfect. She turned back toward the front door expecting Pharoah to open it. When he didn't she went to the living room window that faced the driveway. Pharoah had a garden hose out and was rinsing the car off. She tapped on the window but he didn't notice her. His soiled coat lay on the grass beside the car and and she noticed a dark spot on his shirt over his shoulder. Shelly went to the couch to wait. She knew something was wrong and thought it best to let him finish alone.

Pharoah put the garden hose away and pulled the Eldorado into the garage. Closing the door he picked up a rag and dried the car off. When he was finished, he peeled off the blood stained shirt and stuffed it into a garbage bag with his overcoat. His mind reeled with memories of his younger brother and how he had died so young.

They had both been in high school with Pharoah two years ahead. Pharoah and his brother had been lazy students, with Pharoah involved in one band or another. Pharoah had been playing drums for a good band. Everybody had assumed that a record contract was only months away. Tommy, his little brother, had the same bright future. Everything was rosy 'til their dad was laid off by the factory. He had been too old to find a new job, so Pharoah and Tommy had to help out.

Jobs were scarce in Watts and Pharoah finally managed to get work after school sweeping up at a supermarket. Tommy wasn't as lucky and felt bad about it. They both knew the kids in school who dealt drugs and Pharoah knew the small change he was making wasn't enough to support the family. Pharoah formed a plan.

He and his brother would start a small dealing operation with Pharoah handling most of it and Tommy helping distribute the stuff to the kids at school. It worked better than Pharoah expected and soon business was booming. They were making an average of three hundred dollars a week and Pharoah, who decided to keep the job at the supermarket as a cover, was having trouble findng enough time to meet his connections. His mother was proud of her son and didn't question him when he told her that he just kept getting raises and working late at the store.

One night Pharoah had to stay late at a rehearsal for the band and audition for an agent. He was excited at the prospect of going big-time with the music. His parents came to the rehearsal to meet with the agent and were happy to hear that their son had a very good chance of getting a deal with a record company. Pharoah had a drug deal going down with a street gang the same evening. He called them to put it off but they wanted their drugs and and demanded a meeting as promised. Pharoah didn't want to blow them off as they were good customers, so he agreed to send Tommy with the goods.

Tommy took Pharoah's pistol with him to the meeting. The three gang members were pleasantly surprised that they were dealing with someone who was so green. They waited until Tommy had given them the drugs, taken the money and was starting to leave. They jumped him in the stairway of the abandoned apartment building and beat him to death. That was was the story that the police and Pharoah put together. The gang members wanted the drugs and the money too. Unfortunately when the police investigators checked out the scene of the crime, they found a number of pills. Pharoah was booked on suspicion of narcotics possession and his hopes for a contract with the group went up in smoke. He had been dealing ever since. It was his way out of the ghetto.

Pharoah put the cash and the pistol in his pants pocket and slowly walked into the house. From the hallway, he saw the candles that had burned halfway down on the table. Shelly jumped off the couch in the living room and rushed over to him.

"Pharoah, are you all right?" she asked, seeing the bruise on his shoulder. "What happened?" Pharoah kissed her gently and walked past her into the living room.

"A little trouble, is all," he said tiredly, collapsing on the couch. "Get my robe, would you?" Shelly dashed upstairs and returned with Pharoah's large terrycloth bathrobe and some ointment for the bruise. She cleaned the cut and after putting a bandage on it, helped Pharoah put the robe on.

He walked over to a small desk in a corner of the room and dumped the money and pistol in the drawer and locked it. From another drawer, he took out a base pipe. He dropped a pellet of base in and returned to the couch to smoke. Shelly curled up on the opposite end of the couch and waited till he was finished.

Pharoah felt much better with the base in his lungs and racing strength all over his body. His thoughts became a kaleidoscope of images from the fight at the factory and other parts of his life. He made himself the hero of all the pictures, defeating his enemies and feeling the triumph of victory. He imagined himself the biggest and best dealer in the whole country. He felt strong and powerful. Invincible. He looked over at Shelly, one of his battle prizes and smiled.

"Dinner ready, girl?" he said sofly. "I am starving." She beamed at him, sensing that all was well again and dashed to the kitchen.

"Go into the dining room, honey. I'll bring it right out." Shelly answered, disappearing into the kitchen.

It was almost three in the morning. Pharoah needed rest badly. He would have preferred going straight to bed, but here was this dinner that Shelly had made for him. He managed to feign enthusiasm for the over-done roast and the almost dehydrated vegatables.

"Is everything okay?" Shelly asked, knowing full well that everything was overcooked, but hoping he would lie to her.

"Yeah, it's fine baby," Pharoah replied. "Tell me something."

"What, honey?"

"Is this the recipe you got from N.A.S.A.?" Pharoah smiled and Shelly looked puzzled.

"No wonder more people don't volunteer to be astronauts," Pharoah laughed. Shelly was still confused.

"Dried food, baby," he chuckled. Shelly became embarassed and her face flushed. She looked at her hands. It was one of their private jokes. Her cooking wasn't very good but she tried, oh, how she tried. There had been chocolate cakes that mysteriously turned into bricks in the oven and cheese souffles that looked like frisbees.

"I'm beat. Let's go to bed, sugar," Pharoah smiled, stroking her hair. "It was fine, really!" He tried to keep a straight face, failed and burst out laughing again. He rose from the table and pulled her up. They kissed and headed upstairs to bed.

They slept in each others arms until four the following afternoon. Shelly had been exhausted from jet lag and Pharoah needed to heal his body with rest. She awoke first and checked the clock. Shelly remembered the party at Marcellus' mansion and tried to decide what to wear, idly stroking Pharoah's thigh. She found him irresistible and forgot about choosing a dress as her hand moved up his thigh to his cock. She gently kissed his slowly breathing chest and stomach, her hand gently massaging his balls. Pharoah sighed in his sleep. Shelly slipped her head under the sheet and kissed his cock. It began to slowly stiffen as she licked the length of it. Pharoah sighed again and shifted his legs. Shelly took her hand and held his cock up to more easily take it into her soft, warm mouth. She rested her head on the thick mat above his cock and softly sucked.

Pharoah was gradually waking up to this pleasant sensation, a smile forming on his lips. He rubbed his eyes and looked at Shelly's smooth back, curled up beside him. He started to move his hips to meet her lips. She wasn't ready and suddenly released his cock, coughing. Pharoah patted her back.

"Good morning," he said quietly. She came out from under the sheet and wiped her mouth on it. Shelly uncoiled and stretched out next to him, kissing his cheek.

"Hi," she answered, running her arm up and down his chest. Pharoah rolled over to face her and kissed her passionately. He let his hands roam over her fine body, pausing at her breasts to lightly pinch her nipples. His lips left hers and fastened on her neck. Biting and nipping, he felt her begin to writhe against him. She grabbed his hip and ground her pelvis against his hard cock. Pharoah rolled on top of her and spread her legs, bringing her knees up on either side of him. He raised himself on his muscular arms and prodded his cock into her moist opening, withdrawing quickly. He was teasing her. She uttered a low groan and took hold of his ass, lifting her hips to find the cock she wanted inside of her so badly. Pharoah slid halfway in and she gasped. Her hands reached around his back, nails starting to dig in. Pharoah moved slowly. He bent down and nibbled on her hard nipples.

"Please, please," she whispered, out of breath and panting. "I want you so bad."

Pharoah penetrated her a little deeper and sat back, still inside her. He reached out on either side and grasped her ivory ankles. Bringing them up to rest on his shoulders, he leaned forward, driving his cock deep inside her. Shelly screamed and bucked, losing herself in the exquisite pain. Pharoah kept pounding into her, again and again. She cried out. Shelly lost all control when the first tidal wave of ecstasy washed over every cell in her body. She was clawing Pharoah's chest and back now, etching fine red lines on his torso. Pharoah winced as she gouged his bruised shoulder. He rapidly whipped her arms down and held them against the mattress.

Shelly was nearly bent in half, her knees close to the high cheek bones that made her a sought after high fashion model. Pharoah bent to kiss her hungrily, his hips riveting her into orgasm after orgasm. Shelly licked her lips and was muttering incomprehesibly as her head twisted from side to side. Pharoah pulled her arms together by the headboard and held them with one hand. He snaked his other hand down to her ass and stretched her buttocks even wider. Ever so slowly, he eased a finger into her ass. She howled and her pelvis moved wildly. Her stomach muscles knotted with the strain. She breathed hard, like someone suffocating. Pharoah felt the urge for total release welling inside of him. His intensity and speed increased, sweat covering his body and hers. The sheets around the lovers were soaked from their exertions already. Pharoah groaned hoarsly, while their bodies slapped together. Shelly gave a high pitched shriek on his every thrust, tears running down her cheeks. Pharoah's body tensed at the same time Shelly's did. They both cried out in climax. Pharoah collapsed on top of her, kissed her neck and rolled off.

They lay quietly, side by side, chest heaving. Neither said a word for ten minutes. Slowly, they got up from the bed and showered, both in a daze.

Pharoah was the first out of the shower and put on a jogging suit. He walked over to the recliner next to the bed and picked up some record albums. He sat back in the chair and leafed through the albums, trying to decide what he wanted to hear.

Shelly had finished with her hair and sat on the edge of the bed to put on her nylon stockings.

"You'd better get dressed, honey," she said seeing him in his jogging suit. Pharoah looked up from the albums and frowned.

"Screw the party."

Shelly got up from the bed and walked over to him. Stretching herself out on top of him, she gave him a juicy kiss.

"Don't be like that. I want to have fun tonight," she said in a baby voice. Pharoah just rolled his eyes and patted her rump.

"Then go to the party. Nobody's stopping you," Pharoah said, letting the albums fall to the floor. He never liked parties, but especially a party given by Marcellus. That nigger would just lord it over him like king shit. Maybe Marcellus wanted to show off but Pharoah didn't want to be part of the audience.

Shelly was determined and kissed him on the face and neck, talking the whole time.

"But I want to go with you, Pharoah. You're my man and we should go together," Shelly said, stroking his neck. "Please," she begged like a child.

"He's just a jive time," Pharoah began, but was cut off by her finger gently pressing his lips closed.

"For me, Pharoah, please?" Shelly pleaded in a sexy whisper. Pharoah stared hard at her, then a smile crept up on his stern face.

"It'll probably be boring as hell," he finally said.

"I doubt that, but if so you just pull my coattail and I'll see that you get all the excitement you can handle," Shelly giggled, kissing his chin.

"You got a deal, lady," Pharoah replied, smiling. He pulled her close and they kissed passionately. It would

51

definitely take a while for them to get dressed for the party.

4

Evening had come to Beverly Hills. A line of Rolls Royces and limousines was flowing through the tall iron gates of Marcellus Armstrong's opulent estate. The huge Tudor mansion resembled a deluxe private hotel with the gravel parking area filled with row upon row of the most expensive automobiles in the world. Red jacketed parking attendants dashed about the driveway. Their faces told the whole story. The tips for the night would be more than they made in six months.

The rich and powerful from every sphere of society had come to pay homage to the largest coke dealer in the West. Ambassadors from nations around the world were rubbing elbows with stars from the music and film business. The best lawyers and doctors chatted with some of the highest paid athletes in history. They all had one thing in common. Cocaine. Snorting it, smoking it, shooting it, taking it any way they could. Cocaine was the coolest drug invented. It was a drug that only the super rich could afford to get hooked on.

The Fortune 500 of the coke establishment wandered about the estate, comfortable in the knowledge that they were safe behind twelve foot walls with some of the most influential people in the country. The law wouldn't dare put these people away. Prosecuting three Senators, a rising Federal judge, a presidential advisor and several editors of powerful daily newspapers was an impossible idea. The average citizens of the United States had enough problems without discovering that their nation was run by men and women who would sell their mothers for a gram of coke. The alcoholics that turned up periodically were bad enough.

Safety was in numbers. These chic junkies understood that. If enough powerful people were in the club, they would always be safe. Safe from prosecution, at least. They would never be safe from becoming engineers of their own destruction. This fact was making Marcellus richer every day.

Marcellus certainly knew how to bait the trap. His five acre estate, located in the most expensive neighborhood in the world, was meticulously maintained by five full-time gardeners. The gardens were among the most beautiful to be found anywhere. The sweet scent of jasmine and magnolia filled the air. Marcellus had even had the gardeners create a topiary surrounding the pool. The shrubs were all shaped like his favorite animals, the tiger, the lion and the eagle. Every tree on the grounds had been strung with tiny Italian lights for the party.

The television monitors and light beam trip alarms that protected the estate were hidden in all these pretty trees and large bushes. Marcellus' main protection was his private knowlege of the best connections for cocaine in Europe and South America.

Outside of Henry, his white lawyer, nobody knew where he got the stuff. Telling Henry had been part of the deal to have Henry on retainer as his lawyer at all times. Henry merely explained that he couldn't adequately represent Marcellus' interests unless he knew all the facts. If any of Marcellus' distributors discovered the names of his connections he would be dead within twenty-four hours. Henry was a safe bet anyway, being a coke head with a habit far beyond his means. Henry needed the free coke Marcellus gave him. Without it he would have had to sell his house and the new Rolls Royce he drove. Cocaine would bankrupt Henry in a month if he had to pay for it. He was at Marcellus' party for that very reason.

The interior of Marcellus' three story mansion was even more spectacular than the grounds. He had hired three different decorators. One for each floor. The first floor had been decorated by a famous Italian designer and the high ceilinged ballroom was his masterpiece. The walls were covered with paintings by the masters and the floor was dotted with fine sculpture. The black marble fireplace had been found in an Italian villa and brought to the mansion in pieces.

It was the perfect showcase for the beautiful people of society. The women wore elegant designer outfits and the men dressed in the finest clothes for their profession. The music people wore flamboyant silks and the industrialists wore handmade pin-stripe suits. The guests gave the ballroom the atmosphere of a world's fair for the super rich. The pleasant throb of the funky music filled the room as the guests laughed and danced.

A group was gathered around a large table, joking and watching an elaborate toy train set as the little engine chugged around the track. The track was built on several layers, passing through miniature mountains and over high trestles. The center piece of the train set was a large antique silver chalice that stood towering over the city.

"Watch this! You're not going to believe it," a gray haired gentleman exclaimed to his luscious companion.

He pulled her to the edge of the table. She tossed her hair and looked about the room, finally settling her gaze on the distinguished man.

"You men and your toys," she said with a smile, shaking her head. She didn't mind being kept in her penthouse by the owner of six international banks, but watching him get senile was too much. Her gaze wandered over the younger men in the room while she squeezed the arm of her present keeper.

"No really, Diana. Watch the train," he gushed.

The train was making its way through miniature jungle hills toward a tiny European village. There were little toy people leading donkeys on trails beside the track in the primitive section. As the train passed the intricately detailed European villages and cities, several people around the table laughed and pointed at the train. It wound higher and higher until it was headed over the chalice. The train's whistle blew and it stopped, with its coal car directly over the chalice. The doors on the bottom of the coal car clicked open and a fresh load of cocaine spilled into the chalice. The guests surrounding the table erupted into loud laughter at this and the old gentleman turned to his mistress. Her pretty mouth had fallen open and she was staring at the chalice. The little train gave a whistle and started off again.

"I told you this would be the best party you'd ever been to," the man beamed. He was proud that he had been invited to this affair. It would prove to his mistress once and for all that he was one of the hippest men around. He strolled over to the chalice and dipped his gold snuff box in. He cocked his head in the direction of the terrace and Diana obediently hurried after him.

On the second floor, Natasha, Geneva and several other Armstrong models were putting on the final touches in one of the bedroom suites. This level of the mansion had been decorated by a Frenchman with a taste for blue and gold. Natasha had draped her lovely body in a blue velvet chair. She was checking over a copy of the guest list that she had gotten out of Marcellus' study upstairs.

"You should see the people Marcellus has on this guest list! He was right. Everyone who's anyone will be here," Natasha exclaimed, toying with one of her braids. She was radiant that evening. Her large, almond shaped eyes sparkled with gold tinged eye shadow.

Marsha, one of Marcellus' most practical minded girls, was not convinced. She turned away from her mirror and looked at Natasha.

"Any single men?" she asked. "I've had it with the 'other woman' bit." Geneva, who was standing nearby admiring her own voluptuous shape and adjusting her very revealing dress, wagged a finger at Marsha.

"Who cares? It's the money, honey," she admonished Marsha, laughing and shaking her full breasts in the mirror.

"I don't know if he's single, but the Lieutenant Governor is on the list," Natasha said with a wink to Geneva. "Along with three judges, a U.S. Senator and a few people on the White House staff!" Marsha looked at the ceiling and returned to her mirror. She'd been with Marcellus a long time, longer than any of the other girls. She was no longer so impressed with fortune and power, although she enjoyed the benefits of both. Marsha was about ready to settle for love.

"Marcellus really has it covered. I'll say that for him," Geneva trilled, impressed by the list. She faced away from the gilt edged mirror and looked over her shoulder at her reflection. She tugged the short buckskin skirt up to her hips and appraised what she saw.

"Have I gained a few pounds?" she asked no one in particular, stretching the skirt back down over her muscular thighs. Her top was a custom laced creation, also of buckskin, that showed most of her ample breasts. Complete with beaded, knee high boots, she looked like the darkest, most beautiful Indian maid imaginable. If she had been alive in the Old West, the Indians would still own America, probably Europe, too.

Geneva was blessed, or cursed, with an almost intoxicating effect on the male species. Marcellus used to call her his not-so-secret weapon. She had overwhelming sexual magnetism. Her life had been shaped and directed, all because of this beauty. Where Natasha possessed a refined elegance, Geneva's every move screamed of torrid sex.

This phenomenon was not lost on her postman stepfather and was the cause of her being thrown out of the house at age fifteen, by her mother. The strain on the family of all that emerging sexual electricity had been too great. Geneva drifted from one sugar daddy to the next and eventually got discovered by Marcellus at a disco. She was almost nineteen now. Since leaving her middle class home in the suburbs of Los Angeles, her life had been a continual Christmas. Although she was spoiled by the lifestyle that working for Marcellus proided, she was happy that he didn't give her everything she asked for. It was almost like having a father to watch out for her. She still enjoyed bankrupting a rich man occasionally, in his efforts to please her, but she loved coming back to work for Marcellus.

"I still hope he invited some single men," Marsha persisted, while she arranged a pretty gold necklace.

"Why are you so hung up on single men, Marsha? They can't do anything any differently than married men," Geneva shot back. She had forgotten, young as she was, that Marsha was getting older. Marsha was outgrowing her role of the beautiful party girl physically as well as emotionally.

Natasha shook her head at the pair and folded up the guest list. Slipping the list into her bra, she stood up to leave. Sometimes the company of the girls got very tiresome. Natasha strode to the door, her chiffon dress swirling around her shapely legs, and smiled brightly at Geneva and Marsha.

"You know what they say about the difference between single men and married men?" she asked. "Single men use credit cards. Married men deal in cash!" Natasha winked at the now giggling group and left the room.

Outside, in the driveway leading up to the mansion, Pharoah's Eldorado was gliding past the parked Clenets and Auburns. Pharoah took a deep breath and stopped his car in front of the entrance. Shelly was all smiles when Pharoah looked at her. He wished he felt as thrilled by this fantastic show of wealth. Two valets trotted to the car and opened the doors for Pharoah and Shelly. Pharoah locked the compartment that held his base pipe and stepped out, tipping the car hop with a twenty. He knew it was too much, but something inside him made him want to impress the valets. He joined Shelly, taking her arm as they approached the massive double doors that led to the main foyer of the mansion. Pharoah watched while the valet raced off with his car and parked it between a brand new Rolls and a year old Clenet. A scowl passed over his lips briefly and then he forced a smile when he became aware that Shelly was squeezing his arm. He heard the chimes of the doorbell dimly, his mind was elsewhere.

The butler that opened the front doors and greeted them, snapped Pharoah back to the present. They walked into the hallway, the butler taking Shelly's coat. The servant made a gesture toward the ballroom just when Natasha was descending the thickly carpeted stairway to the hall.

"Girl, where've you been? We thought you weren't coming," Natasha cried out, happy to see Shelly.

"You know how Pharoah is about parties," Shelly answered, hugging Natasha. Pharoah was ignoring this girl talk and checking out the well-heeled people talking by the arched entrance to the ballroom.

"Well, I don't blame him! He doesn't want you pawed over by the wolves," Natasha said in mock seriousness to Shelly. Natasha noticed Pharoah's lack of attention to her and patted him on the chest.

"Isn't that right, Pharoah?" she asked winking at Shelly. Pharoah turned his head and looked down at Natasha.

"If you say so, Natasha," he replied, not bothering to conceal his boredom with this line of chat. Natasha took hold of Shelly's free arm and tugged her away from Pharoah, in the direction of the stairs.

"C'mon, Shelly. You gotta see this mink coat Marcellus gave me. It's worth a hundred thousand if it's worth a dime," Natasha said gleefully to Shelly. Shelly made a gesture of helplessness to Pharoah as she mounted the stairs.

"Honey, you go circulate, why don't you. Marcellus is here somewhere. You two should get to know each other," Shelly tried. "I won't be long. Go have fun." The girls went up the stairs together.

"It's all the way live! Everyone's here," Natasha called over her shoulder to Pharoah. "C'mon, girl,"

59

she whispered into Shelly's ear. "You have to see this mink."

Pharoah watched the lightly laughing pair ascend and clenched his fist.

"Yeah, this'll be a real barrel of laughs," he said to himself, squaring his shoulders and striding to the noisy ballroom.

He worked his way through the elegant crowd toward the circle of beautiful people clustered at the toy train table. His eyes stared in disbelief at the giant chalice filled with cocaine. There were at least five people dipping their fancy snuff boxes into the chalice and filling them. He knew that there had to be eighty thousand dollars worth of cocaine in the chalice. Christ, he thought, Marcellus is giving the stuff away. Two of the people at the cup he recognized from the television news as high Federal government officials. Pharoah felt like a child visiting Santa's workshop. The sharp pain of jealousy and ambition was softening. He went to the chalice and took a pinch, thinking the coke must be cut to practically nothing since Marcellus was throwing it away.

"Excuse me," he said to the distinguished Presidential Advisor in the navy blue suit, busy scooping out his second box of snuff. Pharoah had seen him pocket the first box when he thought no one was looking.

"Certainly," the man responded, backing away from the table to let Pharoah examine the chalice. Pharoah touched his tongue with a finger. His tongue tingled, but didn't go numb. There was very little procaine. Taking another small pinch from the chalice, he bent forward slightly and sniffed it into his nose. His head felt a pleasant rush of blood. He nodded his head in approval. Marcellus hadn't cut the stuff much at all, compared to what folks were used to.

"I know you," someone was saying in Pharoah's ear. "I've got all your records. They're terrific." Pharoah turned to see the government official that had been stocking up. He had a stoned grin on his face and was looking right at him. The man's nose was white with cocaine, his expensive silk tie askew. Pharoah blinked once at him and went back to the chalice. Shit, he mused, another honky moron made good. Clown even looks like a pig.

Pharoah left the table and eased his way through a festive group that was dancing to the music. Beyond them, he discovered another spectacular device, a small crowd circled it. The center of the group's attention was an ornate silver fountain that stood six feet high. Pharoah chuckled. His jealousy was melting into open admiration for Marcellus. This was truly unbelievable.

"Hey, handsome, dance with me?" a lovely young woman said to him, tapping his shoulder.

"Hmm?"

"You know," she said, holding her arms up and moving with the rhythm. Pharoah smiled and led her to an open space on the dance floor. They began to dance to a slow tune, moving gently together. She clung to his neck as he turned her in easy circles. Pharoah's eyes caught another woman staring at him from across the room. She smiled and went back to snorting coke lines through a gold tooter. I might enjoy this party after all, he thought, feeling the woman in his arms push her pelvis into his.

In a corner of the ballroom, two of Los Angeles' best attorneys sat in comfortable chairs and smoked a base pipe. The two men were impeccably groomed and tailored.

"The way I figure it, if my clients weren't coke

freaks, I'd be spending upwards of a thousand, fifteen hundred a day for the stuff," one was telling the other and passing the pipe.

"Fair exchange is no robbery," the second agreed, taking a puff and nodding righteously.

"Right," the first pronounced, tugging on one of his gold cuff links.

"I should be that lucky," the second said, holding the pipe up. "I must've spent over a hundred and fifty thousand last year on this." He paused for a moment, in thought. "My wife and kids split. I lost the house." He closed his eyes as he took a long hit from the pipe and held the powerful smoke in his lungs. "Goddamn! There's just nothing else like it on earth," he exclaimed, feeling the rush that had cost him everything. His smoking partner looked at him and nodded.

Pharoah had found what he was after in the solarium. There was a base pipe and many pellets of base in a dish beside it on the table. He settled back in the cushioned chair and lit up a bead. The smoke felt good, filling his lungs. He liked the plant filled solarium. It was more private and quiet. The lights were low. He could lay up here and just enjoy the rush.

Directly across from him, Pharoah saw the young woman laying on a chaise lounge undo the string that held the top of her dress up. The older man, sitting in a chair beside her, took out a snuff box while she rolled her gown down to her waist. Her nipples stiffened with her breasts exposed to the cool night air. The man tapped out some coke on her smooth, high breasts and began to snort it. He licked up the coke that his nose missed. She lay back and looked up at the sky through the glass roof of the solarium and stroked his head. He fondled her breasts and kissed her when he had finished the coke.

She laughed softly in the shadows as he bent over her again.

Pharoah finished four pellets, watching the show across from him and letting the funky music from the ballroom wash over him. He got some soot on his hands from the pipe and rose to wash his hands. He walked back through the ballroom and found a washroom near the front hall.

Pushing the door open, he surprised Henry, Marcellus' lawyer. Henry was carefully chopping up some crystals of cocaine on a large dish with a gold razor blade. He looked up at Pharoah and stopped dicing the coke for a second.

"Care for a one on one?" he asked. He reached into his back pocket and took out his wallet.

"Thanks, but I'm strictly into freebase," Pharoah answered, soaping his hands at the sink. Henry pulled a hundred dollar bill from his wallet and rolled it tightly.

"I base every now and then, but this blow is at least twenty percent, maybe more. Right off the Colombian express," Henry told Pharoah and bent to snort lines. Pharoah dried his hands and opened the door to leave.

"Enjoy the ride," he said, closing the door after him. Henry nodded in his direction and continued snorting the coke.

Back in the hall, Pharoah decided to do a bit of exploring about the house. The hallway was lit softly with crystal wall sconces. Expensive vases, filled with flowers, sat on narrow tables along the walls. Proceeding down the thickly carpeted hall, he came upon a massive, dark oak door with carvings cut deeply into the wood. He tried the brass door knob. It clicked open and the door swung wide open at his touch.

It was a library. The fanciest library Pharoah had ever seen. Leather bound volumes filled the tall bookshelves behind leaded glass doors. Pharoah walked to the desk, spinning a large world globe that sat near it. As he looked at the crystal paper weight and other fine appointments on the leather blotter, he remembered that Marcellus had gone to college somewhere. Shelly had mentioned a school in Europe someplace, before coming to Los Angeles and dealing his way to the top. Pharoah realized that he really didn't know very much about Marcellus. He doubted anyone did. He leaned over and tried the center drawer of the desk. Locked. He heard some laughing voices in the hall outside the door and quickly moved away from the desk. When the voices faded, he slipped back into the passage and quietly shut the door.

In the bedroom down the hall, two very attractive girls were on their hands and knees, combing the carpet for something.

"Why weren't you more careful, Mary?" Sheila asked testily. There was panic in her eyes. They had been searching the deep shag rug for a while with no success.

"Go fuck off! Will you? It was an accident for Christ's sake," Mary spat back. Suddenly, the door to the bedroom opened and Pharoah started to enter. Sheila jumped up and rushed to the door, trying to push him back.

"Wait! Wait! Get out," she instructed him sharply. "Don't come in here yet." Pharoah held the door firmly in place.

"Just looking around," he said calmly. "Why, is this a private party or something?" He watched Mary checking the rug, her rump in the air.

"Naw. Mary dropped some freebase on the rug and can't find it," Sheila explained, releasing the door. She joined Mary on the floor again and began to search. Pharoah looked down at the two of them crawling around the carpet and smiled.

"Thick as this rug is, you may just as well write that pebble off and go cook up some more," he said shaking his head.

"At three grand an ounce?" Mary asked rhetorically, with a shrug. "Honey, I ain't writing off a thing."

"Have fun," Pharoah replied as he left the bedroom. He wanted to check out some more of this fantastic house, not watch two pathetic coke heads crawl around like animals for a lousy pebble.

A sumptuous dinner was being served at a long banquet table in the dining room. The pretty people who could tear themselves away from the cocaine, helped themselves to roast turkey, baked ham and all the trimmings. A wine steward stood at the end of the table, pouring champagne and wine for the guests. Henry, Beverly Hills' most prominent legal gun and Marcellus' business manager, stood next to Natasha. He looked at her admiringly. She was beautiful in her revealing chiffon dress.

"Sure like that dress," Henry smiled at her.

"Do you? Marcellus bought it for me in Paris. It's an Yves St. Laurent," she replied, returning the smile.

"He certainly has good taste. You look very chic," Henry continued, as he served himself and Natasha. She was obviously enjoying his flattery.

"I keep telling him he should open a fashion boutique in Beverly Hills," she added confidentially.

"Well, as his lawyer I know he has a good eye for business, but speaking just as a man," he paused and glanced along the table before returning his gaze to hers, "his eye for the right woman is twenty-twenty all the way down the line." Natasha smiled apreciatively, cocking her head at an angle. She always liked flirting with Henry, he was so sweet.

"I tell him that all the time. That I'm one in a million, that he'd better appreciate me," Natasha sang, patting her hair. Henry smiled and touched the soft skin of her arm.

"Well, if he doesn't, there are a lot of men around who will," he rejoined. Natasha picked up a carrot stick and took a bite, looking Henry straight in the eyes. She performed a little curtsy and winked at him before turning to leave. Henry sighed, wishing he were younger, richer, and not married with three kids. He thought she was the most lovely woman he had ever seen, watching her disappear into the crowd of guests. He wondered idly what all his snobbish friends and relations would think. He shook off the idea and returned to the salad, where it was safe. Marcellus wouldn't be too wild about it either. He seemed to really care for her. Henry popped an olive into his mouth and headed off to find Marcellus.

"My dear Henry," an overweight woman cried out while Henry was attempting to squeeze by her. "How marvelous to see you."

"Why hello, Betty," Henry said, trying not to show his surprise at seeing the Long Island dowager at the party. She must be working extra hard at being chic this year, Henry considered.

"How have you been? What brings you to Los Angeles?" he asked. Henry was already thinking of ways to end this conversation, before she got rolling.

She was going to see her plastic surgeon when she

66

heard about the party and decided to fly out early for it. She managed to tell Henry more than he ever wanted to know about cosmetic surgery before he excused himself. Same old girl, Henry thought. Dressing too young and wearing too many diamonds were her hallmarks. Put her in a store front and you could open a jewelry store.

Pharoah skipped dinner in favor of touring the rest of the first floor of the mansion. As he strolled through a corridor in the East wing, he reflected that he might actually get to like Marcellus. He had to give the guy credit. Marcellus had pulled it off all the way. Pharoah sort of felt like one of the family already. After all, he was living with one of his best models. He heard laughter coming from a room ahead and approached the open doorway of the rumpus room.

Marcellus was sitting at the ornate, circular bar in the center of the room, holding court. He was surrounded by admirers from the upper crust of America. Marcellus was joking and telling stories about the fashion world of Paris. Pharoah stared at the man he wanted to emulate and decided to swallow his fierce pride. As he started for Marcellus, Henry entered the room after him.

Marcellus saw Henry enter and set his drink down on the bar's rosewood counter. He'd been waiting for Henry to appear all evening. There was an important matter to discuss. Marcellus pushed himself off the bar chair and made his way through the chatting crowd to Henry. As he neared Henry, Pharoah held out his hand in friendship and truce.

"Hey, Marcellus, I'm . . ." Pharoah began. Marcellus walked past Pharoah and grabbed Henry behind him. He shook Henry's hand and put an arm around his shoulder, guiding him back into the hall.

"Look here, Henry, I gotta talk with you about

something," Marcellus said quietly into Henry's ear, directing him down the hallway.

The happy group in the rumpus room was chuckling over someone's witty remark and talking loudly. Pharoah could barely hear them. His ears were filled with the roaring sound of his blood surging with anger. His face was a mask of terrible rage. This was the second time Marcellus had snubbed and embarrassed him. He wouldn't alow it to happen again. Pharoah rushed from the room to find Shelly, pushing people out of his way.

Pharoah saw her emerge from the powder room and grabbed her arm.

"We're leaving," he growled, dragging her rapidly down the hall to the front door. Shelly was startled, but was not anxious to leave the fine party.

"But why do we have to go now? We just got here," she whined, not understanding. Pharoah glared at her as they neared the front door.

"Your big time host, that's why," he hissed. "I'll get a case if I stay here one more goddamn minute." Pharoah glanced about the front hall, looking for the butler and not finding him.

"C'mon, get your coat," Pharoah ordered, as they stood by the door. Shelly yanked herself from his grasp and walked to the cloak room.

"Well at least let me say goodbye to Natasha," she called back to him and rushed off. Pharoah put his hands into his pockets and began to pace the foyer impatiently. He couldn't wait to be out of Marcellus Armstrong's house. Pharoah heard a clicking sound behind him and turned to see Juggler's massive silhouette filling the hall. Juggler was tossing the steel balls with one hand, the other resting, relaxed, at his side. Pharoah watched Juggler pass as one might watch an ocean liner clear a bridge at harbor. Their eyes met for an instant and Juggler walked on down the hall. Pharoah checked his watch and cursed under his breath. Where was Shelly anyhow, he wondered, seeing Juggler turn a corner.

He leaned against the wall near a door and took out a cigarette. The door was open a crack, light from inside spilling into the dimly lit hallway. Pharoah heard two voices inside. He lit his cigarette and shifted closer to the source of the sound.

"So I need a legitimate business to dump the bread into. Anything. A fast food franchise maybe." It was Marcellus. Pharoah recognized the voice. Marcellus sounded urgent, worried about something.

"How much money are you talking about?" another voice asked. Must be that lawyer creep, Pharoah figured. He took another puff of his cigarette and listened.

"Hell, I got over a million dollars in small bills stashed in the bar safe, and you know where the rest is," Marcellus was saying. Pharoah was stunned by what he heard. He became very thoughtful.

"A million, huh?" Henry said casually. "Well, give me some time to line something up for you. An art gallery or a film perhaps. I'll work out a deal in the next couple of days."

"Sooner, if you can," Marcellus told Henry emphatically.

Pharoah had heard enough. He pushed away from the wall and walked back to the front hall to meet Shelly. He had things to do.

5

Pharoah's sleek Eldorado cruised down the street to his house and pulled into the driveway. Pharoah stayed in the driver's seat while Shelly got out of the car and closed her door. He thought for a moment and lowered the passenger window, leaning toward it. Shelly stuck her head in and gave him a little kiss.

"You're coming right back, aren't you?" she asked, her eyes searching his face for some sign, clue to his intentions.

"Naw. I got a run to make and a little business to take care of," he answered, his fingers tightening their grip on the steering wheel. "Put my breakfast in the oven if I'm not back before you leave." Pharoah checked his watch. There was an appointment he wanted to make. Plans to be discussed and settled upon. Shelly's body suddenly shuddered in the chill night air.

"Sorry about the party. I thought you'd have fun," she tried to make contact with him again. She worried about him when he became so preoccupied. Pharoah sensed her concern and smiled at her.

"Don't worry about it, baby. Things between me and Marcellus are gonna work out just fine before it's over," he reassured her. He suddenly realized that his left arm was shaking from the death grip he had on the steering wheel and made himself release it.

"I'm glad. I want you to be friends," she said, more relaxed. Shelly leaned close to Pharoah, her lips finding his.

"Don't wait up for me." Shelly smiled and gave Pharoah a coy look.

"What if I do? What will happen?" she asked in a little girl's voice. Pharoah kissed her again. He was relieved that things were back to normal. He had managed to put her at ease.

"What always happens when you wait up for me?" he asked rhetorically with an eyebrow arched.

"That sounds like fun," Shelly laughed and touched his cheek.

"Isn't it always?" Pharoah chuckled.

"Always," Shelly answered. "You be careful." Shelly turned and started walking to the house.

Pharoah flipped the shift into reverse and back into the street. He checked his watch again before taking off. There was a grim smile on his lips now. He had plenty of time to pull this plan together. He gunned the engine and sped off across the dark city to find Rainbow, a local pimp and the partner he needed.

Pharoah ran down the list of places Rainbow would likely be found at two in the morning. He settled on a piano bar on Sunset Boulevard. Rainbow always had a couple of girls working the place and used it as sort of an office. The bartender took messages for him, while he was out collecting from the stable. The cops that had to be paid off with sexual favors more often than not, were dealt with in a back room. Christ, thought Pharoah, with pimping everybody got a slice of the pie. He had no stomach for it. Too many people involved. You never knew who was going to come looking for your ass. Maybe a disgruntled cop, feeling guilty, or some crazed whore with a razor. Pharoah knew of one pimp that was run down in a parking lot with a goddamn dump truck. The police and papers called it a hit and run manslaughter, driver never found. It was a drunk construction worker in a rage over something, Pharoah had heard at the time. Cops never knew what was going on.

Pharoah preferred dealing. It was clean and simple.

The enemies and risks well defined. The money was a hell of a lot better too, Pharoah thought as the neon sign above the bar came into view. He drove to the unlit parking lot behind the stucco building and parked. Seeing no unmarked police cars near the bar, he got out of the car and walked quickly to the screen door in the back.

The cook and the dishwasher didn't even bother to look up as Pharoah passed through the kitchen.

"Hi, boys," Pharoah said before he pushed through the swinging door that led to the bar.

The bartender was wiping the counter on the bar. Only a few rumpled customers were still sitting on the stools, nursing their drinks and their dreams. Pharoah went to the bar and pulled up a stool in front of the bartender.

"Evening, Matt. Rainbow around?" he said quietly.

"Nope. Took two of his broads roller skating, I think," the beefy Irishman answered. "Dead night around here," he added, gesturing at the empty tables with his dish rag.

"Thanks," Pharoah said, standing up from the bar. "I'll catch you later." He went back out through the kitchen, climbed into his car and drove toward Santa Monica Boulevard.

Minutes later Pharoah was paying admission at the ticket booth of Rollers. Once inside the purple structure, he went directly into the rink area. It was difficult to see who was roller skating with the disco lights flashing over the people. Folks, young and old, were whirling around the rink, moving to the beat. One young girl was practicing spins in a corner. Couples, arms linked, rolled past the table where Pharoah sat.

On the far side of the rink Pharoah spotted Rainbow

skating with two very attractive girls in hot pants. He waved to him and motioned for him to come over. Rainbow disengaged himself from the girls and skated to Pharoah. Pharoah watched him a moment and shook his head. Same old Rainbow. It was his taste for extremely gaudy clothes that earned him his nickname. That guy loved flash. The purple shirt with the bright pink scarf that swayed down to his knees went right along with the gypsy earring and the shiny green pants. He was a rainbow all right. The sideshow barker's grin on his forty-year-old face looked a bit worn, the lines beginning to deepen where smooth skin used to be.

The colorful conman skated up to Pharoah and slapped his hand.

"What it is, Pharoah," he smiled.

"Rainbow, you'll never change," Pharoah chuckled, nodding toward the two girls Rainbow had been skating with. Rainbow turned to the girls and pointed at them.

"You mean them?" he asked mockingly, leaning back on the railing. "Gotta earn a living somehow. Here's as good a place as any."

"Check it out," Pharoah said with a slight nod. "Come on back here for a quick second. I got something to lay on you," he continued seriously. Rainbow's expression became a mixture of wariness and curiosity as he stepped behind the railing. They moved to an empty booth by the wall and sat down.

"You always scheming, Pharoah. What is it now? You got some hot furs to unload?" he asked, a twinge of sarcasm in his voice. He'd been through this with Pharoah before. The 'brilliant' scheme build up and then the stupid ass bust. He was interested in anything that made fast cash, but he would have to be convinced. Pharoah ignored his sarcasm and started his pitch.

"Trouble with you, Rainbow, is you're always thinking that small penny ante shit, instead of trying to move up," Pharoah stated, with a shrug.

"Yeah? Well you're last scheme that was supposed to move me cost me eighteen months in the pen, and I don't plan on going back! Not for you or nobody else!" Rainbow retorted.

It was true. Pharoah had gotten Rainbow a job driving a delivery van for Saks Fifth Avenue. He was to work there for several months to establish himself as a reliable and trustworthy employee, then disappear with a truck load of mink and fox furs. Pharoah's part in the plan was to set it all up and then arrange to fence the stolen furs. The week before the heist, Rainbow decided to pocket a few heavy gold chains, worth several thousand dollars. He got popped by a house detective on the way out the door. The end. He wasn't real bright, but that was one of the reasons Pharoah liked to use him. Any possible double crosses from Rainbow would be predictable child's play for Pharoah to unravel and stop.

"You don't have to," Pharoah said, impatient with Rainbow's complaint. "Look, I know where we can lay our hands on a million dollars in cash," he paused to let the figure sink in. "Tonight!" Rainbow's face became serious for an instant and then he sat back in the chair, laughing facetiously.

"Well, all the banks are closed," Rainbow said in mock earnest, touching an index finger to his palm. "And you ain't fool enough to rob no Las Vegas casino." He added another finger to his count. "So you tell me just who you gonna get to give you a million in cash on a Saturday night at two-thirty in the morning," he added after looking at his watch. "This I gotta hear!"

"Gonna get it from Marcellus, that's who," Pharoah

said firmly. Rainbow was shocked at the idea.

"Marcellus? The promoter?" Rainbow said, finding his voice. "The cat who puts on all those rock concerts and beauty pageants and shit?"

"That's right," Pharoah answered with complete assurance. Rainbow laughed in total disbelief, holding his sides.

"Pharoah, you're fucking crazy, you know that? You're out of your fucking mind!" Rainbow paused and drew a slow breath. "As well connected as that nigger is? Shit! Man, the heat would be on us so fast, we wouldn't know which way to turn!" Pharoah took out a cigarette and lit it, smiling at Rainbow.

"Ain't gonna be no heat 'cause it's cocaine money," he said triumphantly. Rainbow realized that Pharoah might actually have a workable plan and became serious.

"Cocaine money? Where?" he asked.

"In his pad behind the bar in a safe. I just left there. He's having a big party tonight. I overheard him talking about it," Pharoah explained, sure that Rainbow would bite.

"Cocaine money, that sure changes the picture," Rainbow said, rubbing his hands together.

"I figure they'll all be coked out in a few hours. We can hit it right after everyone splits," Pharoah continued smiling. He was sure the plan would work. Marcellus was so sure of himself he would undoubtably let his guard down. The plan had both the elements that made odds for its success very good. Speed and simplicity. The first guaranteed surprise and the second left a minimum of errors possible. Pharoah smiled to himself, that cocky nigger Marcellus was riding for a fall.

"Cocaine money," Rainbow repeated, shaking his head slowly.

"Five hundred thousand apiece," Pharoah said

quietly, blowing a puff of smoke toward the ceiling. Rainbow glanced around the rink and leaned close to Pharoah.

"We'll need some fire power and a little help," Rainbow said. Pharoah nodded in agreement.

"We'll get Squeegee. He can handle it." Rainbow rose abruptly.

"Man, let me get rid of these skates and meet you outside," Rainbow said as he went to the railing and skated to the changing room. "Cocaine money, damn," he said under his breath.

Pharoah got up from the table and went to the railing to watch the skaters whirl about the rink. One of Rainbow's girls, Debra, saw him standing alone and skated over to him. She looked almost edible in her pink hot pants. Her breasts swayed free underneath her designer tee-shirt.

"You guys leaving?" she asked Pharoah, letting her breasts brush against his hands as he leaned over the railing.

"Business," he answered, checking her out.

"Got time for a party?" Deborah asked, running her tongue across her upper lip. She knew Pharoah was a successful dealer and wanted some cocaine badly. Her budget in Rainbow's stable didn't allow her to buy any herself. She only got it when her Johns gave her some. Sexual favors for cocaine was a standard practice for cute little girls who couldn't buy it. Musicians called them "coke sluts." Pharoah looked at his watch.

"Yeah, we got an hour to kill. You got a friend?" he asked.

"I do if you have some blow," she said coyly, holding her lips in a soft circle. Pharoah chuckled. She was such a pro.

76

"Is your friend a freak?" he asked.

"She's as kinky as they come," she answered, raising an eyebrow. Debra waved Lottie, Rainbow's other girl, over.

Lottie was a complete hammer. She skated gracefully over to Pharoah and Debra. For the first time Pharoah realized how tall the girl was. She was six foot four inches in her roller skates, her large afro making her appear even taller. Slim hipped, she was all legs and huge breasts.

"Hi," she smiled to Pharoah. "What's happening?" she asked Debra.

"We're going to party with handsome here and Rainbow," Debra answered. "Over at Rainbow's place. This guy's Mister Blow in Los Angeles." Lottie smiled and nodded approvingly at Pharoah.

"Pleased to meet you. I'm Lottie. You've already met Debra," she said.

"I'm pleased to meet you, pretty ladies," Pharoah said simply. There was no need for them to know his name, he thought. "Let's get a move on." Pharoah hurried them toward the entrance and went to meet him.

"I gotta make a quick call. There a phone in this dump?" Pharoah asked Rainbow. Rainbow pointed to the door marked 'MEN.'

"Pay phone," he stated. Pharoah walked past small laughing groups of skaters who were leaving and into the men's room. Waiting until two stoned teenagers left the room, he dropped a dime into the slot and dialed Squeegee's number.

The red phone, with it's jangling ring, in Squeegee's bedroom interupted the passionate moans of the fat woman laying in the bed. She seemed alone, her hands moving under the covers, her heavy breasts covering half her bulky torso and arms, rolling in gentle waves.

"Goddamnit. Why does this happen?" a man's angry voice cried out from beneath the covers. The phone continued to ring.

"Oh, answer the damn phone, Squeegee," the huge woman groaned. Suddenly the covers on the bed rose up about four feet as Squeegee stood up to his full height, and let the sheet fall around his shoulders like a miniature Caesar. The woman picked up the phone from the night stand and handed it to him.

"Yo! Do you have any idea what time it is?" the angry midget yelled into the phone." Squeegee got very quiet as Pharoah explained what was to go down that night. He agreed without a moment's hesitation to help with the plan and hung up.

"What are you gonna do, my little giant?" the woman asked as Squeegee knelt by her side.

"Business," he said with finality, wrapping both hands around a swollen nipple and climbing back aboard his overheated mountain of flesh.

Pharoah returned to meet Rainbow and the girls in the rink's lobby.

"All set, Rainbow," he said to his gaudy partner, leading the group to the door and outside. The girls just looked at each other and shrugged, each one hanging onto one of Pharoah's arms.

"Guess they figured out who's got the blow, huh?" Rainbow cackled. "Let's stop by my place. It'll be more comfortable than their motel rooms," he said getting into his well maintained sixty-four Cadillac convertible. "Get over here, Debra." Reluctantly, she let go of Pharoah and got in beside Rainbow. Both cars drove off into the night for Rainbow's house.

It was a run down cottage in a poorer section of the city. Rainbow made out, but not all that well. The house could've used a paint job and Pharoah noticed the yard was a jungle of weeds. God, he was glad he wasn't a pimp. All that trouble for this.

The four went into the house. The girls excused themselves and went into the bedroom, while Pharoah and Rainbow sat down on the dilapidated sofa in the livingroom.

"I'd like a drink. How about you?" Rainbow asked, getting up and opening his liquor cabinet.

"No, thanks, I want my head clear for the action," Pharoah answered, not looking up from the small mound of cocaine he was preparing on the small coffee table. Rainbow poured himself a whiskey and put on some music.

"My, my, that looks good," he smiled at the cocaine on the table. Pharoah was cutting it into lines in a tarnished silver dish.

The girls emerged from Rainbow's bedroom in matching baby blue nighties. Their eyes widened at the sight of the coke as they padded to the table and got comfortable. Debra knelt before Pharoah and Lottie curled up beside him on the couch.

"Just a taste girls," Rainbow walked over to the couch and produced a tightly rolled twenty dollar bill as he sat down.

Rainbow bent his head to the dish and snorted a line of the dust.

"This stuff is great. Where'd you cop this?" Rainbow asked, handing the tube to Lottie. Pharoah sat back and ran his hand under Lottie's top when she bent over the dish.

"'You'll see," Pharoah smiled at Rainbow, giving each of Lottie's full breasts a hard squeeze. When she

79

finished she gave the rolled up twenty to Debra, but didn't change her posture so Pharoah could continue kneading her.

Debra greedily snorted up a line and, seeing Pharoah occupied, was going to whiff another when Rainbow slapped her. She let out a small cry and went over to Rainbow. "I'm sorry, daddy," she said, pouting. Rainbow took the rolled bill from her and snorted another line. Debra watched jealously, but knew what she had to do before she would get any more coke. When Rainbow had finished the line, she moved closer to him and reached for his belt buckle.

Pharoah sighed from the talented attentions of Lottie and thought about the night's work that lay ahead of him and his two partners.

6

Pharoah's sleek gray Eldorado entered the gates of Marcellus' mansion and stopped. Pharoah looked down the long gravel driveway that led past the main house and saw that most of the fancy cars were gone. Better still, the car hops had been sent home already with their fat tips. Pharoah nodded to Rainbow, who was sitting beside him. and slowly pulled ahead with his lights out.

Squeegee was in the back seat hunched over his .357 Magnum, loading the barrel. The heavy bullets clicked into place and he snapped the barrel closed.

"You got that hand-cannon ready, Squeegee?" Rainbow whispered nervously, his eyes darting over the grounds of the estate.

"You got it," Squeegee answered in a normal tone of voice, hefting the weapon with both hands. The pistol, which was usually too large for men over six feet to handle comfortably, was larger than Squeegee's forearms. He sat back, resting the barrel in the crook of one arm, two fingers on the trigger.

The Eldorado glided quietly past the well-lit front entrance toward the garages beyond. Both Pharoah and Rainbow strained their eyes into the shadows, checking for guards. There was no one. Pharoah turned the car around to face their escape route back down the long driveway and parked behind a cluster of giant palms. The car would now be out of view from the house.

Pharoah flipped open the center glove compartment and pulled out three ski masks and silk stockings. He tossed a mask and stocking to Rainbow and Squeegee.

"All right. You got everything, Rainbow?" Pharoah asked. Rainbow nodded and pulled the front of his sweater up. Neatly cut lengths of rope were strung over his belt and two mail sacks were stuck in his pants and folded against his chest.

"How about ammo for the riot guns?" he asked, gesturing to the two sawed-off shotguns on the seat next to Rainbow.

"Both loaded. I got a box worth of cartridges in my pockets," Rainbow said tensely. He was nervous. His last visit to prison had been bad enough, but he knew judges liked to stick long sentences to three time losers. A bead of sweat trickled down Rainbow's neck and he flexed his arms to calm his muscles.

Rainbow and Squeegee had put on their ski masks and were pulling the nylons over them when Pharoah noticed something in the rearview mirror. A light had flashed on in one of the garages and then gone out before he could really focus on it.

"Stay here. I'll be right back," Pharoah hissed, "and get down." He slipped out of the car and disappeared into the shadows, moving closer to the garage where the light had come from. His heart raced as he crept closer. He was not going to lose that million dollars because of some damn nosey fool, he thought. There was a movement to the side of the garage, a lighter shadow moving against the darker background. Suddenly a tight beam of light shot along the far side of the garage. It was a security guard. Pharoah was relieved that the guard wasn't stalking his car. He was just making his rounds. Pharoah darted across the front of the garage and peered around the corner.

The guard was facing away from him, relieving himself by some bushes and idly pointing his flashlight about the lawns. Pharoah moved fast. He leapt upon the guard like a huge cat, knocking him flat. In one smooth motion Pharoah had him by the throat with one arm, swept the large flashlight from his hand and brought it down on his head with enough force to smash the glass. The guard only had time to grunt when the air was forced out of him as he crumpled beneath Pharoah. Pharoah jumped up and, seeing that the guard was laying still, trotted back to the car.

Pharoah climbed back into the car and put on his ski mask and stocking.

"You can sit up now, Rainbow," Pharoah chuckled.

"What was it, man?" Rainbow whispered, from beneath his mask. "Are we still on?"

"A security guard is all. I took care of him," Pharoah answered. "Squeegee, you stay by the door. Anybody comes, buzz us on the intercom."

"Bring back enough for me," Squeegee returned.

"It'll be the easiest hundred grand you ever made," Rainbow joked, trying to convince himself more than anyone else. He cracked open his shotgun, checked the shells for the tenth time and snapped it closed.

"Talk is cheap," Squeegee replied. He'd been on enough stick ups to know that a lot of big cash promises get made in the planning, but the reality of the take is usually disappointing.

"Not in this case," Pharoah said seriously as he took his shotgun from Rainbow. "You ready?" His partners nodded.

The trio slipped out of the car and, with Pharoah in the lead, moved into the bushes that were along the wall of the mansion. Creeping forward, they were almost to the front door, when it swung open and two young couples came out laughing. Pharoah waved Rainbow and Squeegee down and waited. The group was headed for a Continental that was parked near the entrance. After a brief argument about who was going to drive, Pharoah let out a breath of relief as the couples finally drove away.

Pharoah had considered that there might be a few unforeseen obstacles, but he didn't like wasting time like this. Speed was everything in a well executed stickup. If you moved fast and knew what you were doing, the job was over before any of the victims got over the shock of having a shotgun in their faces. He waved his partners on to the front door and rang the bell. All three flattened themselves against the wall on either side of the door.

As the butler opened the door he was greeted by the barrel of Pharoah's shotgun. The butler's mouth fell open and he raised his hands as Pharoah backed him into the foyer. Squeegee and Rainbow followed him and closed the door. The butler was shaking with fear, his lips twisted into a horrified grimace.

"How many people are still here?" Pharoah asked the quaking servant, holding the shot gun an inch in front of his face.

"Hardly anyone," he answered quickly and thought a moment. He wanted to keep these potential killers happy. "Marcellus, his girl, a couple of friends, that's all," he stammered. "Man, please don't kill me," he finally blurted out in a panic.

"If you cooperate, I won't have to," Pharoah said quietly. "Where's Marcellus?"

"Down in the rumpus room, ah, sitting at the bar," the butler answered quickly.

"Good," Pharoah nodded, this was going to be simple with Marcellus already in the room with the safe. "Go check out the rest of the house. You find anyone else, bring 'em down to the bar," he ordered Rainbow. "All the way down to the end of this hallway and to your left."

The servant was visibly startled by Pharoah's knowledge of the mansion's layout. Rainbow cocked his shotgun and headed off into the mansion. He was trembling slightly from nerves and adrenalin, so he kpet shifting the weight of the gun, swinging the deadly barrel back and forth.

Seeing that Squeegee had taken up a position beside the front door, Pharoah stepped aside and poked the butler in the ribs with his shotgun.

"All right, house nigger, let's go see the boss man," Pharoah said in a low growl, pushing the servant toward the hallway that led to the rumpus room. The servant reluctantly moved ahead, eyeing the library door.

"Don't even give it a thought," Pharoah said between clenched teeth, resting the business end of his piece on the back of the butler's neck. The servant shuddered as the cold steel of the barrel pressed into his neck and moved forward again.

"O.K., O.K.," the butler said, gasping.

Rainbow was doing a quick sweep of the first floor and had been very pleased that so far he hadn't found a soul. He trotted in a crouch across the now empty dining room and paused by the door to the living room. He listened and hearing nothing, stepped in. Quickly he moved away from the door and dropped to one knee, the gun at his shoulder ready to fire at anything that moved. Nothing. Good. He saw the glass doors to the solarium and moved to the edge of the drapes that framed them. He eased the door open and stepped in. Following the same procedure as before he dropped down and scanned the room. Empty. Rainbow went back into the house and started up the stairs to the second floor bedrooms.

He stopped climbing near the top of the stairs and lowered himself onto the thick carpet. Easing his head around the corner, he could see the length of the hallway from floor level. There was light coming from one of the rooms on the right. The door was ajar and the giggles of two women were barely audible. Rainbow stepped into the hallway and silently moved to the door. He listened for a moment, his heart pounding in his ears, both triggers on the shotgun moist with his sweat. He placed one of his feet on the door and took a deep breath. Kicking the door open wide, he dashed into the room and leveled the shotgun at the two women.

It was Natasha and another of Marcellus' models that began screaming in that ornate bedroom. The model's blouse was off, her nipples swollen and smeared with

Natasha's coral lipstick. Terrified she stood up and backed against the far wall, dropping the cocaine dish in her hand to the floor. Natasha slowly raised her hands and didn't move from the bed.

"Party's over, ladies," Rainbow said. "Let's move!"

Downstairs a very frightened butler was pushed through the doors of the rumpus room with the business end of Pharoah's shotgun. Pharoah gave the butler one last jab forward and surveyed the room.

"Everybody reach!" he shouted. "Now!" No one moved and a few of the guests laughed, thinking it was a practical joke. "Who is that? David? Bill? What kind of joke are you playing this time?" Marcellus asked, laughing hard at what appeared to be an outrageous joke. Pharoah quickly aimed his gun at the expensive mirrored bar behind Marcellus. He squeezed the trigger and a deafening blast filled the room as the etched glass mirror, imported from an old pub in England, shattered into a million pieces. Marcellus and the guests near him were sprayed with silver fragments of glass and the remains of crystal goblets and mugs. One of the women screamed, seeing the blood from a glass cut trickle down her arm. Pharoah took a step closer to the group and they automatically flinched, expecting another blast.

"It ain't a joke, baby! It's a holdup!" Pharoah yelled. "Everybody on the floor!" The crowd was still in shock and didn't move an inch. Pharoah grabbed the butler by the collar and effortlessly tossed him onto the floor in front of the bar.

"Move it!" Pharoah shouted, pointing the gun at Marcellus' head. Marcellus' face showed real worry now as he slid off the bar stool and down to the floor. The woman with the bleeding arm was crying quietly and being helped to her knees by the man next to her.

Juggler, who was sitting on the stool behind her, figured that her mild hysterics would distract the masked gunman and reached inside his coat for his pistol. The movement didn't escape Pharoah's notice and he swung the shotgun in Juggler's direction.

"Don't do it, faggot, not unless you want to die," Pharoah shouted. "Ease that piece out, put it on the floor and kick it over here to me." Juggler started to reach into his sports coat again.

"Nice and slow, asshole," Pharoah hissed. Juggler pulled the snub-nosed .38 from hs shoulder holster and placed it on the floor. He was a study in slow motion. Juggler pushed the gun toward Pharoah with his foot and got on his knees with the others. Pharoah scooped up the .38 and put it into his jacket pocket.

The sounds of two women crying grew louder near the door to the rumpus room. Pharoah moved back so he could cover the door as well as Marcellus and company. Momentarily a weeping Natasha and friend were shoved into the room by Rainbow. Natasha was in a complete panic and rushed to Marcellus as soon as she saw him. Gently, he pulled her down beside him and embraced her. She was still sobbing uncontrollably.

"Shut that bitch up, or I will," Rainbow screamed, waving his pistol at her. Marcellus whispered some reassuring words in her ear and she began to quiet down.

"Tie them up. All but Marcellus," Pharoah ordered. Rainbow took all the short lengths of rope from his belt and got to work.

"What the hell do you want?" Marcellus asked Pharoah, regaining some of his composure.

"That million dollars cash you got in your safe behind the bar," Pharoah answered evenly. Marcellus shifted his eyes nervously.

"I don't know what you're talking about," Marcellus tried. Pharoah immediately strode over to Juggler's kneeling form.

"Tell you what," Pharoah said, jerking Juggler's head back and forcing the end of the shotgun into his mouth. "I bet I can pull this trigger faster than you can get behind that bar and open it! I'll give you ten seconds. Nine, eight, seven . . ." Marcellus was sweating now and confused.

"Who told you? How did you know about it?" Marcellus asked.

"Six, five," Pharoah continued his countdown. Juggler was drenched with sweat, his eyes wide with fear.

"Was it Henry? That who told you?" Marcellus asked again. He couldn't imagine how this masked gunman could have found out about the money. The frightened sobs of the women grew louder.

"Four, three, two," Pharoah said, his voice rising. Marcellus suddenly jumped up and swung himself over the bar.

"All right! All right! Cool it, okay?" There was a tinge of pleading this time. Pharoah took the gun out of Juggler's mouth and released his hair. Juggler quickly wiped the cold sweat from his brow and raised his hands again. Pharoah moved over to the bar and leaned across it to watch Marcellus.

Marcellus fumbled for the right glass panel, then pressed it. The glass slid into a recess, revealing a large combination safe with several locks. He started to work the first lock.

Rainbow had finished tying up the guests and walked over to Juggler. He pulled out another length of rope and tied it to Juggler's neck. The other end was rapidly tied to his ankles. It was very uncomfortable, but Juggler wouldn't be giving anyone a hard time for a while. Rainbow stood up again and was looking around the room, admiring his handiwork, when the intercom buzzed. Squeegee. He went to the intercom by the rumpus room door and listened.

"Got a couple here who want to join the party," Squeegee said.

"By all means. I'll be right up," Rainbow answered. He looked over at Pharoah and waited for the nod to leave. He got it and dashed out of the room to the foyer by the front door. He felt more relaxed now with everyone in the house tied up. He was even enjoying it, he thought as he admired the fancy decorations along the hallway. Rainbow reached the front door and waved Squeegee aside. Grasping the door knob, he gently turned it and whipped the door wide open. The young couple that he leveled the shotgun at were the picture of shock. They looked at each other and slowly raised their hands.

"What is this?" the young man asked, as Squeegee pushed them into the front hall and slammed the door closed.

"Shut the fuck up and move," Rainbow yelled, gesturing down the hall with his shotgun. "That way." Rainbow could see the attractive young girl's shoulders start to spasm. Not another wailing bitch, he thought, as the girl's first sob filled the hallway.

"Keep her quiet," he shouted, tapping the young man on the head with his gun. The girl saw this and quieted down, stifling her tears. Rainbow hated it when bitches let their noise maker get out of control, he mused, shoving them into the rumpus room.

There was a huge pile of bills now covering the top of the bar and Marcellus was still adding to it.

89

"What is this shit, Marcellus? What's going on?" the young man with Rainbow asked fearfully.

"What does it look like, dummy? A church service?" Rainbow answered for Marcellus. "Lie down on the goddamn floor," he shouted, shoving the young couple to their knees. Rainbow quickly took out two lengths of rope and tied their hands behind their backs. Picking up the young woman's purse, he dumped the contents onto the floor. Sure enough, there was a small white packet. He opened it and waved it in the girl's tear stained face.

"You sure came prepared to party, didn't you?" he asked rhetorically, and shifted his attention to her boyfriend.

"How 'bout you. You bring any toot?" Rainbow asked.

"In my vest pocket," the young man answered hurriedly. Rainbow went through his pockets roughly till he found another small white packet.

"Give me the bags so we can get the hell out of here," Pharoah ordered. Rainbow went to the bar and pulled out the two mail sacks. He handed them to Pharoah and pointed his shotgun at Marcellus while Pharoah loaded the stacks of money into them. Marcellus bent down and produced one last stack of bills before stepping back from the bar counter. Broken glass crunched beneath his three-hundred dollar shoes. There was a clear mixture of disgust and fear on his face.

"Is that it? All of it?" Rainbow asked.

"See for yourself, asshole," Marcellus answered angrily. Rainbow was startled for a moment, then cracked Marcellus in the face with his gun butt. Marcellus staggered back into the shattered wreckage of bar shelves, blood beginning to pour from his mouth and nose.

"Nigger, keep your mouth closed, or I'll paint this

fuckin' room with your brains," Rainbow shouted. Marcellus nodded numbly, while Rainbow leaned over the counter to check the safe. It was empty. Good, he thought, they were almost out of here. He motioned for Marcellus to climb back over the bar with his gun. Rainbow couldn't resist the opportunity and swung the barrel of his shotgun into Marcellus' head, knocking him face down on the floor. Blood now streaming from behind his left ear, he was hog tied like Juggler.

"Let's move it," Pharoah said, stuffing the last pile of bills into a sack. Rainbow jumped up from Marcellus and grabbed a sack, pulling the drawstring tight. Together Pharoah and Rainbow backed out of the rumpus room, with Rainbow flicking off the light switch as they left. The room was plunged into darkness.

"Anybody moves in here is dead," Pharoah shouted as he turned to leave.

At the front door, Pharoah paused to check the situation out with Squeegee.

"Is the front clear?"

"Yeah. Nobody out there," Squeegee said quickly. During this brief exchange Rainbow noticed a finely sculpted figurine on a table near the door. He quickly stuffed it into his sack and raced out after his partners.

7

Pharoah's Eldorado was parked in the driveway of Rainbow's house. A light breeze played over the sleeping neighborhood, rustling the trees softly and dancing shadows across the house. Inside the run down house, Pharoah and partners were dividing up the spoils of the night's robbery. Rainbow's two party girls were gone, as instructed, back to their motel rooms.

"I got to hand it to you this time, Pharoah," Rainbow smiled, wiping some stray coke from his nostrils. Pharoah, seated on the couch, didn't look up from the stacks of money he was counting out on the coffee table.

"Glad you're a believer. Just make sure you don't spend none of this bread for a year," Pharoah said, a tone of warning in his voice. He handed another stack of counted bills to Squeegee and waited briefly for the midget to put a rubber band around it. Squeegee handed the stack back to Pharoah and waited for him to count out the next pile. Neither noticed the incredulous look that Rainbow was giving Pharoah.

"For a year? Nigger, you must be crazy," Rainbow said, shaking his head. "I didn't go through all this, put my ass on the line just so I could sit back and look at it. That's why I got a television," he said finally. He didn't see how anyone could argue with that.

"Yeah, but we gotta be cool about something like this. Don't you know this town will be smoking with stoolies and guys looking for us," Pharoah answered Rainbow, raising his eyes to meet his. "Shit, man, we can't afford to do anything that will draw attention to ourselves. Not for a year," Pharoah stated flatly. Rainbow still couldn't believe his ears and started to say something, but decided to snort another line of coke first. Pharoah went back to counting cash, realizing that convincing Rainbow to be cool with his share was going to be the hardest part of the heist.

"But I got to live the high life, Pharoah," Rainbow

said, sounding like a child that wanted a toy it couldn't have. He was fidgeting in his chair across from Pharoah.

"No. You have to wait, if you don't want to end up dead. Marcellus will use all the hired guns he can to dig us up. Don't be a sucker, a dead one at that," Pharoah said evenly, handing another stack of bills to Squeegee.

"I knew there had to be a catch. I just knew it. We the only niggers in town with a million dollars and can't do nuthin' with it, but wipe our asses," Squeegee said, laughing and tossing a banded stack of bills into the air. Squeegee wanted to relieve some of the tension that was building between Pharoah and Rainbow. They all still had their guns and the last thing he wanted was a shooting after a successful job. His joke worked and Rainbow broke into a smile and began to chuckle as he bent down to the cocaine again. Pharoah continued his hard stare at him, but when Rainbow sat back, laughing hard, he smiled too. Maybe Rainbow had gotten the point after all.

"But did you see the look on Marcellus' face when we came down on him? He didn't know what was going down. That was funny." Rainbow laughed so hard there were tears at the corner of his eyes and he slapped the arms of his chair. Pharoah started laughing too.

"Come on. Let's change out of these business suits," Pharoah chuckled, standing up before the neat rows of bills. "It's all here." Pharoah walked across the living room and quickly stripped off his robbery clothes. He took one of the empty mail bags and stuffed his mask, jacket, pants, and then his shoes into it. While he pulled on his regular street clothes, he was joined by Rainbow and Squeegee. When they had also put their clothes into the bag, Rainbow tossed it over by the door.

"Squeegee, put the empty shell from my gun in the bag too," Pharoah said when Squeegee finished changing. Rainbow just stayed in his underwear. He didn't have to go anywhere, since he was already home, and he could snort more comfortably. Pharoah sat back down on the couch and divided up the money into three separate piles. The smallest was Squeegee's pile of one hundred thousand dollars. Pharoah then reached beside the couch and felt for the handle of his briefcase. He opened it up on his lap and stacked his share, four hundred fifty thousand, inside.

"All right, gentlemen, that does it. Squeegee, put the guns in the trunk of my car," he said tossing the car keys to the midget. "And the hot threads." He watched the midget gather up the guns and pull the sack full of clothes out the door. Rainbow still had his nose buried in the coke and was having trouble snorting because he was chuckling at the same time.

"Pharoah, we did it, baby," he laughed, raising his head. "Shit, I gotta put all that beautiful bread in a safe place." Rainbow stood up, wiping his now runny nose with a tissue and gathered up an armful of money.

"We're set, Pharoah," Squeegee announced, entering the living room of the shabby house. He held a bowling bag in his hand, opening it, and scooped his share of the take into it. Pharoah stood up with his briefcase and started for the door.

"Shit, remember that faggot body guard," Pharoah laughed. "He was shaking in his boots when I put the gun in his mouth." Rainbow carried another armload off into the bedroom.

"Later, Pharoah," he said over his shoulder.

Pharoah and Squeegee went out the door and walked the weed covered path to the driveway. They had one more thing to do before Squeegee got home. Pharoah revved the big engine and left the poor neighborhood behind.

Both men were lost in their own thoughts as the Eldorado streaked along the deserted freeway toward a factory district to the south. Squeegee was idly dreaming of taking his mountain of a wife on a trip, away from Los Angeles. Away from all of Marcellus' heat. Somewhere safe.

Pharoah was thinking about the amount of cocaine he could purchase for sales next year. His lady, Shelly, wouldn't have to work for that nigger anymore. Maybe he'd even get into a little of the concert promotion game himself. His thoughts were interrupted when he saw the exit he wanted.

"This is it," he said quietly to Squeegee, following the exit down to the broad avenue below the highway. He followed the street for several blocks and turned into an alley beside a large factory. At the end of the alley was an industrial trash compactor, top open. Pharoah carried the mail sacks to the machine and tossed them in.

The sun was just starting to rise and its dull orange glow started to fill the eastern sky. A few of the brave birds that lived in the area chirped as they swooped down from the power lines to pick through the garbage on the streets. Soon Pharoah's car was back on the freeway. He would drop Squeegee off with the guns and it would be over. He could go home and get some much needed rest. Pharoah wondered what was happening at Marcellus's mansion; if the hunt had already started or if they were still recovering from the shock of the night's events. Damn, it sure felt good to ace that nigger, with his fancy mansion. He'd gotten soft from having it too easy for too long. Doin' business like that. At a party. Jesus, he must've gotten soft in the head all the way. Pharoah remembered the anger and frustration on Marcellus' bloodied face when he had left him there on the floor.

"He must be one mad nigger," Squeegee said, as if reading Pharoah's thoughts.

"You bet your sweet ass, Squeegee," Pharoah rejoined, stopping the car in front of Squeegee's apartment building. "You stay cool with all that bread now," Pharoah added.

"Don't worry 'bout me," Squeegee answered the warning as he climbed out of the car. "I'll stay so low you won't be able to find me."

"You do that, Squeegee," Pharoah called after him. Pharoah shook his head as he watched the midget struggle to a side entrance with the bowling bag full of cash and the gun case. It looked like the midget was either bowling for bear, or the worst loser in the history of the sport. Squeegee propped the building's door open with the heavy bag and turned to Pharoah's car. He gave a quick salute and disappeared inside.

8

"Why would I rip you off?" Henry, Marcellus' attorney, asked from behind his large teak desk. He was addressing a very angry Marcellus who was pacing back and forth in front of him. The mid-morning sun shone, unobstructed into the high rise office and glinted off the steel balls that Juggler kept in motion by the windows.

Maceo, his other bodyguard, stood against the door that led out into the plush reception room.

"I figure you want a bigger cut," Marcellus shouted, stopping to glare at Henry. Henry was actually nervous for the first time in his dealings with Marcellus. He'd never seen him so furious. He had to think of the right words to calm Marcellus down and show him he was innocent. Henry tried to clear his mind of the hostility now confronting him. He wasn't one of the highest paid lawyers in Beverly Hills for nothing.

"Hell, man, I've already got ten percent! Multiply that by nine other guys in this town and I'm already getting a hundred percent on my money," Henry said, watching closely for Marcellus' reaction. "That's a lot more than the million or so you lost. Besides, I didn't know that you had a million dollars at your pad. You volunteered that information, remember?" Henry said, feeling more like himself as the words rushed out.

"That's right, Henry. You're the only one I told," Marcellus spat out, his eyes slits of anger. Marcellus looked up to the ceiling. "We were alone, right? Nobody else was in the room, right? So you tell me!!" Marcellus was shouting again by the time he had finished his logic lesson for Henry, his clenched fists pounding on the desk.

"Someone must have overheard us, that's all," Henry said, trying to sound casual. Henry was still racking his brain for the right approach to convince Marcellus of his innocence.

"I was in the hallway. Didn't see anyone suspicious," Juggler jumped in. Henry understood that Juggler was fighting for his job and had a big stake in nailing him for the robbery.

"Well, maybe you weren't on the job. It's a big

house," Henry shot back. He hoped that would shut Juggler up. He really didn't want to argue with a damn bodyguard.

"You could have called someone," Maceo threw in from the door. Henry was having difficulty believing this was happening to him. He had to get through to Marcellus.

"Why? Tell me that, will you? If I rip you off and end our arrangement, it means I gotta start all over again with somebody else. Someone I don't know as well," Henry paused to let his words have effect. "I gotta spend time to see if I can trust him, see if he can handle an operation this big. Then I gotta steer clients his way," Henry sighed. "Christ, I'd be out of my ten percent for at least nine, maybe ten months. Goddamn, Marcellus, this is business, man! The last thing I wanna do is lose money," Henry said passionately. He saw with relief that Marcellus' posture had fallen from one of belligerance to the slump of defeat.

"Yeah, Henry, I know. I just can't figure it," Marcellus said sadly as he collapsed into the chair in front of the desk. He touched the bandages on his head and winced from the pain.

"Must have been bad," Henry said, trying to be consoling. Since Marcellus had entered, neither had spoken of the two glaring white bandages.

"Yeah, the clowns that broke in were definitely not cool," Marcellus responded, self-consciously adjusting the collar of his silk shirt.

"Natasha?" Henry asked with honest concern in his voice.

"Fine, fine," Marcellus answered a bit impatiently. He was worried about his million dollars and wasn't in the mood to deal with Henry's badly concealed affection for Natasha.

"Some coffee, partner?" Henry asked, shifting nervously under Marcellus' stare. Marcellus nodded, but his mind was elsewhere. He was tracing and retracing the previous night and the days before, trying to figure out how he had fucked up, what had gone wrong. He tried to picture all the faces that went with the powerful names on his guest list. The most famous came to mind immediately. The music and film stars. Nothing there. They were, as a rule taken care of by rich industrialists, widows, or had made fortunes from their own investments. Anyway, their profile was too high in the media to pull anything like armed robbery. They had way too much to lose. It was the same with the politicians. Nothing there either.

Marcellus' head began to hurt. He rested his face in his hands while the secretary poured some coffee for him. The air conditioner sounded like a jumbo jet was taxiing in the elegant office, right next to his chair. He waited till the office girl had gone to raise his head.

"Got a base pipe handy?" he asked.

"Yeah, sure. Let me get it," Henry said, getting up from his chair and walking to a bookcase full of law books. A slight tug on the law book that was bound in maroon leather and the shelf popped open. Henry pulled a silver pipe from the wall recess with a small silver box. He placed them both in front of Marcellus on the desk.

"Help yourself," Henry offered, handing Marcellus a pipe lighter. Marcellus dropped two pellets into the small bowl and fired them up. He drew long, deep breaths of the powerful smoke down into his lungs, and felt better immediately. The pounding in his skull faded away to be replaced by the accelerated throb of his heart. The pumping in his chest was almost painful, but he felt superhuman.

"Ahh," he sighed. "That's better."

"Good, good," Henry smiled. "We'll get this problem sorted out." Marcellus smiled for the first time since the gunmen had appeared in his house early that morning. It was the smile of someone who was sure he would get revenge.

"Yes. I believe we will," Marcellus mused, settling back into the chair and sipping his coffee. "The problem right now is to come up with a list of possibilities." He felt like he was in total control of his destiny again. Not a victim of a crime, just a genius who had miscalculated. He tapped his forehead in thought and winced in pain when he found the bandage instead.

"No one has ever gotten away with doing this to me," Marcellus said softly, anger edging his voice again.

It was true. No one had so far. Marcellus was brilliant at eliminating enemies before they even knew they were enemies. If a dealer was getting too big for comfort, he disappeared. Marcellus always had plenty of muscle to call upon, some of it legitimate. Dealers or stoolies were easy to set up for a bust if it was inconvenient to kill them. Everyone was vulnerable somewhere in their operation. Marcellus was able to squeeze loyalty out of many of his suppliers through simple blackmail. He knew more than enough about them to get them executed in their own countries, by their own police force.

Marcellus thought about his own operation and tried to imagine that he was outside looking in, trying to bust it up. It would be difficult simply because of his clientele. There were so many powerful people on his list that no police or federal authorities that wanted to keep their jobs would dare touch him.

His mind flashed on the models. Perhaps they were the weak link. They obviously knew about the dealing, but he had always figured that he was ultimately protected by their participation in smuggling. They were accesories to the crime. Why would any of them want to give up the good life for a jail term, he wondered. Women were strange animals though. You could never tell what was cooking in their heads. Maybe jealousy. He had taken all of them to his bed at various times and still did, once in a while. Natasha could be nursing a grudge. No, that wasn't her style. Besides she was well aware of the fact that she could walk out the door anytime and marry some joker that was richer than God. They were actually very fond of each other. She'd been with him two years now and, for the most part, he'd been faithful to her. Natasha saw to that. Along with being beautiful, bright and sophisticated, she was the kinkiest woman alive. One of the others? There was never any way to be one-hundred percent sure, but he didn't think one of the models would have a motive.

"One thing's for sure, Marcellus," Henry said, interrupting his thought. "Whoever it was, was someone on your guest list. Someone you know. Put some feelers out there. With a million dollars loose, someone's bound to make a slip."

"Yeah, I hear you, Henry," Marcellus responded. He stood up and walked to the door. "Let's go boys." Juggler and Maceo snapped to attention and opened the door for Marcellus, letting him go first. After Maceo had closed the door, Henry collapsed in his chair. He was exhausted from the angry encounter and hoped that Marcellus believed him. He pressed the gold button on his rosewood intercom.

"Cecelia, get me the office of Detective Gene Fowler," Henry said into the machine.

"Right away, sir," Cecelia answered. Henry folded

his hands and waited. He'd have to think up some innocuous story. Perhaps a possible theft of a valuable necklace from one of his clients. She, of course, would remain anonymous. After all, she could have merely misplaced the jewels and insurance premiums being what they are, she wasn't about to phone the insurance people until she was positive. A discrete inquiry. Maybe he could tie it after he got Gene on the phone. He was going to do some checking of his own.

9

The alarm clock rang annoyingly next to Detective David "Fisheye" Martin's gray sleeping head. A sharp elbow belonging to his wife jabbed his ribs.

"Turn it off, David," Besty told the drowsy lump underneath the pillow near hers. An insistent foot now joined the elbow. Automatically, a beefy white arm emerged from under the covers and smacked the alarm button to the off position.

"I'll start breakfast, tiger," Betsy said with a coquettish smile, patting the mass of curlers. She always called him tiger the mornings after he made love to her, he thought as he peeked from under the pillow. He watched her pull on her pink flannel robe and recalled an article in the Sunday paper about being "fat and forty." Near fifty, he corrected himself. Did he really have sex with that? Suddenly the alarm started jangling again. David sat upright, his red nose and black eye patch combined with his thick head of grey hair to make him look like a satanic Santa Claus. He focused his watery blue eye on the offending alarm clock and took careful aim. This time he nailed the entire top of the thing. The ringing stopped. He watched it for a moment to make sure it wasn't playing possum. Satisfied, he lifted himself off the bed with a grunt and walked into the bathroom.

After his shower, David came out of the bathroom and sniffed the air. Bacon. Bacon and eggs, with toast. He smiled and went into the bedroom to get dressed in his old suit. He'd been on the Beverly Hills police force for fifteen years and his suit was as close to retirement as he was. The guys at the station had threatened to take up a collection for a new suit. David liked this one though. Sure it was shiny at the pockets and in the seat, but it was an old friend. They didn't think it was good enough for Beverly Hills. Tough luck. He had five more year 'til retirement and he'd wear a potato sack if he felt like it. David clipped his belt holster on and straightened his tie. He glanced at his reflection in the full length mirror that Betsy had stuck on the closet door. There he was, an overweight fifty-year-old Irishman in a dumpy blue suit. The eye patch used to make him look dashing, like Errol Flynn, but that was fifteen years ago when he had transferred from St. Louis to California. He had always been a good cop, some people thought too good. He had been jumped while responding to a call on the South Side. The hoods had put his eye out with a lit cigar. Just their way of saying "take it easy on us, motherfucker." The commisioner himself had arranged the transfer. David, the tough guy, would get himself killed pursuing his attackers. This became an even bigger problem after David realized that he had been set up by other police officers. The brass couldn't get him out of St. Louis fast enough.

"Come and get it, tiger," Betsy sang from the kitchen. David flinched.

"On my way, honey," he called back. He wished it

was Friday instead of Monday. He was tired already and probably running late as well.

He finished his breakfast quickly and, giving his wife a peck on the cheek, grabbed his briefcase and walked to the driveway. The sad little Volkswagon beetle chugged to life and he drove off to the station house. If the traffic on Pico wasn't so bad, he'd only be a few minutes late. His superior, Detective Gene Fowler, wouldn't mind if the most decorated cop on the force was a little late.

David parked behind the station next to the unmarked Ford he was assigned to drive on the job. It was nothing compared to the old souped up Plymouth monsters he used to drive in St. Louis. He had once driven one through the wall of of an apartment building, just to put his man on defensive. Defensive was too mild a word. The suspect, a known killer, had fainted after being struck by a police car in his own living room. David remembered with pride that he had actually managed to get the patrol car back to the station before the engine caught fire and destroyed it. Those cars had more stories told about them than David "Fisheye" Martin had about him and his tactics. Now cops couldn't do jack shit to stop criminals, he mused sadly.

David walked slowly up the stairs to the detectives room and hung his coat on the rack near the door.

"Hey, Fisheye, you're late again," Gene called from his desk on the other side of the large room. Five other detectives shared the room, their desks arranged like a school room, facing the teacher's desk.

"Traffic," Fisheye yelled back. "Impossible." He poured himself a cup of coffee and sat down at his desk, with the morning paper. There were a few official papers on his desk. Nothing important. It could wait another half hour. He'd let the young lions beat their brains out for the paper pushers downtown.

"Fisheye, got another complaint from the D.A. about you," Gene admonished as he approached his desk. Gene was waving some papers at him.

"Let me guess," Fisheye growled. "I forgot to buy some thug an ice cream soda on the way to book him." Gene sat down on the edge of his desk and dropped the papers in front of him. The letter head on each of the pages had the seal of the District Attorney's office.

"I'm serious. I don't want this shit head riding my ass because you have to teach suspects a lesson personally," Gene was almost begging. Fisheye had seniority so anything short of mass murder would only get him a reprimand from the chief.

"Those snivelling little bastards lie, Gene. Sure I rough 'em up when I have to, but you know the score as well as I do. They cry to the damn social workers and shrinks and the D.A. It's all a mountain of bullshit," Fisheye pronounced. "Why I remember one time in St. Louis . . ." he began.

"I know. I know. It was just you, your Plymouth and your blue suit," Gene interrupted. "Look I want you to take an early lunch. See what the word on the street is about that jewelry heist in the Rodeo Drive area that happened last week. I'm getting all kinds of calls from important folks about it." Fisheye scowled and shook his head. He'd had a bellyfull of important folks. They always got in his way somehow.

"Try to get a line on the fence if you can," Gene added, rising to return to his desk.

"What do they figure the street value is?" Fisheye asked, taking another sip of his coffee.

"A million. Give or take a few," Gene answered over

his shoulder. Fisheye was only half listening. His eye had fastened on the bold headline at the top of the sports page. "Lakers Drown Knicks."

"Hey, you owe me five bucks," Fisheye folded up his newspaper, put on his coat and left the room. He would put the word out and then wait in his favorite coffee shop for his stoolies to show.

Cultivating stoolies was a brutal art that Fisheye enjoyed. He liked having the power to force one sleaze to inform on another. You had to have a coward. Guys who were only able to summon up the balls to sell pot at the beach or stole small items like car stereos. It was best if they had no family living out of state and had already been to jail a few times. With no family to run to and a terror of facing prison again, Fisheye could put the squeeze on. These guys really got around, between stealing their wares and selling them. They saw and heard much.

Fisheye was truly one of the last of the old style hard nosed cops. Most of his contemporaries had been weeded out of their departments across the country. They had been either forced into early retirement or dismissed for misconduct. These men were easily as brutal as the criminals they sought. They would break bones for information and murder if they were crossed. Fisheye, like the rest of the dinosaurs, believed in God, country and apple pie, but he also believed that fire should be fought with fire. The new philosophy of police science, as it was called, had little value for such men. Like the lawmen of the old West, Fisheye was being pushed aside by civilization. He was allowed to do investigative work with the low-life element, but little else.

This jewelry heist was turning out to be a tough nut to

crack. Fisheye put the word out and waited for six weeks to get a lead. None of his informers had come up with anything. He began to feel that the robbers had made a clean escape, right out of the country. Gene was getting very impatient. Fisheye figured that someone was putting pressure on him to produce suspects.

Fisheye called an informer he knew simply as "Snitch" one hot afternoon and it was agreed that they would meet at Fat Burger in Beverly Hills. Maybe he would know something. He was such a poor dealer and thief that he had to occasionally do an honest day's work. Some of this honest work included ratting on his fellow criminals.

Fisheye took a small table at the hamburger stand and started to eat lunch. He pretended to read his newspaper while watching for Snitch's arrival. Momentarily a man in his mid-thirties sat down at the table next to Fisheye's with a soft drink and hamburger. The man was nervous and he rocked back and forth on his seat, his eyes darting over the people at the stand and in passing cars.

"Heard you wanted to see me," Snitch opened, looking straight ahead.

"Need some information, Snitch," Fisheye responded, wiping his hands with the paper napkin. Snitch's eyes flashed angrily at Fisheye and he turned away.

"I hate that name," he said in a low voice.

"You earned it," Fisheye chided him with a grim smile. He picked up his paper and pretended to read.

"Suppose I stopped earning it?" Snitch retorted. Snitch crossed his legs. His right foot wagged rapidly up and down. It seemed like he would explode from all the nervous tension he evinced. Fisheye watched him squirm and smiled to himself.

"Then I put you back in jail, that's all," Fisheye said casually. "Look, see what you can pick up on that jewelry robbery that went down. They figure it'll turn a million on the street and anyone that fat with cash had to move it."

"I'll look around. What's it worth to you?" Snitch asked, sipping his soda and crossing his legs the other way. He hated dealing with cops, especially Fisheye, but sometimes the money was good.

"I'll buy your hamburger next time," Fisheye chuckled.

"You're so generous," Snitch said sarcastically and stood up. He remembered something that might be worth some bucks and made himself sit down again near this pig. "There is one thing. Ever hear of a dude named Rainbow?"

"Yeah," Fisheye answered scowling. "He was a pimp operating off of Sunset last time I saw him. Why?" Snitch began rocking again.

"Been spending a lot of cash lately. You know, new car, new pad, the works. His lifestyle has made a dramatic change for the better," Snitch laughed and seemed to be looking at the sky.

"When did all this happen?" Fisheye asked in a bored voice. He knew all about this Rainbow character and he definitely wasn't important.

"Couple of months ago," Snitch answered quickly.

"So he's dealing now, that's all," Fisheye pronounced, looking steadily at a picture of a girl in a bathing suit advertising a health spa in the paper.

"I don't think so. He ain't got the balls for it. He's stricty a small-time pimp."

"Not according to you," Fisheye said tiredly. "I'll check it out anyway." Fisheye rolled up the hamburger wrapper and shoved it into the small paper bag with the napkin. He slowly pushed himself up from the bench and walked over to the trash barrel.

"See you later, Snitch," he said nodding vaguely toward him. Snitch looked around to make sure no one was watching or listening.

"Don't call me Snitch," he spat out hotly.

"Buy your own hamburger then," Fisheye called back, waving his newspaper at him as if swatting a fly. Fisheye walked the half block to the shady spot he'd parked the car in. He'd have to get himself some new informers. Snitch was his last hope for a lead and the nigger was strictly old news. Christ, Rainbow the pimp. That yo-yo couldn't handle more than two whores at once, let alone actually pull off something big. It was depressing to have to tell Gene that he hadn't found anything yet.

Fisheye started the car and slid it into gear. That was when he noticed the white piece of paper stuck under his windshield wiper blade. Some idiot rookie, not recognizing the unmarked car, had given him a parking ticket.

"Shit," he whispered under his breath, struggling out of the small car to retrieve the ticket. This just wasn't his week.

10

Marcellus sat behind the desk in his third floor study, looking over some achitectural plans. In the weeks following the robbery his face had healed and there were only small scars where the gashes had been. He wore a long silk robe, like a fighter's, and was relaxing with his hobby, building. His businesses were all doing well and he had his personal bloodhounds on the robbery case. He felt he could afford to relax in his private room, something would turn up and he would have his revenge. His pride hurt more than the loss of the cash. Those clowns would have to become a lesson for all the other rip-off artists in Los Angeles.

Marcellus took a sip from the frosty crystal goblet he held and turned over the intricate plans to examine another set. He loved architecture. He had since he was a little boy, watching his father, the carpenter, build modest houses for people. Sometimes, not often, he regretted not finishing his studies and becoming a fine architect. His parents had been so proud to see their son off to Paris with a partial scholarship to one of the best schools in the world for builders. Marcellus smiled at the memory of his mother's tearful goodbye at the Kansas City airport.

Paris had been all new and exciting for the handsome young student, and his easy mastery of the language made him quite popular. He lived on the Left Bank over a cafe, in a small hotel for students. He was poor, but he was studying much too hard to notice or worry about it. That is until he fell in love with a model who had social aspirations. The tall beauty was named Onda Duquesne, her name well represented her African-French ancestry.

She would visit him whenever she was in Paris between modeling assignments. Marcellus would put his books away and take her to the museums and little cafes around Paris. They had a wonderful time, laughing and telling each other their dreams for the future.

Inevitably they would end up in Marcellus' room in each other's arms, much to the chagrin of the old woman who sat at the front desk. Onda was very experienced in lovemaking and Marcellus was an avid apprentice. She taught him how to dominate a woman, take her to the brink of both pain and orgasm; draw out the pleasure till she screamed for release. More than once the hotelier had, upon hearing them cry out, climbed the narrow staircase and rapped sharply on the door.

"Monsieur, monsieur. C'est impossible," she would shout.

Once he had even come back to the hotel and found that the lock had been changed. He went downstairs and with some embarrassment and a lot of charm, got the old woman to give him the new key. She was just lonely, Marcellus had decided at the time. Before long the old woman would smile and wag a finger when he brought Onda to the hotel. She was having fun, being a co-conspirator in his love affair.

Life was very sweet during his first year in Paris. Marcellus' letters home became less frequent and by the summer recess he had explained to his parents that he would be staying in Paris, not going home as planned. He told them that he had lucked out and found a summer job with a good firm right in the heart of Paris on Place Vendome. In truth, Onda had invited him to spend a month with her and some friends at a beach house in the south. He was to take the train south as soon as school was finished and join her.

It was lovely. The house was a white stucco mansion in the Moorish style. Marcellus was happily reunited with Onda and spent many hours roaming the strange house and walking along the high terraces overlooking the turquoise Mediterranean sea. She mentioned that their host and his party would be arriving at the house during the weekend. Marcellus looked forward to the meeting. He thought that the man who owned the place must be very interesting indeed, if his tastes ran to Moorish castles in France and the house guests he didn't know.

That Sunday a black Mercedes limousine drove up the winding drive. A tall, dark man in flowing robes emerged laughing and greeted Onda and Marcellus in a booming bass voice.

"I'm so glad you both decided to come," the giant said. Marcellus realized that the man must be almost seven feet tall. He towered over him and he was over six feet tall himself.

During the next week Marcellus became good friends with the giant man called Sotar. Sotar liked the young man's company and decided to let him try some of the glorious white powder he had brought back from his trip. There was plenty of cocaine and Sotar encouraged Marcellus to make a pig of himself. Sotar thought the handsome young man had potential and formulated a plan.

Toward the end of Marcellus' stay. Sotar feigned illness and asked him to do a slight favor for him. A client was expecting a delivery of the white powder and Sotar felt too weak to make the trip. Marcellus didn't have to think twice about a chance to repay Sotar's kind hospitality and readily agreed to take the powder to the client.

Sotar gave the willing young man a locked, leather briefcase as Marcellus got into the huge limousine.

"The case will return with you, my friend will know the combination and remove the contents. He will also have an envelope for you," Sotar rumbled and shut the door.

Marcellus delivered the goods to a chateau in the mountains to the east. It was a long ride, but he was puzzled that Sotar had asked him to do it rather than just have the chauffeur drop the stuff off.

A servant in livery greeted Marcellus at the front door and showed him into an ornate office to await the master of the house. Shortly, an elegant old gentleman appeared in a velvet robe bearing a coat of arms. He introduced himself as a viscount and took the briefcase to the desk. The old viscount fumbled with the locks to no avail.

"You must forgive an old man," he said with an embarassed smile. He slid out a drawer in his desk and rummaged around in it until he spied what he was looking for.

"Et voila," he said exultantly. It was the combination for the locks on the briefcase. He opened the case and removed four large plastic packets of cocaine, setting them in another drawer.

He called Marcellus to him and handed him an envelope just as Sotar had said he would. The phone rang on the desk and the Viscount answered. He smiled and handed the phone to Marcellus.

"Hello," Marcellus said, still surprised.

"Bonjour, my friend," Sotar's voice rumbled. "Did you get the envelope?"

"Yes."

"Well, open it lad. It's for you. For helping me," Sotar said. Marcellus flipped open the envelope and found five thousand American dollars inside. His eyes showed even greater surprise.

"What is this for?" Marcellus began to object.

"Not a word. You will deeply hurt my feelings if you do not accept it. Have no fear. My profits from the transaction you helped me with are a hundred times that," Sotar boomed. Marcellus just stared at the cash and thought of all the ways he could use the money to help with his studies.

"Thank you, Sotar," Marcellus stammered.

The rest of the summer passed quickly. Sotar kept Marcellus busy delivering cocaine and gradually all thought of finishing school faded into the background. Marcellus had promised himself that he would only deal for Sotar for a year and then stop when he had a nice nest egg saved. He applied himself to learning Italian and German for both dealing and to help him when he became an architect.

He never did finish his studies, of course. Greed for the easy money of cocaine and the power that he was gaining over people were all important. There was no way, as Sotar knew, that he could ever stop dealing.

This path had led to California, where Marcellus had become an American Sotar. So here he sat, staring at the plans he had drawn himself for his dream house. He planned to build it on one of the Hawaiian islands some day. He had changed the detailing on the drawings a hundred times. It wasn't because there was anything wrong with the plans. Marcellus just loved to putter endlessly with them. There was a soft knock on the door to Marcellus' study.

"Yes," he called out. Natasha opened the door and walked to his drawing table, smiling. She was wearing an extremely sheer purple nightgown with nothing on underneath. She looked ravishing.

"Hi, baby. Still working on that house, huh?" Natasha spoke softly, letting the gown fall open as she stepped around the table to Marcellus's side.

"Yeah," he sighed. "I was thinking of building an atrium in the guest house. The weather's warm enough for it in Hawaii," he continued, placing a hand behind her knee and stroking upward along her shapely thigh. She shivered at his touch and smiled at him.

"Why, I think you have some wonderful ideas," Natasha purred. Marcellus marvelled at her smooth skin and squeezed her inner thigh. She had been leaning on the work table, resting her weight on one foot with her other leg resting on the toe of her high heel shoe. She shifted now, standing on both feet, legs apart.

"I think I'll be able to retire from dealing in a couple of years," Marcellus said thoughtfully. He was still dreaming of a life in which there were no bodyguards and he could spend his days working on the plans for new buildings.

"That would be wonderful," Natasha said soothingly. She had gotten to know Marcellus better than any of his previous girl friends and felt she understood him. Most of his other girl friends had never been allowed into his private sanctuary. He had shown her his high-school for design with a glowing pride. Even a copy of the letter that announced his chance to study in Paris hung in a frame on the study wall. She understood that this was where Marcellus the idealist lived in the mementos and drawing that spanned fifteen years. If any of the little boy dreams still breathed in him they were all kept hidden in this room.

Marcellus appreciated Natasha's understanding, even if his dreams stayed shut up in this room.

"My investments have done very well. You can't deal forever. The odds just don't allow it," Marcellus said, flicking the transparent robe Natasha was wearing over her curved back. His hand idly traced the line of her back to her perfectly curved behind.

Natasha shivered again and, unable to stand Marcellus' teasing electric touch, turned and kissed him. Marcellus always drove her wild. Her hands moved to his neck muscles underneath his robe and massaged them.

"You get so tight, honey," she said, sitting down on his lap. They kissed again, passionately. Marcellus stroked her soft belly slowly. "Let's take a sauna before we go to bed."

"Good idea," Marcellus said, lifting her off his lap by the waist. He took one last sip of his drink and stood up behind the table. He allowed himself to be led by the hand to the door and took a last look around the room as he switched off the light. Closing the door behind them, he thought about how good Natasha was for him. He was dimly aware that his dream to retire and finally become an architect would most likely remain just that, a dream. This dream was important to him though and Natasha respected that. She was a loving confidant.

They padded down the thick carpet into the bedroom. Natasha had recently redecorated it with the deep reds and black lacquer of the Orient. It was spacious and uncluttered. The large king-size bed sat on its low legs to one side. The headboard and glossy black night tables on either side concealed a stereo system and a wide variety of oils and other paraphernalia for exotic lovemaking. Beyond the tall silk screens were the closet and a glass door that led to the master bath and sauna.

They shed their robes on the floor near the bed and holding hands, continued into the sauna. Marcellus opened the sauna door and was greeted with a cloud of thick eucalyptus scented steam. He pushed his way past an overgrown jungle fern and stepped down into the rolling hot tub. Natasha sat on the edge, dangling her legs into the hot water.

"Mmm, this feels good, baby," Marcellus smiled as she massaged the taut muscles in his shoulders and neck. He figured that she was the best geisha possible, so attentive to his needs.

A rough, natural sponge lay nearby with a bottle of body shampoo. Natasha finished massaging Marcellus' upper arms and began to lather and scrub his shoulders. The lotion gave Marcellus a tingling sensation and he settled back against the edge of the tub. Natasha then reached under his arms and helped him out of the tub and onto a long padded mat beside it. Marcellus sighed contentedly and stretched out on the soft cushion, closing his eyes.

Natasha poured the shampoo over his chest and, giggling, let some of the cool liquid fall on his relaxed member and balls. Marcellus chuckled at this and felt her hands rubbing his chest with the sponge. She circled his strong chest muscles and slid the sponge along his powerful arms. His breathing began to slow as he let the tension go. In such capable hands, his worries about his business interests and even the robbery ebbed away.

Natasha was extremely thorough. She gently twisted his fingers with her soapy hands and kneaded his arms. She briefly rubbed his stomach with the sponge and moved to his thighs, avoiding his genitals. Marcellus was treated to this titillating massage over his front, on down to his toes. Natasha then rolled him over and repeated the process, sweat and steam making her body glisten. Small drops formed and dropped from her large, pointed nipples to fall on her wet thighs.

She soaped her own body with the sponge and climbed on top of Marcellus' back. Sliding up and down, she further massaged him with her breasts, arms and thighs. Marcellus groaned in pleasure as she moved. Satisfied that his back was done, she rolled him onto his back again. This was her favorite part of the massage. Starting at his feet she rubbed herself all the way up to his genitals and let her breasts gently brush his member. She quickly moved along his chest, stopping at his face and swirling her perfect nipples over his closed eyes.

Natasha took hold of a small hose near them and tested the temperature of the fine needle spray that shot from it on her thighs. Lukewarm. She sprayed herself, rinsing the bubbles off and then washed Marcellus off. When he was rinsed she put the hose away and bent over his genitals, kissing his stiffening cock and his full balls.

She stopped long enough to position herself on his knee and gently rubbed her pussy on it while she licked and nipped his groin area. His cock was rapidly becoming gorged with blood and she held the base with both hands, licking the head like a delicious ice cream cone. Marcellus groaned and shifted his free leg and stretched his arms. Natasha placed the head of his now erect cock into her warm mouth and started to softly suck. Marcellus raised himself up on an elbow and opened his eyes for the first time in an hour. He watched her lips slide more of him into her mouth and listened to her little moans mix with the sucking sound. Her hips were rocking in rhythm with her bobbing head. She released his thick shaft and cupped his balls with both hands, her head taking longer strokes as he penetrated more deeply into her throat. Marcellus reached out and placed a broad hand on the back of her moving head. Forcing her down, he rotated her on his cock. He flexed his buttock muscles to meet the thrust of her mouth.

Several minutes passed till Marcellus released her hair and sat up. She raised her lips to his and they kissed deeply, while he tugged on her hard nipples. Natasha moved close to him and placed herself over his erect cock, standing with her knees by his hips. Marcellus fastened his mouth on one of her nipples and slowly pulled her down onto his cock. A cry escaped her lips as she sank her pussy onto his shaft. They rocked gently, both sitting with straight backs, until Marcellus was inside her completely. They kissed, their tongues snaking between their mouths.

Natasha's breathing became short gasps and her rocking accelerated. Marcellus grabbed the cheeks of her wet ass and pumped her up and down forcefully. Her gasps grew into shrieks as she began to have orgasm after orgasm, each one bigger than the preceding one. At last, with an ear splitting scream, she fell back onto the foam mat and let his still hard cock slide out of her dripping pussy. Her chest was heaving from her efforts to catch her breath and her sobs. Marcellus smiled at her and slid back into the hot tub. He would save his release for later, when she had recovered a bit. He sank down in the foamy water to his chin and chuckled like a man who had wanted everything the world had to offer and gotten it, twofold. The aggravations of his business and the search for the jerks who stole his money could wait until tomorrow.

The following afternoon Natasha had Shelly, Marsha and Geneva out to the mansion for lunch. She had slept very late and wore a beautiful house robe. The four women were sitting in the solarium, all eyes riveted on an expensive necklace that Geneva was wearing.

"Girl, you hang on to him, understand?" Natasha said with a laugh.

"That's right, 'cause generosity in a man is rare nowadays," Shelly added lightly.

"Is he married or single?" Marsha asked seriously.

"There you go again with all that married and single

stuff! Hell, I don't know, Marsha, and don't really care. Not as long as he treats me right," Geneva said with a wink to Shelly and Natasha. They all were laughing when Marcellus walked in carrying an attache case, Juggler close behind.

"Hi, honey. We were just talking about Geneva's new boyfriend. Look what he gave her," Natasha said, pointing to the jewels about her friend's neck.

"Nice," Marcellus answered, fixing himself a drink at the portable bar. Juggler sat down in a chair at the side of the group.

"Yes, honey, this man just loves to spend money," Geneva explained, smiling. "A month ago he went down to the Cadillac dealer with a briefcase full of money and paid cash for the car! I swear! I saw it with my own eyes," she said and looked at her audience with big eyes. "Then the nigger went down to the marina with the same briefcase and bought a yacht, cash." Marcellus chuckled and held his glass up as a toast to her.

"You're very lucky to have someone like that," he said.

"It's not me, it's Rainbow with all the luck. That's his name, Rainbow," Geneva said happily. "Why do you know just two months ago he was poor as a churchmouse. I mean the nigger didn't have a dime to his name! Now he's living like a millionaire." Marcellus stopped drinking and exchanged a look with Juggler. Juggler let the steel balls fall into his hand and leaned forward, listening intently. Marcellus moved from the bar and sat in a chair opposite Geneva.

"Two months ago you say? He sounds rather enterprising. What line of work is he in?" Marcellus asked trying to be offhand about it. The throbbing in his chest told him that he was suddenly much closer to finding the robbers.

"Now, Marcellus, you know I'm not about being nosy," Geneva scolded him playfully. Marcellus raised an eyebrow and took a sip of his cool drink.

"I guess what you don't know won't hurt you," he said quietly.

"I heard that," Geneva laughed. Marcellus set his glass down and stood up to leave while the women were all giggling with and at Geneva.

"Well, I'll leave you ladies to your gossip," Marcellus smiled, picking up his briefcase. He nodded to Juggler as he passed him to follow.

The two men stopped in the hallway off the solarium, out of earshot.

"You know this Rainbow character?" Marcellus asked in a hushed tone.

"Never heard of him," Juggler answered.

"Well, you and Maceo check him out, understand? Anyone who was poor two months ago and now buys yachts for cash is somebody I want to know," Marcellus stated firmly.

"Or kill," Juggler nodded.

11

"Don't you know somebody named Rainbow?" Shelly asked Pharoah from the kitchen. Shelly had heard Pharoah mention many names offhandedly when he was doing business. She thought she remembered that name. Rainbow.

They were preparing a barbeque in the backyard. Pharoah was starting the charcoal in the metal grill as she spoke. He tossed a match onto the lighter fluid soaked coals. The flames leapt up and roared briefly before dying to a slow burn.

"What, baby?" he called to her as he walked to the back door.

"Rainbow somebody. Don't you know him?" Shelly asked innocently. She handed him a bowl of potato salad to put on the picnic table. Pharoah felt his throat tighten. He hoped that she hadn't noticed the quick start that the name Rainbow had caused. He hadn't been in touch with him. That was all part of the plan. Pharoah recalled their last conversation on the night of the robbery. Now Shelly was talking about him. He set the bowl on the red-checked table cloth and returned to the back door.

"Here you go, honey," Shelly smiled handing him a pitcher of rum fruit punch and two tall glasses. She didn't seem at all preoccupied with the subject of Rainbow, but she had been over at the Armstrong mansion yesterday. He had to find out what she knew about Rainbow and where she heard it.

"Yeah, I've run into the guy once or twice a long time ago," Pharoah said, pouring himself a drink. He had to seem casual. "Why?" He closed his eyes slowly, waiting for an answer.

"Oh, no reason really. Can I get one of those?" she said indicating his glass of punch. He poured her a glass. "You know Geneva?"

"Yeah. She models with you, right?" Pharoah said. He watched a butterfly dart across the yard and waited. He felt like striking her, she was so oblivious. He took a deep breath and reminded himself that she should always be ignorant of the kind of information he carried around inside his head.

"She's dating the man."

"I figured she had better taste," Pharoah replied with a forced laugh. He let his nervous system relax a tiny bit. Perhaps Rainbow was following the plan, after all.

"Well, apparently the guy struck it rich. You should see the diamond necklace that he bought her," Shelly laughed lightly and continued talking. Pharoah didn't hear much of the rest. A wave of total panic passed through him. Rainbow had blown it. The stupid nigger couldn't wait a year. Pharoah caught the words Marina Del Rey and excused himself to make a phone call.

The call had two purposes. The first and most important, to locate Rainbow. The second was to arrange to receive a phone call in ten minutes that would call him away on business. He had to talk some sense to Rainbow or they could all end up dead.

Pharoah returned to the yard and put the chicken on the grill to cook. It seemed like hours before the phone call came. He tried to make small talk and led the conversation onto less explosive topics. When the phone finally rang, he let Shelly answer it.

Shelly walked out to the picnic table and told Pharoah that it was Mr. Lenox. Some business. Pharoah made his how-can-anyone-disturb-us face and went inside. He momentarily returned with the news that a very important deal was happening and he had to be there.

"I shouldn't be more than a few hours," Pharoah said, giving Shelly a kiss.

"I'll miss you," she called after him, alone with her barbeque.

Pharoah tore off in the Eldorado, to an address he had written on a scrap of paper. He was doing close to eighty miles an hour when the Marina exit came into view. Crossing three lanes of traffic, he shot down the exit ramp and squealed around the corner toward the Compton Towers.

He ran two red lights and screeched to a stop in front of the luxury high-rise's lobby. Pushing the parking valet aside, he ran to the elevators. God, the fucking penthouse, Pharoah thought. He was much more angry than afraid.

He banged on the penthouse door. No answer. He rushed back to the elevator. Maybe the girl at the desk would have an idea.

"I think he's on his boat, sir," the girl answered brightly.

"Where?" Pharoah shouted, frightening the poor girl.

"The yacht marina, sir. I don't know what slip he's in," the girl answered. She searched his face to determine whether she should summon security. Pharoah turned and ran out of the lobby doors. The parking attendant held out his hand, determined to get a tip one way or another. He was nearly knocked flat as Pharoah brushed him aside and got into his car. Pharoah had roared away before the attendant had time to curse him.

The Eldorado raced through the narrow streets of Venice to the large marina parking lot. Pharoah squeezed into a parking place at the back, overlooking the boats. The yachts of the rich rocked gently in their slips. Pharoah scanned the rows of large pleasure cruisers. Rainbow would have gotten one of those, he thought. A sailboat would have been too much work.

Pharoah got out of the car and walked down the gangway to the first row of boats. He walked halfway out along the dock and turned back. Nothing there. He walked to the next row and spotted something at the end. Flying above the cabins was a flag. It was the colors of the rainbow. That had to be it.

Pharoah ran down toward the far end of the dock and stopped near the cabin cruiser with the rainbow flag over it. He stayed out of sight behind the boat next to it. He didn't want to be seen with Rainbow by Geneva or any or the other models who worked for Marcellus. Moving to the edge of the cruiser he saw Rainbow sitting at a table. Rainbow was sipping a beer as if he were King Tut. Pharoah waited several minutes, until he was sure that Rainbow was alone.

Rainbow looked up, squinting into the sun at the tall figure standing on the deck of his boat.

"Hey, man. Welcome aboard the good ship Rainbow," he said laughing. Pharoah just stared at him, too angry to speak. Rainbow held up a beer for Pharoah. Pharoah smacked the bottle out of his hand, sending it crashing on the deck.

"You dumb shit," Pharoah hissed, shaking his head.

"What you mean, man? Calm down. You gotta relax more, Pharoah," Rainbow offered nervously, gesturing at the tranquil surroundings.

"I mean this is crazy, man!! We just hit the dude little over two months ago and already you're living like a king," Pharoah said disgustedly.

"Yeah, I feel like one too," Rainbow smiled, patting his stomach. Pharoah began to pace the deck in front of Rainbow.

"Where is your brain, Rainbow? Don't you know this is how they catch niggers like us? Just waiting till we start to spend big?" Pharoah shouted, slamming his fist down on the table. Rainbow suddenly looked worried and leaned forward.

"Thought you said there wasn't gonna be no cops?" Rainbow asked like a child. Pharoah was so angry and frustrated that he picked up a chair to smash it over his partner's head. He thought better of it and set it down gently in its place on deck. His gaze met Rainbow's.

"You still got to use common sense! Hell, Marcellus' probably got every one of his goons in the street, trying to get a lead on us," Pharoah shouted, sweat rolling down his forehead. Pulling a handkerchief from his back pocket, he wiped his face and tried to collect his thoughts. He knew he had to get through to Rainbow.

"Yeah, but we got away clean, didn't we?" Rainbow chuckled. His laugh grew into a drunk cackle.

"It ain't no laughing matter, Rainbow. You got to get rid of all this stuff, quick, fast and in a hurry. You won't enjoy this stuff dead," Pharoah yelled hoarsely.

"Bullshit," Rainbow cried, the king-pin insulted. "I ain't getting rid of a goddamn thing! I earned the right to have it and I intend to enjoy it. If that nigger Marcellus comes anywhere near me I'm gonna kick his ass," Rainbow shouted bravely. He started laughing uncontrollably. By the time he had recovered from his laughter Pharoah had already gone.

Pharoah slammed his hands on the steering wheel of his Eldorado. He had to come up with a plan that might protect him from Marcellus. That dealer was smart. It was why he was one of the biggest in the country. Rainbow had gone soft in the head and hung a bullseye around his neck. Pharoah considered the results of killing Rainbow and decided that it was too late. The word would be all over town. It didn't matter how careful you were. Someone always saw something and it would be enough to lead Marcellus back to him. No, murder was out of the question. Pharoah wondered how much

Marcellus and his cronies had found out. They couldn't have missed the clues that the voluptuous Geneva was dropping.

Pharoah started the car and drove out into the traffic that cruised along the little street by the marina. He would tap the grapevine himself and see what he could find out, see what others had found out. The information would help him formulate his next move. There had to be some place in Marcellus' empire that was a weak link.

Pharoah knew full well that since the robbery, an assassin wouldn't be able to get close to Marcellus. He had to think of another way to eliminate him as a threat. Information. It was a life and death power in the city, the slyest weapon of all.

12

The sparkling black limousine belonging to Marcellus Armstrong moved gracefully through the Beverly Hills business district. Marcellus was seated in the back, Juggler next to him and Maceo sat facing them. Maceo was flipping the pages of a small notebook he held in his hand. He stopped and looked up at Marcellus. Marcellus nodded for him to start.

"As far as we could determine, he has no bank accounts, at least none in his name," Maceo said. He cleared his thick throat and turned the page. "The guy's a small time pimp with three or four girls in his stable. Blows all his bread on toot and pot. No dealing in hard drugs and no rap sheet to speak of." Maceo could have been reading a grocery list he was so cool. Marcellus pushed his sunglasses back on his nose and listened for the rest of the report.

"He did eighteen months in the pen a few years back for a small jewelry job. Been clean ever since. He's strictly into cunt money now, small potatoes all the way," Juggler added, playing with the steel balls.

"At least he was," Maceo said looking at Juggler and Marcellus.

"Meaning?" asked Marcellus, brushing a piece of lint from his tailored sportscoat. He was anxious to get to the bottom of the Rainbow biography so he could make a judgement. Maceo turned another page over.

"He's lived pretty much hand to mouth all his life. Never owned anything and owed just about everybody. Then about two and a half months ago he suddenly cashed in his chips, sold the stable and paid everyone off with interest," Maceo finished the page.

The limousine was speeding through Westwood now toward the beach. At every stoplight, pedestrians and other motorists tried to see through the tinted glass into the back seat. Most assumed it was another Arab on the way to his mansion.

Marcellus lit a cigarette and exhaled the smoke slowly. He leaned forward and pushed the button for the driver intercom that was attached to the side of the bar.

"Hector, you can stop at our destination right in front. We won't be there long," Marcellus said into the microphone.

"Yes, sir. We're only a block away," Hector answered turning slightly in his seat to acknowledge Marcellus' order.

"Gentlemen, this will have to wait a minute. A delivery has to be made up here." Marcellus smiled and pointed to the large granite building that sat on Wilshire Boulevard.

The limousine pulled up directly in front of the building's glass doors. The brass plaque to the right of the door read Holden Land Corporation. It was one of the most successful land development enterprises in the West, and its owner and founder Phillip J. Holden had a coke habit that would tax the trunk of a bull elephant. He'd already had to have an operation on his nose.

The delicate tissue in the nose called the septum can only take so much cocaine. It had begun to disintegrate six months earlier. Phillip J. Holden's nose had started to gradually collapse. A very expensive plastic surgeon had constructed a new septum out of some space age plastic and made Holden promise to lay off the coke. Permanently. It was a promise that was impossible to keep.

Juggler opened his door and stepped out onto the busy sidewalk. Marcellus gracefully slid across the seat and stepped out into the sun beside Juggler. He reached inside as Maceo handed him his briefcase.

"Maceo, you can stay here. This won't take long," Marcellus said.

"All right, boss," Maceo answered, trying to casually resume his seat by the bar. Maceo watched Marcellus and Juggler push through the doors and shook his head. He still felt like he was on the outside of Marcellus' operation. Juggler got to go everywhere with Marcellus. Maceo rapped his fingers on the bar and then pulled out his note pad again. If this Rainbow dude was the right one, he thought as he thumbed through the notes, he could perhaps be allowed into the inner circle with Juggler.

Marcellus and Juggler nodded to the security man sitting at the desk in front of the elevator banks. The guard recognized Marcellus immediately

"Nice to see you, Mr. Armstrong," the guard said with a grin.

"Nice to see you, old buddy," Marcellus said warmly. "They treating you all right around here?" The guard basked in the attention of this important man.

"They can't dish out anything I can't deal with," the guard said, puffing out his chest.

"Glad to hear it. Glad to hear it," Marcellus nodded and stepped into the elevator, which had opened behind him.

Marcellus watched the numbers blink toward the top floor on the gold panel. The elevator slowed and stopped on the sixteenth floor. The gold doors slid aside and Marcellus and Juggler stepped into the cavernous reception area of the Holden Land Corporation. A single receptionist sat in the vast expanse of grey carpet. There was only a telephone on her desk. No typewriter, no paperwork.

"Good day, Mr. Armstrong. Mr. Holden is expecting you," the receptionist smiled with some strain. She was an attractive woman, just over forty, but she had an inkling of the kind of business that Mr. Holden and Mr. Armstrong transacted. She really didn't approve.

"Thank you," Marcellus said, watching her rise from her desk to lead him back to Holden's lair.

The entire reception room resembled the lobby area of a large hotel. Groups of chairs and sofas were clustered around low tables across the room. Marcellus stood at the tall doors that led into the office and motioned for Juggler to wait outside, by the door. The receptionist rapped softly and led Marcellus in.

"By God, good to see you, Marcellus," cried out the

ruddy faced young man behind the desk. Phillip leapt out of his chair and bounded to shake Marcellus' hand.

"Good to see you, Phillip," Marcellus grinned. "It's been a while, hasn't it?" Phillip waved him over to a group of comfortable chairs.

"You may go, thank you, Miss Ekhart," Phillip said. "I don't think she likes to see us get together," he laughed, nudging Marcellus in the ribs. Marcellus waited till she had closed the door behind her and then set his briefcase on the coffee table. Phillip rubbed his hands together and looked at the briefcase hungrily.

"I thought I had lost you, Phillip," Marcellus said, spinning the tumblers of the combination locks.

"Only for a while, compadre. You know how it is," Phillip laughed tensely and tapped his nose, "The scars are almost invisible now." Marcellus clicked open the locks and drew the case open. He nodded to Phillip.

"Silly Doctor wants me to give up this stuff," Phillip sighed. "I just told him to give me an industrial strength nose. The standard equipment isn't that good," Phillip laughed. "Say do you want something to drink?" Phillip was most anxious to please Marcellus. He was the best connection in the West. It had taken a bigger screening process to get to Marcellus than it had to get into Harvard.

"No, thank you, Phillip. You like to try a bit of this?" Marcellus offered him a small silver tray and silver tooter. There were several small lines of coke cut on the silver.

"Don't mind if I do," Phillip chuckled and took the kit from Marcellus. He snorted all lines in a flash and brought his head back up, brushing his red hair off his forehead.

"Wow! That's great, Marcellus," Phillip cried.

131

"How much can you spare?"

"Well, not a whole lot to tell you the truth. This batch is very high quality. All this is spoken for I'm afraid," Marcellus gestured to the stacks of plastic wrapped coke in his case.

"I can certainly understand that. Can you spare ten bill's worth? I'd really appreciate it," Phillip tried.

"I think I can for a good client," Marcellus smiled. Phillip smiled in relief and rose to go to his desk. While Marcellus pulled out a bag and relocked his case, Phillip came back to the sofa with an envelope. There were ten one thousand dollar bills inside. Marcellus didn't have to count it. He knew that his clients wouldn't risk offending him and losing their supply. Besides it was a matter of great pride to these people to be able to spend fantastic sums of cash on cocaine. To prove to themselves how rich they really were.

"Thank you, Marcellus," Phillip said earnestly as Marcellus handed him the small bag.

"Anytime, Phillip, Anytime. Hope you can make my next party," Marcellus said, walking to the door. Phillip's eyes lit up. He hadn't been invited to one of Marcellus' great parties until now. He felt like a kid on graduation day.

"I'd love to," Phillip answered, opening the door for Marcellus.

Marcellus stepped back out into the reception room and winked at Juggler. Juggler sprang up from his chair and followed Marcellus out. All the way down to the car Marcellus considered how strung out his better clients were. They couldn't stay off the stuff unless they were absolutely broke. Enough of them had quit that way. First the wife and kids bailed out, after the wife discovered that some jewelry had been sold and the Rolls

Royce traded for cocaine. Eventually the house would have to be sold, and, finally they would lose their companies and jobs. Fortuanately, there was always someone who had just made a fortune begging to become one of Marcellus' clients. Begging to be chic.

Juggler followed Marcellus into the limousine and sat down next to him on the seat.

"Gateway Recording, Hector," Marcellus spoke into the intercom. The limousine glided away from the Holden Land Corporation and headed east on Wilshire Boulevard. Maceo sat impatiently for Marcellus to ask him for the rest of the run down on Rainbow.

Marcellus was preoccupied for a moment with his next delivery. The buyer was a prominent rock star of the sixties. The musician, who had brought joy to millions of people, was trying to make a comeback album. He was too strung out to even attempt it without cocaine. The manager had called Marcellus in the middle of the night begging for him to come over to the studio with some coke. The star was on the floor of the sound booth, weeping uncontrollably, unable to finish a brilliant track. Marcellus had sent a few grams over with Juggler and was himself to deliver the bulk of the order today.

Marcellus doubted that the album would ever get finished. The manager had sold some of his own cars to buy studio time and coke, but it wouldn't be enough. There could never be enough time or coke. This one time star was a perpetual nervous wreck from drugs. He'd either have a complete nervous breakdown or die from an overdose. There were too many loyal friends around to protect him from an overdose, so he'd probably end up in a padded cell somewhere.

Marcellus took out a cigarette and watched the traffic

as the limousine turned up Doheny Drive. His attention was drawn back to the present by Maceo's flipping through his notebook again.

"All right, Maceo. What else have you got?" Marcellus asked.

"This Rainbow paid three hundred thousand for a condominium with cash," Maceo stated and looked up from his notes.

"In small bills," Juggler added, emphatically.

"He took the money to the real estate office in a large suitcase. It took 'em all day to count it," Maceo continued. He didn't want to be upstaged by Juggler and flipped to another page, hoping to locate his other notes before Juggler could jump in again.

"He also spent fifty thousand on a small cabin cruiser and another twelve five on a Fleetwood. He paid for them right out of his suitcase," Maceo announced proudly.

"He's been flashing cash all over the place," Juggler added. "Nightclubs, jewelry stores, you name it." Maceo nodded agreement and closed his note pad.

"Of course we got no proof it's your money," Maceo said. Marcellus looked out the window and became thoughtful.

"It's mine," he spoke quietly.

Marcellus rubbed his temples as the flush of anger reached his head, making it ache. He had been doing well, holding the rage in check, but he couldn't this time. Some stupid nigger named Rainbow was going to have to answer some questions and maybe forfeit his life.

13

Fisheye stood in the middle of the pasta aisle in Ralph's Supermarket on Sunset Boulevard. He was scratching his head and looking from the crumpled shopping list he held in his other hand to the shelves of spaghetti, macaroni, manicotti and twenty other varieties. His wife, Betsy, had only specified pasta, he hadn't the vaguest idea which one. He shrugged and picked up the box of spaghetti as thick as pencils and threw it into the cart. Walking down the aisle, he promised himself that the next time their second car was in the shop he'd just give her cab fare and write it off as an informer bribe. He couldn't remember exactly how Betsy had roped him into buying the groceries on his lunch hour, but it was too late to worry about that. He was almost finished and a good thing too. Apparently supermarkets had become very paranoid since he'd last been in one. Some fool security guard that had been following him, casually peeked at him from around corners on every aisle. Maybe it was time to retire the blue suit after all.

Fisheye pushed the cart to the end of the aisle and sure enough, there was the guard. He was pretending to study a stack of taco shells now.

"Excuse me," Fisheye said making the guard jump. "I can see how busy you are, but I thought you might want to see this," Fisheye smiled, pulling out the badge and shoving it into guard's face. "I'm here if you need me," he whispered. When he put the badge back into his jacket pocket he held the jacket open so the guard could see his .38 cradled in his shoulder holster.

"Thanks, officer," the guard stammered. He still

wasn't really sure if Fisheye was a true cop or a nut case in full costume. Either way he didn't want to mess with him and he walked away to another aisle to examine soup cans.

Fisheye could understand the guard's paranoia. This particular supermarket was locally famous for it's collection of weirdos and loonies. It always looked like a cast party from hell was in progress.

Fisheye placed some beer into his shopping cart and walked to the checkout stand. The girl in line ahead of him was wearing white go-go boots and a black miniskirt. Her outfit was topped off with a black turtle neck sweater and a pixie hair style that was almost white from peroxide. He watched her read a national gossip magazine and felt disgusted. Then he felt something else. She actually had great gams and a terrific ass. He sighed, knowing that the closest he'd probably ever get to that kind of action was busting her on a heroin charge. Her long sleeve sweater was a giveaway. Kids were so crazy now, who could tell. Fisheye repressed the urge to bust her, visions of a strip search dancing in his head. He closed his eye and tried to think of police business. God, that's right. Snitch. He was supposed to meet him at the hamburger stand.

Fisheye made it through the check stand and hurriedly rolled his cart to his police cruiser. He put the groceries in the trunk. No need to upset brother officers by having the back seat filled with shopping bags. He didn't need Gene jumping all over him either.

He checked his watch and calculated that he would only be fifteen minutes late for his one o'clock appointment with Snitch. The little weasel had better come up with something good, he thought. There hadn't been any breaks in the jewelry case for weeks. He shot the car out of the parking lot and headed for Beverly Hills.

Ten minutes later, Fisheye was cruising past the hamburger stand to see if Snitch had showed up. He spotted him, hunched over a burger in a corner of the stand's outdoor table area. Good. Now he just had to find a shady spot to park the car in.

The place he normally used was empty. So it should be, he thought. It was a no parking zone. Executing a perfect U-turn, he guided the car into the spot and parked. He could see parking tickets on the two cars on either side of his. That little jerk that worked for the traffic division certainly was efficient. The guy must stay up all night writing out the tickets in advance for the location so all he has to do is fill in the specific car's license number.

Fisheye walked down the street to the hamburger stand. Seeing that Snitch was still there, he went to get a burger and a soda for himself. He paid for the lunch and went over to where Snitch was fidgeting.

"Howdy, Snitch," Fisheye said, sitting down.

"Don't sit here, man," Snitch answered. "Everybody can see us."

"What's the matter? You don't want your buddies to know what good friends we are?" Fisheye grinned and started to eat his lunch. Snitch's eye's darted around the stand back to Fisheye.

"I guess it's all right," Snitch said finally, his foot tapping rapidly on the pavement.

"I ain't got all day," Fisheye stated impatiently.

"You check out Rainbow yet?" Snitch shot back with a smile. He liked to put Fisheye on the spot whenever he could.

"I'll get around to it. Why?" Fisheye asked. Snitch smiled a little bigger. Fisheye obviously hadn't put anything together about this Rainbow dude yet and it could mean money for him.

"My expenses are just terrible this week," Snitch said, looking away from Fisheye.

"Get a job," Fisheye said flatly. "If you want to stay out of the slammer, you'd better cooperate... *Snitch*." Snitch winced this time when he heard the name. His hatred for this cop that wouldn't play by the rules, wouldn't pay for information, was growing every time he had to deal with him. Other cops paid for tips. Why couldn't this asshole.

"Go ahead, Snitch," Fisheye grumbled, staring at him.

"Sombody else has noticed his extravagance. Been asking a lot of questions around town," Snitch responded hesitantly, crushing his empty soda can in one hand.

"Probably the IRS," Fisheye dismissed the idea with a shrug.

"That's not the word on the street," Snitch continued.

"Oh? Who then?" Fisheye asked with more interest. Snitch hesitated again. He hated giving away this choice information for free. Who ever heard of a stoolie turning in people for nothing. This son of a bitch never got off his back.

"Who, Snitch?" Fisheye asked again, slamming his hand down over Snitch's wrist.

"Ever heard of Marcellus Armstrong?" Snitch asked.

"Concert promoter?" Fisheye chuckled and released his arm. Snitch couldn't believe how dim this old cop was. The badge in this pig's pocket should have his name on it.

"You want to take a ride to the station," Fisheye stated, sensing the other man's reluctance to go on. Snitch sort of collapsed and decided it was best to get this conversation over with.

"The same. Word has it he's dealing cocaine," Snitch said, throwing the crushed soda can into a trash barrel.

"Everybody knows that. We haven't got enough on him! Tell me something I don't know," Fisheye said looking at his watch.

"Well, it seems that Marcellus got ripped off at his pad about two months ago. Three guys supposedly walked with a million in cash. Marcellus seems to think that Rainbow's new-found wealth is his," Snitch stated and watched a smile form on this old pig's face.

"Cocaine money? Well I'll be goddamned," Fisheye chuckled. "Who were the other two?"

"Don't know. Don't nobody know," Snitch answered, anxious to leave.

"Find out for me and I'll treat you to dinner at the Playboy Club," Fisheye offered, still smiling.

"Can I bring a date?" Snitch asked as he rose to leave.

"Who would go out with you, Snitch?" Fisheye laughed. Snitch turned back toward the table with a smile of his own.

"Your mama."

14

The funky music throbbed through the Marina Club's private disco, high above the marina docks. It was a haven for the super-rich from all over the globe. Oil sheiks, in custom tailored suits from London, danced with beautiful women in designer clothes from Paris. Texas oil barons mixed with industrialists from all over the United States. The dance floor, under the bright strobe lights, was jammed with wildly gyrating couples. The Marina Club had truly become the new playground for the rich, their playmates, and their children.

The lights on the docks far below, sparkled in the night air. Huge yachts and motor cruisers looked like toy boats, as they bobbed in their berths. If Heaven had a price tag and your credit was good, this was the place.

One of the pretty young waitresses squeezed past some young gentlemen sitting at the bar and picked up her order of drinks. The young man nearest her tried to flirt, but she had ignored him. She had a table that good tips had been flowing from all night. At the rate she was accumulating cash, she'd have gotten over two hundred dollars by the time the night was over. Holding her drink tray aloft, she maneuvered between the dancing couples on the edge of the dance floor. Blocked by some elegantly clad gentlemen who were deep in a shouted conversation, she deftly elbowed one in the ribs. He moved swiftly, still unaware of her existence, to avoid the sharp pain. Moving around some couples, she at last reached the party that was so generous.

Rainbow sat, like a happy king, in the center of the booth, surrounded by several attractive women, including Geneva. The waitress set the drinks down, returning this generous man's smile, and placed new coasters under each of the drinks. She picked up another twenty from the center of the table, performed a small curtsey and moved back into the milling crowd at the side of the dance floor. Rainbow raised his glass and the others followed suit.

"Cheers, ladies." They all touched glasses and drank.

"You sure know how to treat a woman," Geneva said, taking Rainbow's arm and snuggling up close.

Rainbow chuckled and turned to her, his hand sliding between Geneva's legs. She opened her legs slightly and tilted her hips up to meet his probing fingers. Rainbow leaned to her face and they kissed hotly.

"It's all in the touch, baby. It's all in the touch," Rainbow spoke into her ear, still playing with her.

"It sure is," Geneva answered, squeezing her thighs around his hand. The two other girls exchanged a knowing glance and laughed.

Rainbow sat back, his head rocking with the beat of the music and looked at Geneva. She sure was something out of a fantasy. Much better than most of the tired hookers he'd had before, he mused. Geneva had class, being an international model. There was justice in the world after all. After a poor life of running whores and being small time, he'd struck it rich off Marcellus Armstrong. He'd not only copped a million bucks, but stolen one of his women as well. Rainbow felt like the big shot he had always dreamed of being. He was rich and had more women than he could bang in a lifetime.

The music blaring out of the speakers had been mixed into a new tune and the dance floor was shifting gears. Geneva took a drink from her glass and looked at Rainbow.

"Let's dance, Rainbow," she said, stroking his thigh. The two girls sitting with them had been asked to dance by some promising young men and rose to go to the dance floor.

"The next one, okay?" Rainbow answered. Geneva just smiled and put her head on his shoulder. She watched the couples on the floor and gave Rainbow a playful squeeze. She was having a great time with this guy, however long it lasted, she thought. These things never went on forever. She had reconciled herself to that. The guys always went broke, or back to their wives, or she found someone she liked better. God, it was fun while it was happening. Rainbow had bought her the diamond necklace she was wearing as well as the tight silk dress with the plunging neckline. She always made out okay in the end, truly enriched by each relationship. This nigger was one long good time, she thought. Geneva even got a kick out of his wild clothes. He really was a damn Rainbow.

On the far side of the club two rather serious men entered. Maceo and Juggler. The steel balls seemed to keep time with the funky music as they spun in Juggler's hands. They both scanned the room until Maceo spotted Rainbow and Geneva sitting in a booth. Maceo pointed them out to Juggler and they started to make their way to the table. Maceo went ahead like a coast guard ice breaker, people jostled aside in all directions. Juggler followed, saying 'excuse me' to the more ruffled patrons. Nobody was actually interested in testing their manhood against these two and they gratefully accepted Juggler's token apology. One young man, too drunk to realize what he was doing, threw a punch at Maceo. Maceo caught the man's fist and quickly pulled it down with a twisting motion. The young fool staggered away into the packed dance floor, his cry of pain buried by the loud music.

Geneva spotted them as they neared the table and waved them over, smiling. Rainbow was occupied with watching a pair of very young girls dancing together and didn't noice their approach until they were standing at the table. Juggler was blocking the view. The steel balls seemed oddly familiar.

"Juggler, Maceo, I want you to meet a friend of mine. This is Rainbow," she said, grinning. Rainbow looked up as he shook the outstretched hands. He searched their faces for some clue. Why should he know them? Suddenly the image of Juggler and Maceo tied up on the floor at Marcellus' mansion exploded before his mind's eye. This was impossible. Rainbow took a long drink from his glass and tried to compose himself. He was no Shaft. He couldn't kill these two and stroll off into the sunset with his arm coiled about Geneva's waist. Quelling his fear, he tried to tell himself that this meeting was an accident. They couldn't know. Rainbow saw Juggler's sadistic smile as he stood, towering over him.

"Any friend of Geneva's is a friend of mine," Rainbow spoke, trying to sound casual, but his throat tight and dry. He took another big gulp of his drink.

"What are you drinking?" Rainbow asked the men. They were just staring at him, like hungry panthers.

"Thanks, but I'm on the wagon," Juggler answered, the evil smile still in place.

"Same here," Maceo added. "Nice club."

"First time here?" Rainbow asked, his mind reeling with images of the robbery. He took a deep breath to calm himself. He considered lighting a cigarette, but could feel his hands shaking. He kept them in front of him.

"Yeah, it's our first time. Lotta pretty girls," Juggler said, the disinterest obvious in his voice.

"Well of course," Geneva burst out. "How do you think I met Rainbow, Juggler?" she laughed. Juggler smiled with a barely disguised cruelty at Rainbow. His eyes burning with fury. Rainbow could not hold the stare and dropped his eyes to his hands that were now locked around his glass.

"Rainbow certainly has good taste," Juggler said. Rainbow looked at him and lifted his glass.

"I'll drink to that," Rainbow said, finishing the

drink with one swallow. He wasn't about to make it through this without another one so he motioned for the waitress to come over.

The waitress, hoping for another twenty, quickly left the table she was waiting on and stepped to Rainbow's. Clearing the glasses away, she looked to Juggler and Maceo. Both of the men shook their heads in the negative and returned their gaze to Rainbow's damp face. The waitress shrugged and left to get the new round. Probably wouldn't have meant a larger tip anyhow, she thought.

Juggler and Maceo rose from the table. The steel balls were in motion again.

"Figure we'll circulate a bit," Maceo told Rainbow.

"Lotta action out there. Maybe you'll get lucky tonight," Rainbow said. The relief that he felt when the two started to leave was written all over his face.

"Yeah, maybe," Maceo said, with more meaning than he intended to convey.

"See you around then," Rainbow said, hoping that they would go away forever.

"You can bet on it," Juggler said ominously, before turning to follow Maceo. Rainbow mopped his brow, which by this time was covered with beads of perspiration. He watched Juggler and Maceo disappear into the crowd.

"Where do you know them from?" Rainbow asked Geneva. He was desperately trying to understand what was happening to his perfect life. He had to test her. Geneva laughed.

"Now don't you go getting all jealous! They're not my type. They work for Natasha's boyfriend, Marcellus. She and I talk all the time and they're always in and out of the place," Geneva responded gayly. Rainbow stared hard into her eyes for a moment and then decided that she wasn't part of a set up to nail him.

"Let's dance," Rainbow said. She nodded and he led her onto the dance floor. Rainbow felt safer with all the dancing bodies surrounding him. He desperately wanted to forget that Marcellus' thugs had appeared.

Geneva's voluptuous body, dancing close to his went a long way in helping him out of his depression, but he was still sober enough to realize that he had to do something. He needed time to think.

Rainbow decided to get rid of all the women for a night and do some driving, maybe visit an old friend. He'd figure out what to do later.

Many floors below, at the entrance to the massive complex, Juggler handed a parking ticket to a blue jacketed attendant.

"What do you think?" Maceo asked.

"That voice," Juggler said, remembering. "Even through the mask and shit, I know the voice."

"I didn't pay much attention to it," Maceo shrugged.

"I did," Juggler stated seriously, watching for the Mercedes Benz 600 E to come up from the garage.

"It ain't much to go on," Maceo said doubtfully.

"It's a start," Juggler retorted. The parking attendent screeched up out of the underground garage and stopped the Mercedes in front of Juggler and Maceo. Juggler handed the attendant a five and got into the car. Maceo trotted to the passenger's side and hopped in.

"So what do we do now," Maceo asked as Juggler put the car into gear and drove out of the Marina gates.

"We wait," Juggler said simply. He'd done this many times and knew that patience was generally rewarded. He guided the car into the flow of traffic going north toward Santa Monica. Maceo watched him in silence, not sure he wanted to spend all night waiting for a possible suspect to do something out of the ordinary. Christ, he thought, the real robbers were probably in another state living it up.

"It could be a long night," Maceo said, a little discouraged. Juggler shot a look of distain at Maceo.

"We're getting paid for it," Juggler snarled. Juggler figured that this was a chance to make it up to Marcellus. His efforts would demonstrate his loyalty even if this Rainbow asshole turned out to be innocent. Juggler had the feeling that this nigger was the right one. The voice was right.

Juggler had been with Marcellus when he started in Los Angeles. Marcellus had chosen him to be his lieutenant from hundreds of security men. Juggler had been drifting since Vietnam, unable to pull a civilian life together. He had even worked for a small circus that worked out of Florida. A clown named Eddie had taught him to juggle. After bumming around the country, Juggler ended up in L.A. doing security work for a factory. Marcellus had plucked him out of the wage slave routine and given him a life. Self respect. Juggler felt that he would always owe Marcellus for that. He loved the man. This robbery was the first real trouble that Juggler hadn't been able to take care of in twenty-four hours. Juggler knew that Rainbow could be the key to solving the crime. And revenge.

15

Three hours after Juggler and Maceo had left the Marina Club disco, Rainbow felt safe to leave. Nobody would wait around that long, he figured. He left the waitress another twenty and searched the disco from his table to see if he could spot the other two girls he brought.

"Where are they?" he asked Geneva. She kissed him on the cheek and started giggling. She was very drunk.

"I dunno. Maybe they left," she answered, slurring her speech and bursting out with a laugh.

"Well, I'm gonna take you home, at least," Rainbow said. "C'mon baby, I'll help you up." He slid around the table and reached back for his tipsy date. She got unsteadily to her feet and leaned on his shoulder for support.

The disco was still jammed at this hour, but Rainbow's two other guests saw them when they got up from the table. The two girls caught up with Rainbow and Geneva as the pair neared the exit of the club.

"Figured you two got lucky," Rainbow chuckled. He was practically carrying Geneva now. He nodded to the attendant by the elevators and the man pressed the button for the lobby.

"I'm afraid I got business to do, girls. I'll take you home," Rainbow said smiling. The visit by Juggler and Maceo had completely sobered him. He wanted to be clear headed so he could think.

While the four of them rode down in the elevator, Geneva half asleep on his shoulder and the two other girls talking softly, Rainbow decided that he would call

Pharoah again. He had tried to reach him from a pay phone at the disco, but Pharoah and Shelly hadn't been home. What bad luck, Rainbow cursed to himself.

The elevator door opened on the ground floor and Rainbow managed to get Geneva to walk to the main doors and out to the sidewalk. They looked like the last contestants in a dance marathon. She was draped over him as they waited for the Fleetwood to be brought up from the garage.

He walked around the front of the car and poured her into the passenger's seat. The two girls hopped in back. Propping Geneva up long enough to get into the car, Rainbow inserted the key and started the engine. He was anxious to be rid of the women and sped down the driveway and into the traffic headed for the city.

He didn't notice the Mercedes 600 E that was always a discrete distance behind him from the moment he left the Marina Club driveway, till he had dropped off the last girl. Rainbow was in a hurry and had formulated a plan. It wasn't much, but it was the best he could do. He'd phone Pharoah later.

The Fleetwood turned the corner on the dark residential neighborhood and pulled up in front of his dilapidated old house. He wanted to find out if anyone had been poking around. He had been meaning to rent the house, but never got around to it. He wished he had now, as he walked across the scruffy lawn to the front door. He pulled an old key from his pocket after he discovered the door intact. Good. The place hadn't been vandalized. He made a mental note to try and sell the place soon.

As Rainbow entered the dark house and closed the door behind him, another car moved slowly down the empty street. Juggler had switched off the running lights on the Mercedes after turning the corner and parked it a hundred feet in back of the Fleetwood so it couldn't be seen from the house. After five minutes had passed, Juggler decided that it was allright to make the next move.

"Maceo, get the cardboard box out of the trunk and tin can him. We've done enought tailing for one night," Juggler said with a grim smile. Maceo jumped out of the car and went to the trunk to retrieve the box full of empty tin cans with long strings tied to each. While Maceo trotted off to set it up, Juggler watched and drummed his fingers on the dashboard. This mother fucker was trapped, he thought.

Maceo set the box down by the Fleetwood's rear bumper and rapidly began to tie the strings to it. When the six strings were attached, he played out several feet and set the carton on the curb beside the right fender. It would appear to be someone's rubbish and Rainbow would figure that he just hadn't noticed it, if he saw it at all. The trap was set as Maceo withdrew into the deep shadows nearby and pulled out his .357 Magnum.

Inside the rundown house, Rainbow was checking the second floor. The first floor, he had happily decided was clean. Nobody had broken in to do a little detective work. He felt much better about the whole thing. Maybe that pair of Marcellus' goons had really been at the club by chance.

The upstairs rooms were just as he had left them. A mess, but a mess that he knew. Anyone poking through the junk in the bedrooms would rearrange the junk, while looking. Rainbow looked at one of the stained mattresses and felt a bit nostalgic. A lot of pussy had worked in these beds. He almost missed the never ending hassles of running a bunch of whores on the street.

Perhaps he would open a classy cat house, he thought to himself. Of course, he was retired now, but a man needed hobbies. Why not a profitable one that had all those fringe benefits.

Rainbow found himself in a much better mood than he had been in for hours. If Marcellus actually had something on him, this house would have been ransacked. It wasn't, so he was safe. He'd call Pharoah later and tell him what a chickenassed son of a bitch he was. Worrying himself to death over nothing. The robbery had been pulled off perfectly. Shit, Marcellus would never find out who ripped him off, Rainbow smiled to himself.

Rainbow flicked off the lights upstairs and descended the creaking stairs to the front door. Taking one last look around he stepped out onto the porch and locked the door behind him. Time to go home and enjoy those new silk sheets he'd had Geneva pick out for him.

He crossed the yard, passing within three feet of Maceo, and got into his new Fleetwood. Rainbow sniffed the air in the car. Perfume, liqour and leather upolstery. Smelled like rich success, Rainbow thought. He revved the engine and started to pull away, but heard something that sounded like his muffler had dropped and quickly applied the brakes.

"Shit, a brand new goddamn car," Rainbow muttered, getting out of the car and walking to the back. He saw the box and the tin cans tied to the bumper.

"Damn punks," he said angrily and bent to rip the strings. He had snapped all the strings but one, when he felt the cold steel barrel of Maceo's .357 press into his temple. Rainbow simply froze and slowly looked up at Maceo.

"You," Rainbow choked out. Maceo motioned for him to snap the last string and stand up.

150

"Get in the car, please," Maceo said softly. He didn't want Rainbow to panic, here in the middle of a residential street. Rainbow was both relieved and puzzled by Maceo's polite tone, as he walked around the car.

"What's with the hardware?" he asked, trying to sound unafraid.

"Don't make me use it," Maceo answered quietly, waving to the driver's door of the Fleetwood. Rainbow searched Maceo's face for a clue to his intentions, but found nothing. Maceo's expression was poker faced. There was no anger, but also no casualness about him. He was definitely serious. Rainbow turned to the car door and opened it.

Maceo moved past him and slid across the seat first, his gun always trained on his target. Rainbow briefly considered running, but knew Maceo would gun him down before he took two steps. Rainbow climbed into the car and shut the door.

"What the hell's this all about?" Rainbow asked. It didn't seem like Maceo was bent on violence so Rainbow decided to try a little righteous indignation. The put upon innocent. Maceo just stared at him for a moment.

"You ask too many questions. Drive to your place," Maceo ordered. He checked the rear view mirror as Juggler turned on the Mercedes' headlights and pulled up directly in back of Rainbow's car. Rainbow put the car into gear and eased the Fleetwood into the road. No need to antagonize them, he thought.

"I think you're making a mistake," Rainbow said, glancing from the road ahead to Maceo's face.

"If so, I'll apologize," Maceo stated calmly.

"That's reassuring!" Rainbow smiled slightly and felt more confident that he wasn't going to end up dead in the trunk of his own car. "Are you the heat?"

"Curiosity killed the cat," Maceo answered. He was geting impatient with all of Rainbow's chatter and hoped he shut up after this thinly veiled warning.

"But, I don't . . ."

"Shut up and drive," Maceo ordered. "We know where you live, so don't try anything."

"O.K., O.K, I just . . ." Maceo jabbed the .357 into Rainbow's ribs, causing him to grunt from the pain. The drive to the condominium was silent the rest of the way.

Rainbow was very frightened and sweating again, as he had in the club. He wished that he had called Pharoah before going to the house. Pharoah would know how to get him out of this jam. Maceo had bruised his ribs with the gun's barrel and there was a dull ache in his right side, throbbing.

The 600 E was never more than fifty feet behind all the way to the Marina exit. Juggler followed the Fleetwood down the off-ramp, his hands flexing and relaxing on the steering wheel. The strange smile that had been on his lips at the Marina Club disco, was in place again. The green light from the dashboard made him look ghoulish, like one of Satan's own flesh eaters.

The Fleetwood slowed in front of the towering condominiums and drove down into the subterranean garage. Juggler followed and parked in the space next to Rainbow's. He quickly stepped out of the Mercedes and the steel balls were instantly in motion. He joined Maceo and a terrified Rainbow by the Cadillac.

The two men and their prisoner walked to the elevator. Juggler pushed the button for the penthouse suites and the doors opened. The glass enclosed elevator quickly rose above the garage and lobby levels, giving the occupants a view of the city lights spread out below.

Rainbow was determined to act cool, so he lit a cigarette and took a slow puff.

"You really got a thing for them balls, don't you?" Rainbow said, looking at Juggler. Juggler's face didn't register anything. He kept staring at Rainbow with his evil smile, silent. Rainbow felt an involuntary shudder race up his spine and looked away.

The elevator reached the top floor and Rainbow was hustled to his door to open it. He fumbled with the keys, found the correct one, and let them in. His mind was racing for a way to escape, but there was none. This condo had no private service entrance and the fire escape, since this was the top floor, was a stairway in the hall, leading to the roof. No, he had to think of a real good story. Juggler nodded for Rainbow to sit on the couch and took a seat at the bar.

"You live pretty well," Juggler said, his eyes not moving from Rainbow's.

"I manage," Rainbow answered. "What can I do for you?" he asked, watching Maceo wander in and out of rooms off the living room.

"Suppose you tell us just how you manage," Juggler continued, his voice threatening. Rainbow looked around the room nervously and shrugged.

"Got lucky at the track, Vegas, a little poker here and there," Rainbow answered. It was the best he could do. He hoped it would be good enough. He saw Juggler slowly close his eyes and inhale deeply.

"Stealing," Juggler stated with assurance.

"Stealing? Stealing what?" Rainbow asked. He would play dumb, lying was too complicated.

"Money that don't belong to you!" Juggler retorted, his voice getting louder.

"I don't follow."

"I think you do," Juggler smiled as Maceo returned to the living room.

"Nice pad you got. What did it set you back?" Maceo asked, standing over Rainbow.

"A lot," Rainbow answered quietly.

"About three hundred grand?" Juggler asked with a sneer.

"I got lucky. I told you," Rainbow was almost whining. This wasn't going well and he knew it. He stared at the floor and noticed something. His telephone was under the table, out of the sight of the inquisitors. Maybe he would be able to reach Pharoah still. He slipped off his right shoe with his left and asked if he could have a cigarette to cover the sound of him knocking the receiver onto the floor.

"Sure," Maceo answered. "You told us you got lucky already." Rainbow pressed the number seven and prayed that it was the correct speed-dialing code. Maceo paced in front of the low table impatiently.

Across town, in an affluent neighborhood, a phone rang. Pharoah, still up and watching an old western on the television, wondered who could be calling at such a late hour. He reached over and pressed the button on his speaker phone.

"Yeah?" Pharoah waited for an answer. None came. Probably some joker playing games, he thought. "Yeah, who is it?" he tried again. He started to push the disconnect button on the side of the speaker box, but out of idle curiostiy turned up the volume instead. This western wasn't that good. Picking up the remote control, he switched off the sound of the television. John Wayne was madly waving two six guns at a group of attacking Indians. It became a pantomime.

Rainbow sat on the couch in his penthouse, looking from Juggler to Maceo and down to the phone. He prayed that Pharoah was home and would do something. Rainbow wasn't sure what Pharoah could do, but he needed help.

Maceo suddenly stopped pacing and, reaching for Rainbow, pulled him by the jacket to his feet. A rough push was all it took for Maceo to propel Rainbow over to Juggler. Juggler had already placed the steel balls in his pocket and was holding his .357 when Rainbow's body landed on him. Juggler squeezed Rainbow's arm tightly and pressed the gun into Rainbow's ear.

"You lying ass motherfucker. You ain't told us shit," Maceo shouted, pointing his pistol at Rainbow's chest. Rainbow winced, expecting him to shoot.

"You ain't got much time left, Rainbow. Better use it wisely!" Juggler hissed into his ear, smiling sadistically. "Now, someone hit Marcellus for a million in cash just about the time you got so lucky!!" Juggler said sarcastically, pressing the Magnum harder. Blood began to trickle from the cut on Rainbow's ear.

"Well, it wasn't me," Rainbow cried out, flinching from the pain in his head.

The speaker phone in Pharoah's living room was working well. Pharoah leaned closer to make out the words exactly and recognize the voice.

"Bullshit, it wasn't! I never forget a voice! Never!" a metallic voice came over the speaker.

"I don't know what you're talking about," said another voice that Pharoah recognized as Rainbow's. Pharoah blinked in concentration trying to picture the faces that went with the other two voices.

"Who else was in on it, Rainbow?" an angry voice shouted. "I want to know his name! Don't nobody stick a shotgun in my mouth and get away with it." Pharoah closed his eyes.

He knew who the voice belonged to now. It was that

bodyguard, Juggler. The image of Juggler kneeling with Pharoah's shotgun rammed into his mouth was vivid.

Pharoah felt sick to his stomach. They knew. He twisted the volume knob to the maximum, and hoped to God Rainbow wouldn't tell them his name. It would mean his death warrant if he did.

Rainbow was still in the grip of Juggler, the ear with the gun pressed to it bled down his neck onto his bright yellow sport coat. Maceo took a step toward Rainbow and hit him hard in the stomach. Rainbow grunted and Juggler let him fall to the floor.

Maceo looked at Juggler. Neither one of them was sure if they had the right man. Maybe the stupid nigger really did get lucky. He and Juggler had given him quite a scare, thought Maceo. The creep obviously had no guts. He should have tried to implicate someone else by now. Maceo idly looked about the room while considering the situation. Rainbow was doubled up on the floor with Juggler's foot planted firmly on his back.

Maceo noticed something across the room and walked over to a bookcase. The shelf that had caught his attention was filled with cheap pottery sculpture. Black ceramic panthers stalked through tall plaster grass and glass girls in hula skirts were in frozen postures of the dance. It wasn't all this junk that interested Maceo, it was a fine figurine of a woman. It belonged to Marcellus.

Maceo placed his .357 back into his holster and picked up the small statue. He looked at it for a moment and walked back over to Rainbow's prostrate form. Juggler nodded with a smile. They had one.

Maceo quickly reached down with one hand and pulled Rainbow up to his knees. He shoved the figurine at Rainbow's face.

"You lying son of a bitch!" Juggler yelled. "This is

one of a kind. Where'd you get it?" Juggler asked rhetorically. Shock was in Rainbow's eyes as he tried to think of an answer that would save him.

"Huh? Oh, that. Well, uh, some guy sold that to me. He said it came from ..." Rainbow stammered, twisting his head at an ugly angle to answer Juggler. Maceo interrupted the answer by snapping Rainbow's head down by the hair and smashing his knee upward into his face. Maceo pulled his head back up. Blood was streaming from the corners of Rainbow's mouth and his nose.

"Bullshit! Bullshit! You ripped this off from Marcellus the same night you hit the safe, didn't you," Maceo shouted.

"I'm telling you I had nothing to do with anything," Rainbow mumbled, a loose tooth falling from his lips. His breathing was hard and rattled with all the blood in his nose and throat.

"You lying motherfucker," Juggler boomed, standing up. Rainbow was on all fours, just shaking his head to the negative.

Rainbow hurt too much to think beyond simple denial. The front of his face felt like it had collided with a baseball bat. He was still dizzy from the impact on his skull. The rug seemed to roll like an ocean, far below.

Juggler cocked a powerful leg and kicked Rainbow in the ribs. Rainbow groaned as the air was knocked out of him and he landed on the coffee table. Slowly Rainbow tried to get off his back, falling to the floor again in the effort. Juggler rushed over to him, a big smile on his face, and stood him up. Before Rainbow could collapse to the floor again, Juggler whipped his fist into his jaw with a loud crack. Rainbow spun into an end table, smashing a lamp. His jaw broken, Rainbow could only groan like a wounded animal.

On the street below the condominium, an unmarked

police car cruised by. Passing the building it stopped, backed up, and slowly drove into the underground garage. The car parked along side the Mercedes 600 E and a scruffy man in an old blue suit got out. Fisheye had a piece of paper in his hand and he checked it before pushing the elevator button. He was going to check that fool Snitch's tip for himself. Maybe the stoolie would shut up about this Rainbow character then.

The elevator arrived and Fisheye stepped inside and pushed the button marked Penthouse. Fisheye shook his head ruefully. How many times had they tried to build a case against Armstrong? There was never enough concrete evidence.

Maceo grabbed Rainbow's arm and stood him up, twisting it and forcing it up to the braking point behind his back. Rainbow screamed as he felt the bone give way and snap. Maceo heard the dull popping sound and started on the other arm. Rainbow shrieked again.

"Who was your partner, Rainbow," Juggler shouted, "who's got the other half?" Rainbow lifted his head slowly.

"I told you. I don't know what you're talking about," Rainbow mumbled through a broken jaw filled with blood and loosened teeth. The words weren't clear, but Juggler understood the tone of Rainbow's garbled answer.

Juggler smiled wide and took out his huge .357 pistol. He put on the safety and turned it around so he could grip it like a ripping hammer. Rainbow shrieked and screamed as Juggler battered his face and skull. The butt of the heavy gun sliced deep and crushed the bone it met. Rainbow could no longer scream. All his energy was spent. His face had become a Halloween fright mask painted in blood. His nose flattened over a cheek bone, his eyes swollen shut. The fatty tissue of what used to be an eye brow dangled precariously by a thread of skin.

Downstairs in the lobby, Fisheye was headed back to the elevator after a brief interview with the night manager. The night manager had been doubling as a security guard that night and had run into Fisheye in the elevator. Fisheye had definitely looked like a suspicious character and the night manager had told him to come with him to the office or he'd call the cops. It took a phone call to the station house to convince the man that the bum standing in front of him was, in fact, a detective. Fisheye had heard the laughter on the other end of the phone after the night manager described him. He'd settle that officer's hash later.

Fisheye got back into the elevator and continued on his way to the penthouse as he'd originally planned. He lit a cigarette and leaned against the railing by the window. The view was spectacular, he mused, and so was the rent these people paid. He'd heard that they paid in a month what he earned in a year. Nobody can make that much money honestly.

Maceo stretched Rainbow's head back and shook the bloody mass.

"Tell us who it was, Rainbow! Who planned it with you," Maceo shouted. Rainbow's lips moved, but nothing came out.

"I said, I don't know anything about..." Rainbow's whisper trailed off to a sputtering sound in his throat. Juggler moved in with another deadly kick, this time to Rainbow's groin.

Rainbow bent in half and tumbled into a bookcase, knocking the books and cheap ceramic sculpture onto the floor in a shower.

"You two bit lying punk," Juggler said between clenched teeth. He bent down and lifted Rainbow as if he weighed nothing and hurled him at the plate glass window. The force was enough and Rainbow's battered body shattered through the window and fell thirty stories to the ground.

In the glass elevator, Fisheye heard the crash above and raised his eyes. He saw Rainbow's body plunging down and flash past the elevator in a shower of broken glass. Small fragments of glass rained on the roof of the unique lift. Fisheye frowned and drew his gun.

"Jesus Christ," he muttered, pushing the button for the penthouse.

Juggler went to the window to look and quickly turned back to Maceo.

"Let's get the hell out of here," Juggler said, suddenly quiet after all the violence.

"What do we tell Marcellus?" Maceo asked. He was afraid that the boss might be upset to know they had executed their prime suspect without finding out who the accomplices were.

"That half of his problems are over! We'll get the other one, don't worry. Money buys a lot of information," Juggler answered, as they walked briskly out the door of Rainbow's apartment. Maceo pressed the button and was relieved to see that the door opened right away.

As the elevator door closed on the two assassins, the next elevator's door slid open. Fisheye stepped onto the floor cautiously, his revolver at the ready. He slowly worked his way to the apartment and gently pushed the door open. There wasn't a sound, except the wind through the shattered window.

Fisheye looked around the living room and knew that

whatever was going on in here was all over. Whoever threw that person out of the window was gone. He went to the window and cast his eyes down to the pavement below. Rainbow's broken body looked like a toy in a growing pool of blood. Just then Fisheye's attention was drawn to the car that was speeding out of the garage. It was a Mercedes 600 E.

He tiredly surveyed the living room. There was blood all over the rug and broken furniture. He sat down on the couch. He wanted to think before the boys from the Santa Monica police arrived with L.A. homicide. He noticed a phone under the table with the receiver off the hook. Fisheye picked up the phone with his handkerchief.

"Hello?" The connection was still open. "Hello? Hello?"

Pharoah listened for a moment and pushed the disconnect button. The line went dead. His face was twisted with fury. He was going to have his revenge. That pimping nigger Marcellus was going to pay and pay. Pharoah already had the information he needed. Now he would put it to work and destroy the murderer and his muscle.

16

Fisheye went to headquarters much earlier than usual the morning after Rainbow's brutal murder. He hadn't felt like this in years. There was a chance that he could break the biggest drug dealer in Los Angeles, send him to prison for a long, long time. It felt like the old days in St. Louis.

Fisheye had arrived early to check the files on Marcellus Armstrong. Very little was in the yellow folder. Police surveillance had compiled something that resembled an international flight schedule, but no hard evidence. Armstrong's legitimate businesses accounted for enough of his money it seemed. It didn't warrent spending the tax-payers' money on watching him. The frequent trips all over the world were justified by his concert and contest promotions.

Fisheye shoved the file back in its place in the file drawer and slammed it shut. He sat on the edge of the desk that was nearby and took a drink from his coffee cup. There was really nothing of value in that damned file. The vice squad and drug divisions had come up embarrassingly empty-handed. That's all changed, Fisheye thought. There was a corpse now, and word on the street that Armstrong was the executioner.

Fisheye doubted that Marcellus Armstrong had been in Rainbow's apartment last night, but he probably gave the order. No fingerprints had been found yet, which surprised Fisheye. The attack and murder of Rainbow had the viciousness of a genuine assault by a psychotic.

Fisheye shook his head and heaved himself to his feet. He would have to try Snitch again for more information. The little weasle may have been holding something back. Fisheye decided to apply pressure on him to break him down.

There was a pay phone in the basement, outside the file room. Fisheye picked up the receiver, put a dime in, and dialed. Five rings later, Snitch answered.

"I want to talk to you. We have to talk. Usual place and time," Fisheye said forcefully. He quickly put the phone back on the hook. He was in no mood for Snitch's whining and wailing.

Fisheye slowly climbed the stairs, pausing to catch his breath at the top, and continued into the detectives room.

"You're late again," Gene yelled over the general office noise. Fisheye held up a hand and shook his head to the negative.

"Early in fact. Been down in the files," Fisheye answered. He poured himself another cup of coffee and sat in a chair beside Gene's desk.

"What are you looking for?" Gene asked, shifting stacks of legal forms from one place on his desk to another. "I'm losing the paperwork battle," he laughed. "Have something to do with that murder last night?" Gene handed Fisheye a series of reports.

"Yeah, I've got an idea of who was behind it," Fisheye said.

"Who?" Gene asked.

"I don't want to say anything till I'm more positive," Fisheye answered, his good eye fixed on his coffee cup.

"Well, put it in your report," Gene stated flatly. "I need those reports back by tomorrow for the homicide division."

"I'll have them for you as soon as I can," Fisheye said, rising to leave.

"Tommorow, Fisheye. I mean it!" Gene yelled after Fisheye's receding back. Fisheye just dismissed him with a wave of his arm and took his coat off the rack.

"Stay out of it! It's homicide's case!" Gene barked and went back to his mountain of paper work. When he looked up a few minutes later, Fisheye was gone.

Fisheye knew it was homicide's case, but he also figured that they would never crack it. He felt that the strings would eventually lead back to Marcellus Armstrong and the police had long ago reconciled themselves to living with Armstrong. As far as they would be concerned, it was only his wild hunch, nothing more. He needed proof for his theory and hoped he would be able to squeeze it out of Snitch.

Fisheye took his assigned, unmarked car out into the traffic on Wilshire Boulevard and sped toward his rendevous. The sunny, palm lined street was bustling with the elite doing their shopping and heading for early lunches. Fisheye scowled at the thought that none of these folks in their expensive cars would be heading for the hamburger stand.

Fisheye headed north through a residential area and the hamburger stand came into view ten minutes later. He parked near the low budget eatery, so he could leave in a hurry if he had to. Getting out of his car, he walked to the order window.

"Burger, plain and a Seven-up," he said to the white capped kid inside.

"Yes, sir," the kid answered. Must be new here, Fisheye considered. In a week he'll be as rude as the rest of his workmates. The kid came back with the hamburger and soft drink in three minutes. Fisheye opened the bun to spread some mustard on the bread and check for foreign objects. Satisfied with the quality of the hamburger, he put the bun back on and looked at his watch. Snitch was running a bit late. Fisheye scanned the people eating at the counter and at the outdoor tables. He heard the sound of a roller skater coming up behind him and turned. It was Snitch.

"You're late, Snitch," Fisheye said quietly.

"I told you not to call me that!" Snitch spat back, trying to hold his position on the inclined concrete. Fisheye wrapped his hamburger in some wax paper and picked up his soda.

"Let's go for a ride, Snitch," he said firmly. It was an order, not a suggestion.

"Man, I can't afford to be seen with you! Besides, I got skates," Snitch complained.

"No shit!" Fisheye smiled, sarcasm in his voice, and gave Snitch a shove with his elbow. Snitch had to roll right to Fisheye's car to avoid falling, his hands grabbing the roof to stop himself.

"Get in," Fisheye said. "Or I put you away so far, you'll forget where you came from." Snitch quickly resigned himself to the inevitability of this car ride and awkwardly climbed into the car. Fisheye started the car and drove west.

"Where are we going, man?" Snitch asked, shifting in his seat restlessly. Fisheye didn't answer.

They drove for half an hour in silence. Fisheye had driven all the way to the Pacific Ocean. He pulled over onto the sandy shoulder of the road and stopped. Snitch nervously fidgeted in his seat. Fisheye casually unwrapped his hamburger and began eating it, while he watched the surf crash along the beach, and the people on the sand.

"I need some names, Snitch," he said finally. He figured that Snitch would be nervous enough by now to cooperate.

"I'm hungry," Snitch said indignantly. He wanted to get something out of this pig that had practically kidnapped him from the hamburger stand.

"Dinner at the Playboy Club," Fisheye answered calmly, still watching the shapely topless sunbather he'd spotted. God, she was built. Fisheye considered how hot this young number must be and nearly bit his finger off when he took another bite of his hamburger.

"Fuck the Playboy Club!" Snitch retorted.

"Okay, so we got to MacDonalds. Names, Snitch," Fisheye persisted. Jesus, the girl on the beach was sitting up. Couldn't be more than eighteen, not a day, Fisheye guessed. He knew that it was about time to get ugly with Snitch and put the fear into him. He'd get what he wanted.

"My memory gets short when I'm hungry," Snitch whined. Fisheye took a deep breath and put his hamburger down on the dash board, still not looking directly at Snitch. In a flash, Fisheye drew his pistol and pointed it at Snitch's skull.

"You goddamn cocksucker! If I don't get some names, your life is gonna be short," Fisheye shouted. Snitch blinked and pressed himself against the passenger door, considering a run for it. He shifted his feet and the extra weight on his legs reminded him of the roller skates. There would be no dash for freedom with these things on.

"Why are you so interested in this thing with Marcellus? Just because your man got blown away, don't blame it on me!" Snitch scolded. "I told you about him, remember? You blew it, Fisheye, not me!" Snitch shook his head and held up his hands. He had done his part. He felt he'd given this crazed pig all the help he deserved.

"Have it your way then," Fisheye said, shifting the gun to his left hand and starting the car. Keeping the .38 pointed at Snitch, he drove a quarter of a mile further along the road. He turned the car around in an empty picnic area and parked close to the edge of a sandy cliff. The wheels on the passenger's side were almost over the tar lip of the rest area. Snitch looked anxiously to the bottom of the cliff below. Fisheye put his .38 back into his shooting hand and cocked the hammer. Snitch stared at the gun and swallowed hard.

"Hey look, Fisheye, maybe I did hear something, you know, just rumors, that's all," Snitch said quickly, trying to placate Fisheye.

"You're wasting my time, Snitch," Fisheye said with smoldering anger in his voice. He moved the gun closer to Snitch's head.

"They say the lookout was a guy called Squeegee," Snitch spoke hurriedly.

"And the other one?"

"No one's saying! Nothing! Honest," Snitch said, his face filled with fear.

"Give me an address!" Fisheye knew that he was getting all that this poor sniveling wreck knew. The stoolie was afraid that he would kill him.

"An apartment somewhere in Hollywood. That's all I know, I swear," Snitch cried. Fisheye believed him now. Snitch knew nothing else that could be of use.

Fisheye reached across him and opened the passenger door.

"Get the hell out of my car," he shouted. Snitch looked down at the cliff below.

"You know you're crazy, man. You're fucking crazy," Snitch hissed at Fisheye. The detective raised his right leg and gave Snitch a hard kick, knocking him out of the car.

"See you later, Snitch," Fisheye said softly, watching him tumble down the steep bank to the beach. He yanked the door closed and started the car. Sqealing onto the road in the direction of Hollywood, he picked up his microphone and got headquarters.

"Detective Martin. I need the address of a previously convicted felon, nicknamed Squeegee. Should be in the Hollywood files. I'll call in half an hour for the adress. Out." Fisheye knew he was getting closer to unraveling the case. He only worried that someone else might be a step ahead of him, like the marina. He pushed the gas pedal down and hurried to Hollywood.

Back down on the beach, Snitch had picked himself up and was brushing the sand off his clothes.

"You chicken-shit motherfucker!! I'll get you for this. You'll see," Snitch screamed. He attempted to walk a few steps, tripped in the sand and fell. He'd find a way to punish Fisheye. Punish the pig who humiliated him so often.

17

One hour later, Fisheye was standing down the street from Squeegee's apartment building. He had left his car parked around the block to avoid tipping anyone off to his presence. He was determined to not blow this lead.

He walked slowly down the sidewalk, a man enjoying a day off perhaps, and around to the side entrance. This time he would use the stairs. He crept up three flights silently counting the floors by the landings. The lights on each floor had all burned out or been stolen. It was completely black.

Fisheye felt the door that would open onto the third floor hallway and tried the knob. It wasn't locked. He opened the door a crack and saw the shabby hallway with it's dim flourescent lights overhead. Seeing no one in the hall, he quickly stepped through the door and let it close behind him.

Squeegee's apartment door was the second one on his left. He listened at the door and heard no sound coming from within. Drawing his .38, he took a step back and charged it. The cheap locks snapped when his shoulder hit the door and it swung wide open. Fisheye went inside the unlit apartment and felt the wall by the door for the light switch.

He moved cautiously to the rear of the apartment to another door. He kicked this open, bracing himself against a wall, waiting for gunfire. Nobody. The bathroom was empty.

Fisheye next moved to the kitchen and found it empty as well. Maybe that jerk Snitch had given him a bum steer. Snitch might be smarter than he gave him credit for and a better actor. Fisheye checked the refrigerator. He had to step back and cover his nose from the stench of curdled milk and rotting meat and vegatables. Christ, this Squeegee had been gone for over a month. Disgusted, he walked back to the living room and to another door. An empty closet. A few wire hangers jangled inside as he slammed the door closed.

Fisheye was getting very frustrated. He had believed Snitch and still did. He put his revolver back into it's holster and sat down at the table. He wondered if somebody had gotten to Squeegee long before they had discovered Rainbow. There were papers scattered on the table and Fisheye idly leafed through them, hoping to find some clue.

Several bills from the cleaners were crumpled under bills from the major department stores in the area. Squeegee had gone on a shopping spree, he noted. Then he saw them. Beneath the flattened bag from some drug store were several travel folders. Fisheye picked them up to have a better look. Oh, Christ, they were for places all over the globe. Squeegee could be absolutely anywhere in the world by now, except the United States. It had been well over a month judging by the powerful stench in the refrigerator. The airline personnel wouldn't remember a man with two heads, let alone a dwarf. Christ! The trail was too damn cold to follow. There was no way he could justify a worldwide manhunt with no evidence. There was no way he could convince anyone of the connection to Marcellus Armstrong yet.

Fisheye gathered up the travel folders and other papers and put them into his pocket. His face told it all. He was totally disgusted. One big bust was all he wanted. Send the biggest cocaine dealer in the West to the slammer for twenty years and add murder conspiracy for good measure. Fisheye figured that he could retire to his fishing a happy man if he closed this case successfully.

Fisheye left the apartment door open on the way out and walked down the corridor to the elevators. No need to worry about spies now he thought, pressing the button.

The elevator doors opened and a rush of childish laughter greeted Fisheye. Several little children were playing in the lift. Fisheye stepped inside with them and tried to ignore the loud giggling and theatrical screams. They were playing robber. One of them held a small toy gun in front of the other two who now held their arms up. The little boy with the dark eyes who held the gun, pretended to take valuables from the two victims. The elevator reached the first floor and the three children ran out ahead of him, shouting happily. Their chase was on. Fisheye watched them disappear down a dingy hallway and felt the beginning of a headache creep into his temples.

Fisheye left the building and walked briskly to his car. Sitting inside, he found the aspirin he kept in the glove compartment with his flasher and handcuffs. He gobbled three of the white tablets and drove back to the station.

Once back at his desk, Fisheye spread out the pamphlets advertising exotic getaways and tried to guess where the hell Squeegee went. The pain in his head was worse, He reached into a drawer and pulled out another bottle of aspirin. The pain of these headaches always seemed to center on the destroyed eye beneath the eyepatch. The doctors had told him it was because of the nerves that would never heal or go completely dead. He popped a couple of aspirins in his mouth and went to the soda machine for a drink.

Fisheye noticed that Gene was at his desk at the back of the room and walked over. Gene sat back and lit a cigarette, while Fisheye made himself comfortable in a chair nearby.

"I think I'm in the wrong racket," Fisheye said. He was attempting to relax, but the strain showed on his face and in his slumped posture.

"How so?" Gene asked, exhaling a cloud of cigarette smoke. "Hate the reports, huh?"

"No, Gene, I mean, here I am riding a desk for eight bills a month and some clown with half a million in cocaine money is taking life easy on some deserted island half way 'round the world," Fisheye answered.

"Yeah, but at least you sleep at night. The other guy is looking over his shoulder every five minutes," Gene chuckled. Fisheye shook his head in agreement and took a swallow of the soda as if it were whiskey.

"I guess your right. Man, I sure wanted to bust up Armstrong's cocaine empire," Fisheye mused.

"You may get your chance yet," Gene responded, sitting up. "With a much better chance for collecting some hard evidence."

"What?" Fisheye asked as he watched Gene shuffle through some papers on his desk.

"We got a tip," Gene smiled, handing Fisheye one of the papers. Fisheye started to read the list with great interest which quickly turned to amazement. He whistled in surprise.

"Some list, huh? Everyone there was at a cocaine party he hosted some months back. When we start pushing buttons, look out," Gene said, almost sadly. He knew that a lot of pressure would be put on the city to perform a cover up, lose the list and forget he ever saw it.

"Is your informant reliable?" Fisheye asked, giving the list back to Gene.

"It wasn't an informant. It was anonymous. He sent that through the mail a couple of days ago. This morning we got a phone call that told us that Marcellus smuggles his cocaine in the trophies his beauty contestants win. If he's not reliable, we'll know in a couple of hours. The fellas are downtown now, getting warrants to search his house."

"Was it a local call?" Fisheye asked, agitated.

"What the tip? Yeah. It was a local. Why?" Gene asked, but Fisheye was already walking away.

"That means he's still here," Fisheye said over his shoulder.

"Who's still here?" Gene asked, confused.

"Forget it! Look, I gotta run. Talk to you later, okay?" Fisheye half yelled. He grabbed his coat from the rack and rushed out of the police station. In a few minutes he was speeding south, out of Beverly Hills toward a poorer section of town. There was a certain pool hall where he figured he could find his old buddy

Snitch. The little asshole had been holding something back. If he had known the names of the two, he had to know the name of the third robber. He was a pretty good actor after all, Fisheye decided.

When Fisheye burst into the smoke-filled pool hall, flashing his badge, it only took him a second to spot Snitch. He had been bent over a table, lining up a shot. He was with two of his sleezeball friends, Moochie and Romero.

"Nobody moves," Fisheye shouted. "Spread 'em out. All of you." Reluctantly the three men bent over the pool table and spread their arms and legs.

"What is this shit, man?" Moochie asked in a stoned daze.

"Yeah, you lonely or something? Looking for company?" Romero chuckled.

"Nobody gave you permission to speak," Fisheye growled, frisking Moochie. He found a familiar shape in Moochie's pocket and pulled out a .45 pistol.

"You got it registered, punk?" Fisheye yelled. Moochie didn't answer. Fisheye hit the side of his head, drawing blood.

"I said, is it registered?" Fisheye asked again. Moochie began to raise a hand to his head to check the cut, but Fisheye slammed the butt of his own gun down into the small of his back. Moochie went sprawling, face down on the table, from the impact.

"No! No, man, it ain't registered!" Moochie cried out.

"You're goddamn right, it ain't registered," Fisheye exclaimed, moving over to Snitch. Fisheye put the .45 into his pocket and patted Snitch down for weapons. He felt into the recesses of Snitch's jacket pockets and withdrew several marijuana cigarettes.

Fisheye slapped the joints on the pool table and pulled Snitch's arms behind his back.

"What else you got on you, punk?" Fisheye shouted, pulling handcuffs from his belt.

"You put that on me, Fisheye. You dirty motherfucker!! I was clean when I came in here, man. I was clean," Snitch cried out.

"Sure you were," Fisheye exclaimed, slapping the cuffs on. Fisheye had the man he wanted and started dragging him to the door. Planting the joints on him protected his identity as a low life criminal.

"What are you doing, man? Why you always hassle me?" Snitch shouted.

"Because you're such an asshole, that's why," Fisheye growled, shoving Snitch through the door into the street.

"You planted that stuff on me, man. I was clean," Snitch yelled, as he was shoved over to Fisheye's car. The old detective opened the door on the passenger's side.

"Shut up and get in the goddamn car!" Fisheye shouted, muscling him down into the seat and closing the door. He quickly ran around the car and jumped in. The tires squealed and left smoking patches of rubber on the street as Fisheye took off.

He drove to a parking lot behind a warehouse, a few blocks away. Nobody would see them there. Fisheye parked the car and lit a cigarette.

"One day somebody's going to put a contract out on you, Fisheye, and I'll be the first one to dance on your coffin," Snitch scowled. Fisheye exhaled some smoke and looked at him.

"You're on these streets by a wing and a prayer, Snitch. Don't push your luck with me," the detective warned, taking another puff. "I figured the folks who hit Marcellus were long gone, but I was wrong. They're right here! Whoever it was just tipped Marcellus' hole card, so he's gonna be on ice for a while. That means it was a set up all along. Someone's looking to get Marcellus out of the way and fill his shoes," Fisheye stated, watching for Snitch's reaction. "I wanna know who it is, Snitch," Fisheye suddenly screamed.

"I told you not to call me that," Snitch retorted. Fisheye grabbed his head by the hair and slammed his face into the steel dashboard. Blood trickled down from both Snitch's nostrils and he groaned from the pain that shot through his face.

"You goddamn son of a bitch, I could kill you right now and nobody would be the wiser," Fisheye shouted, smashing Snitch's face into the dashboard repeatedly. "Now I want a name, Snitch! When Marcellus goes to jail, there'll be a vacuum and I intend to see it stays that way! Understand?" Fisheye yelled. Snitch didn't respond. His face was banged into the hard steel again. There were abrasions bleeding all over his face now. His jacket was dotted with blood and the dashboard smeared with it.

"Do you understand?" Fisheye screamed. Snitch was groaning constantly by this time but managed to shake his head affirmatively.

"Good! Now get out!" Fisheye growled. Snitch stumbled from the car and sat down against a brick wall. Fisheye took some napkins left over from lunch and wiped up most of the blood from the dashboard and the floor mat. Tossing the red napkins out of the window, he started the car and raced out of the warehouse parking lot.

Snitch remained huddled over, trying to let his head

clear before he tried to stand again. His whole head hurt and his face burned. He took off his jacket and attempted to blot up the blood which covered his face and was coagulating in lumps over the cuts.

Blocks away, Fisheye stopped at a gas station to wash off the dashboard completely. The last thing he needed was more brutality charges. He could imagine what the stupid rookies would think. They'd probably want to lock him up and charge him. The fools didn't understand that you had to be as heartless as your quarry to ever stand on an even footing with them. As it was, it was always a matter of catch up, the police always just behind the criminals.

Fisheye finished washing the car and headed back for the station. He was tired, but happy. It really was like his younger days. He was putting the pressure on insignificant thugs to trap the big ones. This was the way he loved police work. You didn't get to do it like this anymore. Had to wait till some psycho had gunned down eight people standing around you before you could get tough. Even then you had better read the animal his rights or it wouldn't get to trial. Ninety-nine percent of it was all bullshit nowadays, mused Fisheye.

Fisheye felt confident. He had put the fear into Snitch, but good. Snitch wouldn't want to risk another beating like that. He'd deliver something very soon.

18

The police timed their search of the Marcellus Armstrong estate well. Twelve hours after a Los Angeles judge granted the search warrant, eight police vehicles arrived on the doorstep. A certain detective in Beverly Hills had assumed that with all the powerful friends Marcellus had, there would be a tip off about the raid. Only two officers that he was sure could be trusted and the District Attorney knew of the raid, besides Fisheye and himself. The narcotics division was informed just one hour before the raid would take place. Gene wanted to make sure that it was as difficult as possible for any cops on the take to "lose" evidence. He also didn't want normal police procedure to get in the way of this bust. He knew exactly who to call upon.

At approximately five-thirty in the morning, Fisheye had parked his unmarked car down the street from the Armstrong estate. The quiet street was still cloaked in darkness. His heart pounding, Fisheye stepped out of his car and walked into the moist ground cover that grew along the high walls. He carried a small bag of tools that if discovered, would have any case against Armstrong thrown out of court immediately. It was a well equipped lock picking kit.

His footsteps came too close to a family of doves that were drinking water from the wet leaves and they shot up into the trees. Fisheye jumped at the sudden noise and paused to slow his breathing down. His pulse was still racing when he continued.

Fisheye reached the huge stone pillar that supported one of the heavy iron gates and peered around the corner and down the driveway. He knew that there was probably a closed circuit camera trained on the gates from one of the trees inside, but hoped that the only reason anyone would look at the screen was a ring of the bell.

There was no activity outside the house at all. Fisheye walked to the middle of the gate and looped the long strap of the black bag over his neck. Unsnapping the clasp, he took out a mirror and a fine jewelers screwdriver with a tiny flashlight attached. By holding both of these tools in one hand he would be able to see all sides of the steel lock box comfortably.

He was familiar with locks of all kinds and knew that the locks on most of these big gates were designed to look impenetrable, but be accessible for quick maintenance. The California rainy season played havoc with even the best electrical systems and often it shorted the circuits. The super rich didn't appreciate being prisoners on their own estates and got extremely irate with their security companies. Thus the gates had lock boxes that were more like a magician's trick than a locked safe.

Fisheye found two promising areas on the box to start with and put on some gloves. There were two seams that ran along the back and a portion of the bottom of the box. If his guess was corect, one of the four welded bolts on the back was a hinge, the other three fake. He looked up and down the street before reaching in through the bars to try to manipulate the panels on the box. The dull glow below the trees on the east side of the street told him dawn was fast approaching. He had to hurry.

The back panel wouldn't budge so he moved his hands to the bottom. After a few minutes of pushing the bottom panel in various directions, he realized that there must be another part to the puzzle. Christ, he wished he knew what the hell it was. Time was running out. The raid was set for just after six.

He took a tiny hammer out of the bag and a slightly thicker screw driver. Again starting at the back panel, he rapped each of the bolts. The fourth one he tapped was a hinge. From the overlapping seam on the bottom edge, he could also tell that the panel rotated downward. He had to get the bottom panel aside if he was going to get into the box.

Rapping on the bottom bolts, he was unable to discern any difference in the sound. They all gave off the shallow ping of a false bolt. This was ridiculous. He had opened a lot of these. He pulled his arms back to check his watch and let the blood drain back into them. There were five minutes left before the eight patrol cars would arrive. If he didn't have the gate open by the time they arrived, they would have to ring the gate bell and wait to be let in. In the long minutes that would follow, every scrap of evidence would be destroyed or hidden.

Fisheye wiped his brow and set to work again. He took the point of the screw driver and tried to pry the seam where the two edges met. Impossible. Christ! Idly, he moved the point of the driver to the bottom bolts and poked at the welds. One of them moved! The one nearest the iron plate on the front of the gate. Fisheye moved the mirror into position and saw the bolt. It had dropped a mere sixteenth of an inch, but it told him what he needed to know.

He rapidly pryed the bolt down and the bottom of the lock box fell to the ground. The back panel rotated downward exposing the simple electrical mechanism inside. He took the screw driver and placed it across the two terminals that controlled the lock. Sparks arced out as it short circuited. He quickly slid the heavy gate lock back into its housing. The gates were open.

He stooped and reached through the bars to retrieve the bottom panel and reassembled the box. He tossed the burglary tools into the case with his gloves and trotted back to his car. He didn't even bother to take the case off his neck until he had driven safely away.

Fisheye drove home. The case with the tools had to be

hidden in his garage and he needed to catch up on some sleep. Age definitely had its limitations.

The police arrived at the Armstrong estate with Gene in the first car. A couple of officers were very shocked when he strode up to the gates and swung them open. They knew that Marcellus always kept the estate locked up.

The mansion was surrounded before anyone in the house was awake. A sleepy butler answered the door bell and stared in surprise at the police convention outside the door. He rushed to the intercom in his nervousness and buzzed the master bedroom.

Gene was pleased when Marcellus' voice came over the speaker and drowsily asked what the problem was. The butler told him that the police were there with a search warrant. The silence on the other end of the intercom was most eloquent.

"I'll be right down," Marcellus' voice blurted and the connection was closed. The wide-eyed butler excused himself to go back to his work and was further frightened by the fact that the police told him he had to remain where he was.

Upstairs in the master bedroom, Marcellus shook Natasha awake and started to dress.

"What is it?" Natasha mumbled, pulling a silk pillow over her head.

"Get up. Now!" Marcellus ordered. "It's the police and apparently they've got a search warrant." Natasha raised herself on an elbow and brushed her hair back from her face. Marcellus had already half dressed when he walked over to the intercom by the bed and pushed the button for Juggler's room.

"Yes, Marcellus. What's wrong?" Juggler asked, trying to sound alert even though the buzzer had wakened him from a sound sleep.

"We're being busted. Get Maceo and clean the house. The cops are here. I'll try to stall them for ten minutes, then you two can split," Marcellus said quickly, pulling on his expensive suede shoes.

"Right," Juggler said over the speaker. Marcellus watched Natasha rushing about the room putting on clothes and went to the closet to get himself a shirt.

The intercom buzzed, startling Marcellus. He raced over and pushed the button.

"Yes."

"The detective here says you should come down within five minutes," the butler spoke.

"Yes. Of course," Marcellus answered. While he finished buttoning his shirt with one hand he picked up the phone near his bed and dialed Henry at home.

"Who the hell is this? Do you know what time it is?" Henry groused when he answered.

"It's Marcellus. The police are here with a search warrant."

"What? My God!" Henry gasped.

"Can you take care of it?" Marcellus asked.

"I'm positive I can. Have you got much around?" Henry asked. The intercom buzzed again and Marcellus knew it was the cops in the foyer.

"No. I've gotta go," Marcellus spoke into the phone and hung up. He pressed the intercom button.

"I'm on my way down."

Marcellus found what looked like a small army of policemen waiting for him at the foot of the stairs. While Gene showed Marcellus the warrant, the other officers started their search. Marcellus suggested that they could wait in the solarium and if Gene would allow it, the butler could bring them some coffee and breakfast rolls. Gene agreed and an officer accompanied the servant to the kitchen.

Natasha was brought to the solarium to join Marcellus and wait for the search to be completed.

"Good morning," Natasha said sarcastically. "So this is the holding cell, huh?"

"Sit down and have some coffee, Natasha," Marcellus said firmly. He didn't want her needling the cops all day. He just wanted to get this phase of the ordeal over with so he could start the legal wheels turning.

The search lasted all day and into the evening. The police took the place apart. Pictures were taken out of their frames, furniture dismantled, and electrical outlets pulled from the wall. The mansion looked like an interior demolition squad had been at work.

Marcellus was relieved to get rid of them at ten o'clock that night. Gene was the last one out the door.

"Thank you for your cooperation, Mr. Armstrong," Gene smiled, knowing that they had enough evidence to put him away for a long time.

"Goodnight, officer," Marcellus scowled, closing the door in Gene's face. Gene stopped the door with his foot and smiled at Marcellus.

"Don't worry about your two friends, Mr. Armstrong. We took them down to the station and booked them on suspicion this morning, right after we got here. Good night."

Marcellus thought his head would explode. He slammed the door and leaned against it. The cops must have found a lot of powder around if they nailed Juggler and Maceo.

Marcellus walked to his study and stepping around piles of books left on the floor from the search, went to his desk. He called Henry.

"Henry? Marcellus. What the hell is going on?" Marcellus asked angrily. "They arrested my boys this morning."

"I know. The police have nothing on them. It's just a harassment ploy. They'll be free tomorrow morning," Henry said reassuringly. Marcellus rubbed a hand over his chest. He imagined that his blood pressure must be off the scale.

"What is this about, Henry?" Marcellus shouted, the rage that he had checked all day boiling over. "I want this stopped."

"You don't have to worry about a thing. No matter what the police have found. We'll say you didn't know anything about it. You give a lot of very big parties. Some of your guests must have left the coke, that's all. You can relax," Henry said confidently. He didn't want a big investment like Marcellus to get upset. It made people do foolish things.

"Why?" Marcellus shouted.

"Who knows? The D.A. decided he needed some publicity, most likely. It's for a grand jury probe. I'll handle it." Henry's words did have a calming effect.

"Good night, Henry," Marcellus hung up and sat back in the desk's chair. He needed some base, he decided. Something to ice him out a bit. He couldn't talk to Juggler or Maceo till the morning and he'd sent Natasha to bed with a tranquilizer. It was just as well, he had to think. Alone. He stood up and walked to a wooden panel that had been left intact. Sliding the panel aside, he found a base pipe and several pellets.

Sitting back down at the desk, he fired up the first pellet with his butane torch, swirling the rum in the pipe as he did so. Water cooled the smoke just as well as the rum but the rum added a delicious, heavy sweetness. He inhaled deeply and his pulse raced. Marcellus felt strength return to his tension racked body and clarity to his mind. He knew that he would escape this legal trap and extend his empire further. His enemies would remember when anyone crossed Marcellus Armstrong he stood a good chance of ending up like that Rainbow fool.

19

The district attorney and his staff worked for three weeks to prove to the twelve grand jury members that there was enough evidence to bring Mr. Marcellus Armstrong to trial. The prosecution brought with it a mountain of evidence that had been collected from the Armstrong mansion and affidavits of corroborating evidence was on the side of the D.A.'s office. The jury decided that there was enough evidence to try a case against Mr. Armstrong. Horace Addison, the D.A. was delighted. He was sure that he could win this case and put Armstrong away for a long time.

There had been no testimony in the grand jury hearings in Marcellus' favor. Marcellus hadn't even appeared. Henry thought that it would be ill-advised to have him answer the D.A.'s questions under oath. Henry couldn't imagine the prosecution coming up with enough to try a case against his client, let alone put him in jail.

Natasha and Marcellus were at home the day after the grand jury decided to prosecute and the butler brought them the morning paper as usual. They were having a light breakfast in the solarium when the butler walked in.

"The paper, sir," the butler said. "Would you or madam care for more coffee?"

"No thanks. You can go," Marcellus answered after

Natasha had shaken her head. She was still a bit sleepy and wearing the white silk robe that she had pulled on when she had gotten up.

Marcellus left the paper on the silver tray and took another sip of his coffee.

"Mmm, this is good. That new cook is fine," he exulted with a smile.

"True, darlin'," Natasha anwered, curling up in the wicker love seat. She felt the warm rays of the morning sun heat up her robe and squinted up into it, smiling. She had enjoyed the last three weeks immensely. Marcellus had been conducting his business less and less which meant he was home more often. She loved his company and his loving.

Marcellus took a bite of the croissant roll and reached for the paper. He flipped the folded newspaper open and nearly choked when he saw the headline. "Promoter Indicted In Drug Scandal." A picture with an article about his pending trial. Marcellus threw the paper down and stood up. Natasha opened her eyes when she heard the slap of the paper and saw him dash down the hall.

"What is it, baby?" she asked after him. She reached out and picked up the paper that had fallen face down and focused her eyes on the headline. A small cry escaped her lips and her eyes widened with fear.

Marcellus picked up the phone in his library and rapidly dialed Henry's office number. A receptionist answered in a cheery voice and asked if she could help him.

"Put Henry on! This is Marcellus!" he shouted.

"I'm sorry Mr. Armstrong, he's not in right now. May I take a message?" she answered, determined to remain polite and chipper.

"When's he gonna be back?" Marcellus asked tersely. He had already formed a plan. He wanted to give Henry hell in person.

"I'm not sure, sir. By one o'clock I imagine. It's so hard to tell with these big . . ." Marcellus slammed the phone down. He quickly picked up the phone again and dialed the mobile phone operator. He gave the woman the number of the phone in his limousine and it began to ring a few minutes later.

Juggler and Maceo had been handling a lot of Marcellus's deliveries since the grand jury probe had started. It was best if he layed low in an effort to dig up some incriminating facts. There were almost as many cops on the case as newspaper reporters. All in all, it made sense for him to cool it for a while.

"Yes, sir," Maceo answered.

"Put Juggler on," Marcellus ordered.

"Right."

"Yes, boss?" Juggler said.

"We gotta be over at Henry's by one o'clock. Got it?"

"Yes, sir." Marcellus slammed down the receiver and rose from his desk. He was shaking with rage. His arm flashed out and caught the Tiffany lamp just under the stained glass shade. It flew across the room and hit the book case before crashing to the floor. They couldn't do this to him, he thought. He wouldn't allow it. He'd light a fire under Henry's ass and get him to handle it. There was always a way if you had money, Marcellus figured.

Marcellus stalked out of his library and slammed the door closed after him. He collided with Natasha outside the room, almost knocking her down. He grabbed her arms to keep her from falling to the carpet and brusquely pushed her aside.

"Marcellus, what are we gonna do?" she asked, afraid.

"I'll take care of it," he shouted at her. Her fear reminded him of his own and that made him angry. "I'll take care of it."

Natasha seemed to be reassured. She shrugged as she watched him dissappear down the hallway.

"All right, baby. You know best," Natasha called out. Marcellus had gotten out of tight spots before, since she'd known him. This was just another one he would beat.

Marcellus climbed the stairs to his bedroom two at a time and raced across the room for his closets. He pulled out a custom pin-stripe, white on navy blue. He called it his banker's suit. He tossed the suit on the bed while he took off his robe and pajamas. By the time he was putting the cufflinks into his shirt the buzzer on the intercom went off.

"Yes," he said into the speaker.

"Your car's ready, boss," Juggler's voice answered.

"Good. I'll be right down," Marcellus told him and finished dressing.

Five minutes later, Marcellus descended the stairs to meet Juggler. Maceo was waiting in the limousine out front.

"Let's go," Marcellus ordered. Juggler nodded and followed him out to the limousine out front. Marcellus slid into the soft leather seat and Juggler got in on the other side.

"Hector, I want to see Henry," Marcellus said into the microphone that connected him to the driver's seat on the other side of the thick glass partition.

"What's going on, boss?" Juggler asked.

"I'll show you," Marcellus said in a low voice. He picked up the driver's mike again.

"Hector, I want you to stop at the newsstand on the way. Get today's paper." Marcellus sat back and lit a cigarette. Juggler and Maceo exchanged glances, both wondering what the surprise would be. Marcellus just gazed out at the passing traffic, preoccupied.

Hector eased the limousine up to the curb beside the news stand and hopped out of the car. Marcellus watched him approach the old man that sold the papers and hand him a dollar. The old man smiled gratefully and stooped behind the counter to get one of the last remaining papers. The old man folded the paper three times, like a paper boy would, and handed it to Hector.

Hector returned to the limo, pass the paper to Juggler and continued the drive to Henry's office.

Juggler's face froze when he saw the headline. Silently, he gave the paper to Maceo to read. Maceo gasped.

"I've got a little problem, boys," Marcellus said calmly.

"What can we do?" Juggler asked. His loyalty was an unswerving constant in Marcellus' world. Marcellus smiled at his body guard and friend.

"Henry should be able to take care of it," Marcellus said.

"He'd better," Juggler answered. Maceo was reading the article below Marcellus's picture and shaking his head. If the D.A. could prove what was in the article, it was all over for the three of them.

Hector pulled up in front of Henry's office building and Marcellus got out of the car with Juggler and Maceo. Marcellus took the newspaper from Maceo and led the way into the building.

The security guard looked down at the floor when Marcellus glanced in his direction. Marcellus knew that the poor security guard was frightened of knowing him now. As the three men got into the elevator, he saw the guard turn the page of a newspaper and squint at him as the elevator doors closed. He was trying to check the photograph, Marcellus mused.

The receptionist was startled when she looked up and saw Marcellus and his bodyguards standing over her desk.

"Oh, Mr. Armstrong," she said trying to recover her poise.

"Is Henry here?" Marcellus asked sharply.

"Why, yes, but I don't think . . ."

"Save it," Marcellus said, dismissing her with a wave of his hand. He strode to Henry's office door and walked in. Juggler and Maceo walked in after him and closed the door.

"Marcellus," Henry exclaimed. Marcellus wasn't in the mood and went to the desk and slapped it down over the papers Henry was working on.

"Somebody dropped a dime on me, goddamnit! I want to know who," Marcellus hissed angrily.

"Probably the same person who ripped you off! With the evidence they have, it's got to be somebody you know. I told you that before," Henry answered.

"We've got a lot of money in the street. Something will turn up soon," Juggler added.

"It damn well better," Marcellus growled at Juggler and then turned to Henry. "Where do I stand?"

"At your preliminary hearing we'll plead not guilty. You'll post bond and we wait for the trial. Believe me, Marcellus, when I get through with their evidence, you'll never see a day behind bars!" Henry stated confidently. Marcellus nodded in agreement. He and Henry would be able to handle this one and Juggler would finish the fool that set him up this way. Yes, there was justice, thought Marcellus. You just had to be in a position to pay the expensive legal fees. The main purpose of the courts seem to be lining the pockets of white lawyers and judges, he had observed. It was just a different method of extortion. You either paid or went to prison. The poor were the ones who bore the burden of the lessons to the rich.

"Take care of this, Henry," Marcellus said coming out of his reverie.

"Don't worry."

20

Henry sat alone at the bar inside a posh Beverly Hills restaurant. He idly stirred his drink, lost in thought. It was odd that Horace Addison, the D.A., had called and asked for this meeting. They were old friends, but Horace was never very chummy when they were opposing each other in court. Maybe he wanted to make a deal. Plea bargin the charge down to a simple fine of twenty grand or so. Henry smiled at the idea and tasted his drink. God knows, Horace had attempted to put Marcellus away several times in the past and had always failed miserably. It wasn't that Horace was a bad lawyer, it was just that Henry was the best. Probably wanted to save face, political embarassment, Henry mused.

The thirty year old Scotch went down like velvet fire, warming Henry's stomach and his spirits. He swiveled his chair to see if Horace had entered the restaurant yet. His eyes had become adjusted to the dim light filtering in through the thick stained glass and he could now make out the features of some of the more attractive women at the tables. He was enjoying the view so much that he didn't notice the distinguished D.A. when he entered the bar section.

The silver haired gentleman saw Henry first and made his way around the cocktail tables toward him. Henry noticed the movement and glanced away from the ravishing beauty seated at a table near the bar.

"Hello, Horace," Henry smiled warmly and shook the D.A's well manicured hand.

"Thanks for coming, Henry," Horace replied. His expression was serious. He turned away from Henry and scanned the bar. "Let's get a booth, shall we?" Henry shrugged and picked up his drink. They crossed the room to an unoccupied booth and sat down.

"You know, I'm always glad to talk with the D.A.'s office, Horace," Henry grinned. "Want something to drink?" Henry waved a waiter over to their table before Horace had time to answer.

"Yes, gentlemen?" the waiter asked.

"Another Scotch on the rocks for me," Henry answered, handing the waiter his glass. "Horace?" Horace looked up from the briefcase he had opened on the table, his mind clearly elsewhere.

"Oh, how about a Perrier with a twist of lime," he finally said, going back to his papers in the briefcase.

"I'll come right to the point, Henry. We've got your man this time," Horace said after the waiter was out of earshot.

"Oh?" Henry had heard all this before. He couldn't believe that poor Horace actually felt he could prosecute Marcellus successfully.

"We have a witness that will testify he overheard Mr. Armstrong making a transaction," Horace continued. Henry resisted the urge to roll his eyes.

"Hearsay." He hoped that the trial would at least hold a little challenge. Something to test him a bit and let him exercise his mind.

"It's on tape," Horace stated flatly. Henry drummed his fingers on the table. He tried to imagine how the presiding judge let the grand jury decide to prosecute with such flimsy evidence.

"Inadmissible," Henry said, shaking his head. The waiter arrived back at their table and set the drinks down. The waiter sensed that the two men were having a serious talk and hurried off to tend his other tables.

"Perhaps. Then there's the cocaine we found in the trophies," Horace smiled grimly and took a swallow of the Perrier.

"Circumstantial. You know I'll destroy it at trial, Horace," Henry said tiredly. He was wishing he hadn't accepted the D.A.'s invitation after all. This case would be a snap. Horace pulled a sheet of paper out of his briefcase and held it up.

"You can try, but I don't think you'll have such an easy time of it with this," Horace said, handing the paper to Henry.

"A list of names?" Henry asked, confused.

"Some of them your clients, Henry. Right?" Horace asked rhetorically. Henry wondered what he was up to. "All were at Mr. Armstrong's cocaine party. I understand it was quite an affair." The color had left Henry's face and his hand shook slightly as he took a large swallow of his Scotch.

"Still no proof," Henry tried. The D.A. wouldn't dare implicate the important people on this list. Marcellus, that dumb nigger had to make up a list, he thought angrily.

"Strange your name wasn't on that list, counselor.

And yet there are those who attended who are willing to swear under oath that not only were you there, but were partaking rather actively, shall we say?" Horace smiled. He knew he had him. There were no clever legal tricks Henry could call upon to get out of this one.

"All of this testimony in exchange for immunity, I presume," Henry said acidly and downed the rest of his drink. Horace shut his briefcase and locked it.

"Some people believe in the truth, Henry. Especially if it'll keep 'em from being ruined, or out of jail," Horace added, a note of triumph in his voice. Henry found himself unable to meet his eyes and stared at the empty glass in his hands.

"So what do you want from me?" Henry was resigned now. There really wasn't a thing he could do except salvage the reputations of his other clients. Marcellus might have to go to jail.

"We're not interested in your clients, Henry. They're just good timers. We want Armstrong. I want to put that guy behind bars and throw away the key," Horace said harshly.

"What's the trade off?" Henry asked, handing the list of names back to him.

"The trade off, Henry, is that nobody else gets hurt," Horace answered as he stood up from the table to leave. "Nobody." He started to walk away, but remembered something and turned to Henry again.

"This is your copy, Henry. I've already got one," Horace said, letting the paper fall gently to the table. He left Henry to ponder his next move.

Henry picked up the list of names and started reading. Everyone was on there all right. He shook his head wearily and looked around the bar for his waiter. He caught the young man's eye and pointed down at his empty glass. Henry needed another drink badly. It would help dull the pain of being boxed in by the D.A.

He returned his attention to the list and images of the decadent party flashed through his mind. The toy train ran its course and dumped it precious white cargo into the largest silver chalice anyone had ever seen. The fountain performed it's miracle of spraying cocaine into the silver bowl. All those faces. God, it was a collection of some of the most powerful people in the country.

The D.A. must have really scared those people. Horace probably used veiled threats of scandal that would ruin careers instantly. Politics was not the place for a drug scandal. Entertainers could withstand it. Their public almost expected it. Politicians and industrial titans would be totally crushed by the association.

Henry realized that the waiter already had come and gone. He picked up the glass and drank nearly half of the cold Scotch. He wasn't looking forward to his next talk with Marcellus. Marcellus asked for this to happen, Henry decided. Marcellus and his damn list. Suddenly, he remembered Natasha and smiled slightly. With Marcellus out of the way, he'd be able to test those waters. Henry waved an arm as if brushing the fantasy away and finished his drink. He would see Marcellus tomorrow and then break the news to him.

21

The Armstrong estate was bathed in the soft light of the late afternoon. The sweep of the lawn and the gardens seemed to glow with life. The tranquility of this exclusive corner of Beverly Hills belied the explosive tension at the meeting inside.

Henry had come to the mansion and given a copy of the list to Marcellus. The two sat at the bar in the rumpus room. Maceo and Juggler stood across from them, listening and keeping a watchful eye on Henry.

"What does this mean?" Marcellus asked.

"It means that you're gonna spend some time in jail, that's what it means!" Henry answered sharply. He had considered various ways of dealing with Marcellus and decided that he had to come on strong. It would be best if he could make him think that it was his fault somehow, not Henry's, that he was going to prison. Marcellus blinked from the blunt shock of Henry's words. He was stunned.

"But you said . . ." Marcellus stammered. He felt helpless.

"I know what I said, Marcellus, but you didn't tell me about the list," Henry stated, pointing to the piece of paper in Marcellus's hand. Marcellus shook his head to clear his thoughts.

"I didn't know anybody else had it! There was only one copy and Natasha kept . . ." Marcellus spoke slowly. He was interrupted when Natasha came into the room, loaded down with packages bearing the labels of all the most expensive shops and boutiques. She looked lovely.

"Hello, everybody," Natasha exclaimed, out of breath from carrying all the packages. Maceo quickly moved to help her put them down on the table nearby. "Just a little shopping," she laughed girlishly. Natasha walked to Marcellus and kissed him on the cheek.

"Natasha, where's the guest list from the party?" Marcellus asked quietly. The four men in the room list-

195

ened intently for the answer, while she took off her gloves.

"Gave it to Shelly a few weeks back. Why?" The answer was an incomplete piece of the puzzle. Marcellus' brow was furrowed in concentration.

"Shelly? What for?" Marcellus asked. Henry shifted in his seat, anxious for her reply.

"Said she and Pharoah were gonna have a party and they wanted to invite some of the same people," Natasha shrugged. "What does a lady have to do to get a drink around here?" she laughed.

"Later," Marcellus said sternly. "Pharoah? Who's Pharoah?" Marcellus nodded to Maceo to fix her a drink.

"Her boyfriend, silly! You met him. He was here at the party," Natasha answered. She reached for her drink and realized that she had been grilled for the past five minutes about the party list. "Did I do something wrong?" Natasha asked seriously.

"Not intentionally," Marcellus told her flatly. He snapped his fingers and motioned Juggler and Maceo to him. "Bring the car around!" When the pair dashed out of the room a second later, Juggler was wearing his cruel smile.

Marcellus picked his coat up from the bar and glanced at the list.

"Any of these people could've been charged. Why me?" he asked.

"If you were white and had money, you'd get probation. But you're black and have money, so they're gonna throw the book at you," Henry answered.

"Yeah. See you later," Marcellus said as he ran out of the room.

Henry stood up from the bar stool and lit a cigarette.

It seemed that Marcellus was actually finished, he thought. His big revenge hunt was only going to fix it so he never got out of jail, most likely. The other dealers can take up some of the slack, but there was no way they could cover all of Marcellus' clients. Christ, a lot a cash might be lost.

"Trouble?" Natasha asked, touching Henry's arm.

"Not really. But if I can take you to dinner, I'll tell you all about it," Henry grinned.

"I'm starved," Natasha said, making her eyes big. Henry picked up her gloves for her and slipped an arm around her waist as they strolled to the front door.

"I know a great little French place that you'll love," Henry smiled. Her perfume was making his head light and the touch of his arm on the gentle swell of her hips was electric. He felt like a seventeen-year-old boy with his first real woman.

"After you," Henry said, holding the front door open for her. She smiled shyly at him as they walked to the car. Henry noticed and wondered if it was a smile of mild amusement at his behavior. He never could tell with Natasha, she loved to flirt and have men fawn over her.

They got into Henry's car and drove down the long driveway. The massive iron gates were still wide open from Marcellus's hurried exit. Henry drove through and into the street, heading for the intimate cafe in Santa Monica. Natasha knew where he kept his cassettes and picked one out. Soon, a gentle blues ballad filled the car.

Henry was having trouble keeping his eyes off her, she looked so beautiful in her cream colored suit. He recalled the time two years ago, when Marcellus had found her modeling in Paris. She had been working for a large agency in New York and doing very well. Of course it was nothing compared to what Marcellus had to offer. She had returned to California with him to live in his mansion. Henry had seen the report that Marcellus received from a private detective in Manhattan. She was sophisticated for a good reason.

She was the daughter of a successful doctor, who had his eye on politics. Both he and his wife had sent her to the best schools and drilled her with their values. They had probably struggled to make it, Henry mused and to give her everything. She was a wonderful woman, but spoiled. She expected men to give her everything and they always did.

"Have I been to this one before?" Natasha asked.

"I don't think so. I want it to be a surprise," Henry smiled.

"Good! I love surprises," she laughed. She liked Henry. She wondered what was going on with the legal hassle, but knew better than to ask. Long ago she had discovered that men would tell her more than she ever wanted to know all by themselves. She would wait until dinner. Natasha understood that Henry was more involved with Marcellus than just being his lawyer. Marcellus had gotten angry in the past, but had always done what Henry wanted. The thought crossed her mind that old Henry was actually the biggest dealer on the West Coast and Marcellus his front. If this were true, Henry had to have ten times the money Marcellus had, stashed away in Switzerland or someplace.

"I'm cold," Natasha said to Henry. She slid across the hand-stitched leather seat of the Rolls Royce and let him put an arm around her.

22

By nightfall Marcellus' Mercedes was parked in front of Pharoah's dark house. The driveway was empty. Marcellus sat in the back seat and impatiently smoked a cigarette. Juggler and Maceo sat quietly in the front of the car. They had been waiting for an hour on the dark street. Marcellus wondered if Shelly and this Pharoah had blown town completely. He looked at his watch for the third time in the last ten minutes.

"Well, boys," Marcellus started to tell Maceo to drive off, but saw headlights coming down the street. He watched as the new Cheverolet Nova slowed and pulled into the driveway. Juggler glanced back at his boss, smiling. Shelly stepped out of the Nova and walked toward the front door of her house, fishing for her keys in her purse. Marcellus slipped out of the Mercedes and walked up the sidewalk after her.

"Shelly!" he called out, making her jump fearfully before turning to see who it was.

"Oh. Marcellus!" she said with great relief. "You frightened me," she laughed, feeling a bit embarrassed. "What brings you out this time of night?" Marcellus didn't anwer. He was studying her face.

"Where's Pharoah?" he asked gravely.

"Got me. I haven't seen him in a couple days. Business. You know how that is," she answered and then realized that Marcellus seemed agitated under his cool surface. "Something wrong?"

"Let's go for a ride, Shelly," Marcellus said.

"Sure. Let me clean up first and . . ."

"That can wait. We have to talk," Marcellus interrupted her and took her arm, guiding her to the Mercedes. He opened the back door for her and got in after her.

"Hi, Juggler, Maceo," Shelly smiled. Neither anwered. Juggler turned his head and stared at her with that strange half smile on his face. He nodded slowly. Maceo pulled away from the curb and headed for the freeway.

Once on the highway, the silver Mercedes streaked along in the fast lane. Shelly and Marcellus had placed lines of cocaine on the mirrored bar and were laughing to release the tension she had felt from Marcellus. Everything seemed to be normal now. She figured that Natasha was out and he'd gotten lonely for some feminine companionship. She hadn't made love to him since one afternoon in Europe when Natasha had been too busy with a photo session. He had shown up in her dressing room and taken her right there.

"You like this toot, baby," Marcellus asked in his silky voice with a grin on his lips. She didn't notice his eyes were cold, like a hunter's. Shelly closed her eyes and laughed dreamily.

"Oh, yeah. Yeah, Marcellus. This blow is something else," she said in a low voice.

"Like the kind I got when we were in Italy, huh," Marcellus said softly, watching her. "Why did you want that list, Shelly?" Marcellus asked.

"Hmmmm?" Shelly asked, still laughing and enjoying the rush from the coke.

"The list from the party, Shelly. Why did you ask Natasha for it?" Marcellus asked again.

"List?" Shelly asked herself aloud and opened her eyes. "Oh, that list. Pharoah wanted to give a party. He doesn't know that many people, not like you, Marcellus. He admires you so. I really think he wants to be just like you. Live the kind of life you do," Shelly trailed off.

"Where's the list now, Shelly?" Marcellus pursued.

"I gave it to Pharoah. He bugged me so about it, it was the only way I could shut him up. Give me another hit, Marcellus," Shelly said like a little girl. Marcellus smiled deceptively at her.

"Sure, baby. I'm gonna give you something that will send you out in orbit," he said. Marcellus had a plan. He figured that Pharoah was in hiding, so he had to draw him out. He would leave a warning that would tell Pharoah, where ever he was that he knew he was the one who had ripped him off.

"Here," Marcellus grinned, placing more cocaine on the mirror. "Enjoy, baby." Shelly started to lean forward when she felt Marcellus' hand on the back of her jacket collar. She understood and wriggled her arms out of the sleeves. He put the coat up in the space between the back seat and the rear window, rubbing her back as she bent to the coke on the mirror.

A letter fell from Shelly's coat down onto the seat between them. Marcellus instinctively picked it up and read the addresses on the unopened envelope.

"I see your mother still writes," Marcellus said. Shelly sat back and looked at him in surprise and then at the envelope.

"Oh, yeah. They keep trying to bring their wayward daughter back into the fold," she said and then laughed. "I was supposed to be married to a minister by now and have six kids.

"Doesn't look like she has the right address," Marcellus said. "Here. Why don't you read it." A pained expression crossed Shelly's face. She laced her fingers in her lap and stared at the window, watching the car lights race by on the other side of the freeway.

"I've been meaning to for a couple of months," she said slowly. "It can wait till tomorrow." Shelly didn't want the heartache of another letter from her mother. Her father hadn't spoken to her in years, but her mother still wanted her to come home. Shelly was still vulnerable to her mother's pleas. she felt guilty that she had failed her parents and hurt that they couldn't seem to love her for what she was. She was pretty happy with her life except for these painful intrusions of a past she had left long ago.

"I don't think you should put if off. That never does anyone any good, you know," Marcellus said gently. "When I have something to do that hurts me, I just do it. It's better that way. Go ahead," he said, dropping the envelope into her lap. She glanced at him, the sadness visible in her eyes.

Shelly ripped open one end and blew in it. The envelope popped open and she withdrew the handwritten pages from inside. Her hands were trembling as she unfolded the pages and began to read. She could feel Marcellus watching her.

The letter was dated almost three months earlier in the arthritic scrawl that was her mother's handwriting. "My dearest, Shelly," the letter began. "I pray that this letter is forwarded to you where ever you are working now. I know that your father and I have asked you to come home before, Shelly, but this time if different. Your father had many hard words for you in the past and I cannot say that I approved of your ways either. I think you must know that we have always loved you, perhaps too much or in the wrong way."

Shelly set the letter down. There were tears in her eyes. She could see her mother sitting at the writing table in their living room, struggling to shape the letters. Too many years of playing the piano in damp little churches had left her hands gnarled. Marcellus handed her his handkerchief.

"Thanks," she said, embarrassed. "This always happens to me," she tried to laugh. Marcellus turned away and she returned to the letter.

"This time I'm not asking you to come back home, Shelly. I'm begging you. Your father's heart trouble has gotten very bad. They took him to the hospital two days ago. He has been asking for you, Shelly. The doctors say that he'll be alright, but I don't think so. He's dying, Shelly, and wants to make some kind of peace with you."

Shelly began to sob quietly, her breath coming in short gasps. She hadn't heard the words Marcellus had spoken to Juggler or felt the car pull over to the side of the freeway. She didn't see Juggler's huge frame approaching her door.

23

Pharoah had been staying in the dilapidated Midnight Motel up the coast from Los Angeles. He had decided to disappear for a few days, at least until Marcellus was tried and sent to jail. It was best for Shelly too. She'd be out of danger if Marcellus or one of his goons associated him with any of their troubles. She didn't know anything anyway.

Pharoah had become bored with sitting in the shabby motel room by nightfall and took a drive to a deserted beach. It was peaceful, the only sound the waves breaking on the beach. Pharoah watched the waves breaking on the beach. Pharoah watched the waves and sparkling reflection of the full moon. Gradually the uneasiness he'd felt at the motel began to ebb away. Opening the console between the seats, Pharoah took out his base pipe and torch. He reached into his jacket pocket and found the silver case that held the base pellets. He dropped a pellet into the bowl and fired it with the torch. He inhaled deeply and leaned back in the seat with his eyes closed to savor the rush. That felt good. His entire body felt charged with energy. Marcellus seemed like less of a worry now. Marcellus could be beaten and Pharoah had set all the right gears in motion. Soon Marcellus would be history.

Pharoah opened his eyes and saw the lights of boats moving slowly down the coast. He torched the pellet again and took another puff. He had too much energy to just sit and observe the ocean now.

There was a small portable television in the back seat. Pharoah reached back and set it down on the passenger's seat. He plugged the adapter into the cigarette lighter outlet and turned the set on. He felt like talking to someone, but this would have to do. Pharoah flipped the dial until he found a news program. A picture of Shelly flashed onto the screen. Startled, Pharoah turned up the sound.

The reporter's voice blared from the tiny speaker. "And in other news, police have identified the body of the young woman found dumped alongside the Harbor Freeway earlier this morning. She is twenty-two year old Shelly Harris of Los Angeles." Pharoah stared at the screen, dumbfounded. This can't be happening, his mind screamed.

"Miss Harris, a model, was a finalist several months ago in the Miss International beauty contest. Police are awaiting the results of the autopsy, but a spokesman told KDC News that it appears to be a homicide. Turning to sports . . ."

Pharoah ripped the television cord from the dash board. The small screen faded to black. "That rotten mother fucker," Pharoah shouted, hurling the base pipe out the car window. It shattered on the concrete. His brain was exploding with rage and pain. "Why Shelly?" he yelled, fighting back tears. He scooped up the television in one hand and stepped out of the car. Raising the T.V. over his head, he ran to the edge of the parking area and smashed it on the rocks.

He stood, fists clenched at his side, glaring at the broken bit of the T.V. that had brought him the terrible news. He kicked the larger parts away and stomped the smaller fragments. His fury spent on this destruction, he faced the ocean. He wanted to drive right to Marcellus' mansion and blow the monster straight to hell, along with his goons. Pharoah imagined the huge estate in flames, the trapped occupants wailing as they burned alive. He could see Marcellus' body crushed under the Eldorado's wheels. Pharoah slashed the air with his fist and spun around toward his car. He walked quickly back to the car and slammed his fist down on the roof before getting in. The force of the blow left a three inch deep dent in the sheet metal.

Pharoah started the car and screeched out of the deserted lot. He couldn't wait for the trial, but he had to be smart. He wanted to make more trouble for Marcellus and company. Pharoah spotted a bar on the side of the coast road and whipped the car onto the gravel, sending the small stones flying. If this worked, Marcellus could get nailed for a weapons possession charge. That pimping nigger would never see daylight again with all the charges against him, Pharoah smiled.

He saw a phone booth at the corner of the old stucco building and jumped out of the car. He found a dime in one of his pockets and ran to the booth. Pharoah thought a moment to recall the phone number. A light flashed in his eyes and he picked up the phone to dial. There was a certain low-life nigger who got around and had connections with both sides of the law. That was his man. Information, true or false, could be a deadly weapon.

24

Fisheye sat at his favorite table on the patio of the hamburger stand. He finished squeezing the mustard onto the hamburger bun and squinted up at the bright noonday sun. It was going to be another scorcher, he thought. He took a sip from his soda and looked down at his newspaper.

One of the columns had a most interesting headline: "Armstrong Pleads No Contest to Charge of Narcotics Trafficking: To be Sentenced Next Week." Fisheye smiled and bit into his hamburger. The bastard was going to prison. If he could nail the other hood that had robbed Armstrong, he'd have a complete case for the D.A. He knew the third member had to be the brains of the operation. The guy was smart enough to set Armstrong up and get away with a million dollars. Maybe the guy thought he was smart enough to move in on Armstrong's action.

A shadow passed over the table and Fisheye saw Snitch sitting astride a ten speed bicycle.

"You eat that shit all day, you'll get cancer," Snitch chuckled and rested a foot on the bench next to the table.

"Man's got to die of something," Fisheye retorted sourly, taking another bite of his hamburger.

"You are most certainly right," Snitch laughed facetiously. Fisheye had a swallow of soda to wash down the burger and glared at Snitch.

"You called me, Snitch?" Fisheye asked impatiently. He didn't want to spend the afternoon trading lines with a fool stoolie.

"You never learn, do you?" Snitch asked, angry.

"I'm not here for a school lesson, Snitch! I want information.," Fisheye stated, finishing his hamburger and wiping his mouth with a paper napkin. Snitch stared down at Fisheye with a cold light in his eyes.

"The guy you're looking for is called Pharoah," Snitch told him softly. After he had spoken the name, he quickly checked out the burger stand's clientele.

"Got an address?" Fisheye asked getting very interested. The pressure he had put on this jerk was really paying off, he thought.

"Don't know where he lives, but he's supposed to cop some cocaine later tonight. A place up in Hollywood. Two ten Crosely Road," Snitch answered, leaning over the table to insure that no one overheard what he was saying.

"What's this Pharoah all about?" Fisheye inquired. He wanted everything that Snitch had on Pharoah. Snitch grimaced and held up a hand.

"You asked for a name and an address. You want a background check, go hire the F.B.I.," Snitch answered sarcastically. Fisheye shook his head and picked up his paper.

"You know something, Snitch? You have a very funky attitude. I sure hope it doesn't get you killed," Fisheye joked tiredly and stood up to leave. Snitch just stared at Fisheye with cold hatred. He watched the old cop walk away to his unmarked car. A crooked smile slowly formed on Snitch's lips as he rode his ten speed away. Part one was finished, now he had to put part two in motion. He would have his sweet revenge after all.

Back by the hamburger stand, Fisheye was sitting in his car and writing down the information that Snitch had given him. He wrote the name and place down on a scrap of paper that was his wife's shopping list. He was relieved that instead of going to a grocery store he would be staking out a drug deal. He put the paper into his shirt pocket and started the car. Fisheye wanted to check this one out himself. If Gene knew what he was planning to do, he'd never allow it. This was to be a pure Fisheye operation. No fleet of regular patrol cars screeching up to a house. No bumbling cops that were more concerned about the suspect's rights than busting a crime. He'd handle this one alone, like the old days.

25

The 600 E Mercedes was driving slowly down a dark street that bordered an empty park. When the car reached a solitary street light, it stopped directly under it. The running lights were switched off, but the engine kept running. There was a slight movement in the shadows of the park and a figure emerged, walking to the car. The figure lingered for a moment by the car window, speaking in hushed tones. Abruptly the figure left the side of the Mercedes and disappeared into the park.

Juggler flicked on the car's lights and drove down the street. Maceo sat next to him, loading a double barreled sawed-off shot gun.

"I told you with all that money on the street, something would turn up," he smiled. Maceo continued to check the gun.

"I'm gonna enjoy this," Maceo said intently.

"We both will," Juggler added, turning onto a freeway ramp.

"Can't you drive any faster?" Maceo asked, anxious for some action.

"Relax. We've got time. Never rush an execution. A man who's about to die, doesn't like to be rushed. Remember that!" Juggler scolded. He shot a look at Maceo and caught the hungry expression on his face.

"The only thing I'm gonna remember is the look on his face when I separate his brains from his skull," Maceo laughed. Juggler started chuckling and soon they both were roaring.

In Beverly Hills, Fisheye rushed down the stone steps of the police station and jumped into his car. The tires squealed as he tore out of the station car lot. He wasn't going to be too late this time. Reaching into his jacket, he pulled out his .38 and flipped the barrel open to make sure it was loaded. He snapped it shut and returned it to his holster in a single fluid motion.

Fisheye's unmarked car flew down the quiet streets of Beverly Hills, past strolling couples and shop keepers leaving their stores late. The traffic at this early evening hour was beginning to thin out and soon Fisheye was streaking through Hollywood. He figured that if he had the information about Pharoah Harris, so did Armstrong's thugs. There was no time to lose.

He finally caught a red light at an intersection near the Hollywood Freeway and cursed under his breath. Two buses were blocking both lanes in a friendly race. The light changed and he shot the car into the turning lane, swerving to avoid the oncoming cars on the other side of the intersection and squeezed back into the lane in front of the busses. The light at the freeway entrance was just turning yellow as he sped up the ramp and onto the five lane highway.

Fisheye took out a pack of cigarettes and lit one. He wanted to at least try to relax. It didn't work. A minute later he was leaning on the horn to get a slower moving car out of his way.

Juggler turned the Mercedes down an unlit street in a poor section of Hollywood. His face was tense. Maceo sat next to him, the shotgun across his lap. Maceo was ready for action, beads of sweat appearing on his unsmiling face.

Juggler saw the abandoned house they were looking for and slowed the car to a stop. Backing up, he passed by the house again and pulled over into the shadows.

"This is it," he said in a low voice to Maceo.

"Let's go," Maceo replied with a nod. They climbed out of the car and quietly closed the doors. They walked cautiously up the sidewalk beside the house. Maceo kept the shotgun against his leg in case anyone drove by. He would merely look like a man with a stiff leg.

Juggler held Maceo back with his arm while he peered around a wall of unkept hedge at the target house. It appeared to be an abandoned, two-story apartment building. The windows and front door were boarded up, the paint peeling from the walls. They could see no lights inside the house.

Juggler stepped around the hedge and into the tall weeds that had taken over the yard. He waved Maceo on and they both approached the front door. Juggler put his Magnum in its holster and took hold of a board nailed over the door. With a quick jerk, the board came loose. Maceo tapped him on the shoulder and motioned that they should go around to the other side of the house. Juggler nodded and set the old board down gently on the ground. They silently moved to the side of the house and began creeping toward the back, weapons at ready.

Fisheye had just turned the corner onto Crosely street and spotted the dark shape of the Mercedes 600 E down the street. He slowly drove up behind the car and parked. This was the same Mercedes he had seen from Armstrong's driveway the morning of the bust. He pulled his .38 and got out of the car. He wished he had taken a riot shotgun from the police station. These clowns played rough. He considered the probable citation that he'd receive for his arrest and felt better about the odds. He still had surprise in his favor and Armstong's boys were already here. Fisheye knew he didn't have to worry about them sneaking up on him.

He walked down the sidewalk in front of the house. Keeping the pistol in his pocket, his finger on the trigger, he stepped with a slight stagger and hummed bit of an old tune. Just a harmless drunk wandering the streets. He kept a careful watch on the house and decided it was safe to proceed to the front door. Any passerby observing this scene would have been amazed at

211

how rapidly this old drunk had sobered. Fisheye made a straight line for the front door of the dark house.

He saw one board laying beside the door and reached for one of the remaining slats across it. It came loose easily and he took hold of the next one down.

At the rear of the house, Juggler and Maceo were working on one of the windows. Slowly the warped frame gave way to their strength and slid upward. Juggler found a milk crate and placed it below the open window. Maceo and he began to ease themselves into the house.

Fisheye pryed another board away from the door and tried the door knob. It clicked open and the door swung wide. A rush of musty air filled his eyes with dust. He rubbed the soot out of his eyes and stepped over the remaining board on the bottom. Once inside, he crouched with his revolver while he adjusted to the dim light.

Maceo and Juggler walked through the empty apartment and cautiously opened the door onto the hallway. They stepped into the hall and listened. A radio was playing somewhere in the building. Maceo tried to slow his breathing to hear better. It was no use. His heart was pounding in his ears from the adrenalin. Juggler gripped his shoulder and pointed up with his gun. Pharoah must be upstairs. They eased themselves along the corridor, their backs to the wall, till they reached a pitch black stairwell.

Fisheye moved in and out of the weak shafts of light that filtered through the boards over the front windows. He could barely make out fresh footprints in the thick dust. They led off down a short hallway to a flight of stairs. At the bottom of the front stairwell, Fisheye cocked his head to listen. Sure enough, there was a radio playing upstairs somewhere. He strained his eyes, staring into the blackness above, and shrugged. It didn't really matter if there was a lookout posted. The lookout wouldn't be able to see him any better than he could see the lookout. Fisheye started up the steps.

Juggler and Maceo reached the second floor landing and paused. The radio was louder now. Juggler lowered himself before peering down the long dark hallway. He saw a shaft of light spilling onto the hallway floor from the space under a door. He stood up and motioned for Maceo to follow.

Fisheye made it to the top of the stairway and stopped to catch his breath. The excitement and the exertion were tiring him. He leaned against the wall and took out a handkerchief to wipe his brow. The sound of the radio was louder now and he thought he heard a floorboard creak. He began to move down the hall.

Juggler and Maceo had crept to the door with the light and stood silently in front of it. Juggler pointed at the door and Maceo nodded, patting the butt of the shotgun. His face was dripping with sweat. There was no sound from the room except the radio. Maybe the nigger's asleep, Juggler mused. That would make their job a lot easier. The jerk would be blinking himself awake when the death dealing shotgun blew his skull to bits.

Maceo positioned himself and on a signal from Juggler, raised his foot and kicked hard against the door. They crashed into the room, guns cocked.

The room was empty. A single lamp shone on the radio. Juggler and Maceo looked at each other in bewilderment. Juggler saw a bathroom door on one side of the apartment and ran to it. He almost took the door off its hinges as he whipped it open and looked in.

Fisheye had heard the loud crash of the apartment door being smashed and ran around a corner in the black hall. Light was glaring into the hallway. He heard footsteps and another door slam open.

He hoped he wasn't too late. He ran down the hall and stepped into the door way.

"Freeze!" he shouted, seeing Maceo standing by a bed. Maceo turned in an instant and unloaded one barrel of the shotgun into Fisheye. Fisheye was knocked backwards into the wall by the blast, his hoarse scream filled the dingy room. He pulled the trigger of his .38, just as Juggler fired his Magnum.

Juggler felt the slap of hot lead on his neck and forehead as he squeezed the trigger. Screaming, he crumpled to the floor and gasped for breath. The air gurgled through the gash in his throat. His eyes lost their focus and began to glaze with death.

Fisheye was struck in the thigh by Juggler's bullet and knocked to the floor. Half of his upper leg muscle splattered on the wall to the other side of him. His coat was becoming dark as it soaked up the blood from his chest wound. Through a haze of pain he saw Maceo raise his shotgun again, and pulled the trigger of the .38 three times in rapid succession. Maceo's gun jammed. The three bullets pounded into his chest, near his heart. He only had a moment to grunt as he fell back on the mattress and rolled over. Fisheye watched till he became as motionless as Juggler had.

Fisheye knew that he would bleed to death in a matter of minutes if he didn't get to his car and radio for an ambulance. He dropped the .38 and crawled to the door. The pain was excruciating. A growing puddle of blood formed around him. He reached the door and strained to grasp the door knob. No, his brain screamed. He wasn't ready to die. Somehow he managed to take hold of the door knob and place his other arm underneath himself for support. He was getting dizzy and the room spun from his loss of blood. Fisheye tried to push himself up from the floor and a spasm of pain ripped through his chest. He groaned and fell back to the floor.

"Betsy," he called out to his wife. His eyes assumed the glazed look of death and he became still.

26

Pharoah was lying on the bed in his shabby room at the Midnight Motel. He attempted to read the newspaper resting on his knees, but grew too restless and tossed it across the room. He picked up the remote control for the television and turned the set on. Nothing seemed interesting. He flipped through all the stations and dropped the remote control on the bed in disgust. It was the waiting. Not knowing was so uncomfortable. He felt like ants were crawling all over his skin. If his plan worked, he was sitting pretty. If not, he was in even bigger trouble than before. Why doesn't that silly nigger call, he wondered. It was almost eleven o'clock. What went down?

Suddenly the phone rang. Its jangling ring made Pharoah jump. He lunged for the phone, knocking the receiver to the floor. He quickly picked it up.

"Yeah," Pharoah asked, his voice tense.

"Snitch, here," the voice on the other end said softly.

"Well?" Pharoah asked impatiently.

"The eleven o'clock news should be very interesting," Snitch chuckled. Pharoah's brow was knit with worry. He ran the back of his hand across his forehead.

"Any problems get solved?" Pharoah asked.

"One of mine and two of yours," Snitch cackled.

"Permanently?"

"Permanently!" Snitch said victoriously. "Got anything else for me? I can sure use the bread."

"I can pretty much handle things from here on out. We'll hook up down the road," Pharoah smiled. His face relaxed with the great relief he felt.

"It's been a pleasure doing business with you," Snitch said. "Be sure to check out the news!"

"On the one," Pharoah smiled and hung up the phone. He picked up the remote control and changed the channel to the local news. A picture of Fisheye flashed on the screen behind a reporter.

"Funeral services for police officer David Martin will be held later this week. Affectionately called 'Fisheye' by his fellow officers because of the distinctive eye patch he wore, Martin was slain earlier this evening in what police say was a raid on the suspected members of a narcotics ring." Juggler's picture was now flashed on the screen with Maceo's. Pharoah stared at the screen hard, anger on his face.

"Also killed in the raid were Harper P. Evans and Elias Scovan, both believed to be members of that ring with ties to organized crime. In other news . . ." Pharoah turned the set off.

So he'd done it! He'd out foxed the bastards and won. That pimping slime, Marcellus, was already in jail. Pharoah grinned as he walked over to the dresser and poured himself a Scotch. Victory was sweet and revenge felt so good. Those niggers that fucked with him by murdering his woman got what they deserved and the police took care of the execution. Pharoah laughed aloud and sat on the edge of the bed. He took a long swallow of Scotch and looked around at the motel room. It was a dump.

Pharoah guessed it was safe to go by his house now. He could at least pick up a few things and maybe find a nicer place to stay. A place where he could do business.

Pharoah knew that it was almost time for the last phase of his master plan. Everything had worked great, he congratulated himself. An image of Shelly came vividly to mind and the smile faded from his lips It had almost worked perfectly, he thought sadly. Completely obliterating Marcellus and his empire was going to make him very happy, indeed.

Pharoah knew that with Marcellus in the can there was a huge hole in the cocaine network. A tremendous amount of money was being lost every hour that he spent in jail. In two days Pharoah would make an offer that would be impossible for the money man behind Marcellus to refuse. It was all a matter of profit and loss and the equation was finally working in his favor.

27

The walls of the California state prison for Southern California were practically invisible in the heat waves rising from the desert sand. The outer perimeter was a twelve foot barbed wire fence. Guards patrolled the fence in jeeps with specially fitted tires. They needed them to avoid sinking up to their axles every time they drove on the sand.

It was quiet out there. Only the wind roared in the occupants' ears when they were working out in the sand. Special punishment was simple. A prisoner was forced under a rifle to work away from the prison grounds, digging in the desert near the fence. Rattlesnakes and scorpions taught them a lesson of obedience.

The prison was so overcrowded that the administration was happy if only two or three murders occured every month. It was the best anyone could expect with the state budget cutbacks. The warden had told the state legislature that they couldn't get a better system if they were only willing to pay for one guard to every forty prisoners. Rehabilitation was out of the question. It was a matter of controlling that many angry men with a minimum amount of violence. Long ago the situation had reached the point where the guards were terrified of the prisoners and stayed behind thick bars, afraid to mingle with the population in the yard.

The newspapers and politicians all paid lip service to the notion that it was the warden and the guards that ran the prison under the direction of the state corrections board. The fact was that the prison ran itself. The prisoners could be locked into it, but there was no way to control them.

There were factions within the prison population that had more real power than any senator had ever dreamed of. The Mexican Mafia held life and death power over all the Mexicans in the prison. Likewise, the black and white gangster connections ruled their people. The guards couldn't prevent the killings and the other prisoners couldn't give testimony. Much of the time, it was easier for the guards to accept the bribes for favors. They made up to several times their salaries by helping smuggle drugs and letters to the prisoners that were much richer than they could ever be.

Marcellus had been thrown into this situation two days go. He didn't like it but Henry had promised that it would only be for a year at the longest. He could be parolled early for good behavior and get his sentence reduced. Marcellus had decided that the best way to achieve this goal was to keep to himself. He had spoken to none of the prisoners since his arrival and he intended to keep it that way.

He had been let out of his cell for two hours recreation. There were two bunks in his cell, but the prisoner that would have been his cellmate had a fatal accident in the machine shop the week before. Henry had paid the warden a lot of cash to keep the cell single.

Marcellus walked down the long walkway to the recreation room. He had to take small steps because of the crush of prisoners all walking to the recreation room. The sound of heavy prison shoes scraping on the concrete floors echoed off the thick stone walls. Marcellus tucked his regulation prison shirt in. The shirt, like the pants, was made at the prison out of rough cotton. When the laundry got done they could practically cut the flesh of the man that wore them. Marcellus thought of his silk shirts and fine custom tailored wardrobe as he passed into the recreation room. He tapped his fist on the tables as he passed to the front of the room to see the television news.

Henry had gotten word to him about Juggler and Maceo and that cop. This Pharoah dude was clever. The boys probably didn't even know what hit them. Marcellus sat down at a table near the television and listened to the news. His mind wandered over the events that had brought him to this place.

He hated to admit it, but perhaps he had gotten too casual about the whole business, maybe over confident as well. It wasn't too late to correct the errors. He just had to keep a lower profile. Fate might be telling him to retire from the cocaine trade. He could pick up and disappear to Hawaii with Natasha and go back to architecture. Of course, Pharoah would have to be killed first.

There was a loud slapping sound near Marcellus and he quickly turned his head to the source. There was a large brute of an inmate striking an old man. The old man gave his attacker some cigarettes and the hulk walked away. Marcellus turned back to the television and tried to concentrate on the weather report.

The announcer was gushing about how wonderful the weather would be that weekend for the beach and travel. Marcellus shut his eyes for a moment and stood up. There was no news about any of his businesses and he didn't need the torture of a weather report for the goddamn surfers. He wanted to go back to his cell and read some of the books he'd brought with him. He made his way toward the door, past tables full of poker playing cons. Marcellus neared the door and found the giant convict that had been bothering the old man blocking his path. He tried to step around the prisoner and leave along the wall. The convict shot his arm up to block Marcellus again.

"Hey, pretty boy, who do you belong to?" the convict smiled, revealing several missing teeth.

"I don't belong to nobody," Marcellus said in a low voice. He almost made a gesture for Juggler to lay the nigger out, but stopped himself. He would have to think his way out of this one. The con could tear him apart.

"Is that a fact? Then you're up for grabs," the con grinned evilly. "You can call me Victor, baby." Marcellus noticed that several other convicts had gathered around them to watch the exchange. From the smirks on their faces, he knew that they were in on this somehow.

"Naw man. I ain't up for nothing or nobody!" Marcellus stated firmly. He knew he was lost and the victim of a gang rape if he showed any weakness at all.

"Sure talk big for a dude only been here a few days," one of the other convicts added, moving closer.

"Better take him in the head and get him straight," another prisoner said with a grin, placing his hand on Marcellus' shoulder. Marcellus grabbed his hand and removed it.

"Don't put your hands on me! You want me to go to the head, I'll go. But don't ever put your hands on me. Understand?" Marcellus spat out. He knocked Victor's hand from the wall and walked out of the recreation room.

Marcellus walked slowly into the bathroom with the group of prisoners following. He tried to push the snickers he heard from his mind so he could think of something. These animals would kill him unless he could become valuable to them in some way. He entered the bathroom and went to a far wall.

"Speak your piece, man," Marcellus said leaning up against the wall.

"You must not realize where you are! We have rules here. You don't follow them, you're dead," Victor laughed.

"You sure can't make it with the hoogies and the Mexican Mafia would serve you for dinner if they felt like it," another con said chuckling.

"You either somebody's punk, a gambler or a killer, unless you into religion?" a second prisoner asked.

"I ain't into none of that," Marcellus answered, shaking his head. Victor smiled and put a hand on his shoulder.

"Then maybe you should get into me," Victor said firmly. Marcellus knocked the hand off.

"Seems like you got a hearing problem. I said don't put your hands on me," Marcellus shot back. His eyes glared with anger at the group surrounding him.

"Pretty boy, there's fifteen of us in this room. We'll do whatever we feel like to you!" Victor snarled.

"No you won't," Marcellus smiled, shaking his head. He was suddenly secure in the situation. The other convicts saw this and were puzzled.

"And what's to stop us, pretty boy? You gonna pull out your dick and stab us all?" a convict asked sarcastically. All the cons roared at his joke.

"You fuck with me and you lose the pipeline," Marcellus answered calmly. He felt sure that he could control them now.

"What the hell is the pipeline about?" Victor asked.

"I'm into dope. Hash, chemicals, smack, toot, whatever you want," Marcellus replied coolly.

"Can you get some freebase?" a con with scars all over his face asked breathlessly.

"I'm the best cook in America! I can bring back a rock with 7-UP if I have to," Marcellus smiled. He had them. There would be no more trouble from these clowns. Marcellus checked his watch.

"I'm tired, gentlemen. I'll be in my cell. Anybody want to deal, from now on I'm the man," Marcellus grinned and pushed his way to the door and left the bathroom.

"You sure are," Victor said in amazement. He already liked this new guy's guts, even if he was bullshitting. There was plenty of time to find out.

28

Henry was sitting at his desk, filling out some legal forms and sipping his morning coffee. He had been upset about Marcellus having to do a stretch in prison but it had been the only way. Henry figured he was lucky that it hadn't gotten worse. He could've not only lost a lot of clients, but been disbarred and maybe sent to jail himself. His attractive secretary opened the door to his office and stepped halfway in. She looked concerned.

"There's a gentleman to see you, sir. He won't leave his name, but he insists," she said and was pushed out of the way by a tall man behind her.

"The name is Pharoah," the intruder stated. Henry was stunned, the blood drained from his face. The thought crossed his mind that Pharoah was there to kill him, to eliminate any loose ends. Pharoah walked to Henry's desk and stared down at him. In an effort to overcome his feeling of panic, Henry lit a cigarette and leaned back in his leather chair. He was trying to increase the distance between himself and this crazed nigger. Henry motioned for his secretary to leave and waited till she had closed the door before speaking.

"You have an awful lot of nerve," Henry told him. Pharoah smiled and took a seat in front of the desk.

"An attorney with your background shouldn't plead his client No Contest on evidence that a first year law student could destroy at trial," Pharoah said confidently. Pharoah was enjoying this a great deal. He had this white parasite right where he wanted him.

"Meaning?" Henry stammered. He had practically gagged on his cigarette.

"Meaning that you're either incredibly stupid or a part of the deal. I figure its the latter," Pharoah continued.

"It's on appeal. Marcellus will be out in less than a year," Henry retorted. His ego was stinging from that last remark.

"But look how much money you'll be losing," Pharoah said in a friendly voice, gesturing with his hands.

"I'm afraid I don't follow you," Henry responded. Pharoah rolled his eyes in mock disbelief and waved the attorney's answer away.

"I think you do. The way I figure it, you were getting between ten and twenty percent off the top. You made all the arrangements, provided all the cash, Marcellus did all the leg work," Pharoah said calmly. He watched for Henry's reaction and it was there. The lawyer was frozen with fear "I'm here to offer the same deal." Henry nervously snubbed out the lit cigarette and lit another.

"I'm listening," Henry breathed, his eyes darting about the room.

"Only one thing," Pharoah said firmly. Henry had to deal with him whether he wanted to or not. It wasn't just the money. The lawyer didn't have the balls for murder and Pharoah could drop a few more dimes to the police and ruin him.

"And that is?" Henry asked.

"Marcellus is dangerous as long as he has money. I want him broke when he gets out of prison," Pharoah ordered. Henry laughed facetiously.

"Why should I care what happens to you?" Henry asked, still laughing.

"Because it's business, that's why! And after all, the bottom line is money, isn't it, counselor?" Pharoah smiled, knowing he had won.

"Always."

29

Marcellus made friends fast inside the prison with his endless supply of drugs. The inmates had respect for anyone that could manage a drug store behind the walls of a state prison. The group of inmates that had been ready to tear him apart in the first days had become a loyal circle of comrades.

Marcellus had fired up a pellet of base and was sharing it with two other prisoners in his cell. One of the cons took a long pull at the base pipe and closed his eyes for a moment.

"Man, what a rush! Jesus, Marcellus, how you learn to cook this shit?" the con asked, smiling.

"Trade secret, Moko," Marcellus answered.

"Three of the guards on the night shift want some hash, about ten ounces," Victor told Marcellus. His huge frame seemed even larger in the tiny cell.

"Tommorow. Right after visiting hours," Marcellus chuckled. The guards had become his best customers. A loud buzzer sounded and Victor and Moko abruptly stood up to return to their own cells.

"Later," Marcellus said as they left his cell. Soon a metallic clang was heard as the guards threw the switch that automatcially closed the cell doors. Marcellus put the pipe under his bunk and picked up a magazine. He collapsed on his bunk and began to leaf through it.

"Marcellus," a voice called from another cell.

225

Marcellus sat up and heard his name called again. He got up from the bed and went to the front of the cell, his hands gripping the bars.

"Yeah man, what do you want?" Marcellus asked. The prisoner who had called him was locked in the cell next to his.

"Check it out, Marcellus. Sukie's getting out tommorow. Heard about the dude that put you here. He wants to know if he can take care of it for you. You know, if he can handle the contract?" the con asked. Marcellus shook his head and smiled.

"Tell Suki thanks, but this is one piece of business I intend to handle personally," Marcellus answered.

"Yeah, Marcellus, but you might be here for a while," the con pursued. All the cons that had befriended Marcellus knew that he had to be very rich to deal all the drugs. It would be a fat contract and a good start back to work for Sukie.

"I might. It's all the more reason to deal with him myself," Marcellus told him resolutely.

"O.K., just thought I'd pass along the offer," the con said.

"Later," Marcellus said and returned to his bunk. The con might be right, thought Marcellus. This could turn out to be a longer stay than he wished. Still, the important thing was to handle this Pharoah nigger himself. It was the only way to let the other dealers know that he was serious about the business. Marcellus rested his head on the lumpy matress and sighed. It was going to be sweet, that son of a bitch that had messed with his organization. Pharoah was too stupid to take his candy and run. He'd be waiting for him right in the city and probably spreading a lot of Marcellus's money around.

30

Henry and Natasha were seated at a table overlooking the yachts in Marina del Rey. The exclusive sea food restaurant was famous world over for its fine lobster dishes. It was one of those places that didn't bother to list the prices on the menu. If the check made you miss a car payment, you were in the wrong place.

Natasha gazed out over the bobbing yachts at the blazing sunset that had left the sky electric orange and pink. She was thinking about how much she had enjoyed Henry's company in Marcellus' absence. She sensed that he was interested in more than good friendship, but assumed that he would never muster the necessary courage to try anything.

"I propose a toast," Henry said smiling happily. He had enjoyed the last few weeks of candle lit dinners and theater more than anything in his life for years. Still, he didn't want to rush into anything that he might regret, either personally or professionally. Natasha turned her gaze back to Henry.

"To who?" she asked brightly.

"To Marcellus," Henry answered. He wanted to appear the loyal friend till the last.

"Marcellus," Natasha echoed, raising her champagne glass and locking her arm in his. They drank. Henry could not stop himself from kissing her arm before releasing her.

"How's the appeal coming?" Natasha asked.

"It won't be long now, Natasha," Henry answered with his patented brand of confidence. He looked into her sparkling eyes a moment, trying to decide on the best way to present his story. Pharoah had left no doubt that it had to be done. He would lose millions if no one picked up where Marcellus had left off. He drew a deep breath and held her hand. "But there is one other problem."

"What's that?"

"Well, the Justice Department and the IRS are investigating Marcellus' financial status. It's only a matter of time before they discover his Swiss bank account. If they do, he can kiss the appeal goodbye," Henry said with sincerity. It had worked. He could tell she believed him. Why shouldn't she, he wondered. Had he ever lied to her? Natasha withdrew her hand and pulled a cigarette out of her beaded purse. She waited for Henry to light it for her.

"What should we do?" she asked, concern etched on her lovely features.

"He gave you power of attorney, so you'll have to close out the account," Henry responded. This was much easier than he imagined. The trick was to have a creditable first lie and then let the net draw around her slowly.

"But there's over a million dollars in it! What do I do with the money?" Natasha inquired innocently.

"I'll have to invest it for him under a dummy corporation. You sell the house," Henry stated simply, watching her face for any sign of disbelief. He saw only the desire to help Marcellus.

"I don't know, Henry," she whispered, almost to herself.

"Well, it's the only chance he's got to get out without any hassle. They could discover it any day now," Henry said, pushing her further over the brink.

"I know he's always trusted your judgement, Henry," she said, searching his face. "You're sure this is the best way?"

"Natasha, it's the only way."

31

In the months that followed, Pharoah's life took a marked turn for the richer. He moved into a huge penthouse and Henry had found a new supplier for his clients. Pharoah remembered those that had helped him and hired Squeegee and Snitch as bodyguards. The good life agreed with them all. Life became a constant party while Pharoah worked the money machine of cocaine.

Natasha had complied with Henry's request to liquidate all of Marcellus' holdings and moved into an apartment. Henry disbursed the funds that Natasha had given him into various accounts of his own. He knew that in order to keep Pharoah happy, Marcellus had to be broke when he emerged from prison. Henry had maintained his image as a friend to Marcellus and successfully managed to gain his release after nine months in the state prison. The day before Marcellus was to be released, Natasha decided to see Henry and check on the investments he'd made for Marcellus.

Henry was seated behind his desk and reading the Wall Street Journal when he heard a soft knock on his office door. He looked up to see Natasha enter and close the door behind her.

"Natasha, what a pleasant surprise," Henry exclaimed, jumping up from his desk and going to her. He slipped his arm around her waist and kissed her on the cheek. "Hey, how about Marcellus winning his appeal? I told you he would! He'll be home first thing tomorrow," Henry gushed. He escorted Natasha to a chair and returned to his desk.

"I know, that's why I came by," Natasha explained. "I'm going to see him today. You know, to take him a few things and what have you. I was wondering if you would give me the information on those investments you made for him. I haven't mentioned anything to him and I'd kinda like to surprise him," Natasha smiled. Henry frowned and shuffled some papers on his desk. He dreaded the thought of hurting her but it was business.

"Gee, Natasha, I'm glad you brought that up. I was meaning to call you about it. The real estate deal in Mexico filed for bankruptcy and I don't think there's a chance in hell of getting anything out of it. As far as the money I put into the oil and gas drilling, well, they hit a dry hole. I'm afraid there's no return there either," Henry said sadly. Natasha's eyes were wide with worry. She hadn't bother to ask Marcellus if it was all right and now there was trouble.

"Well, just how much is left?" she asked, clutching her purse. Henry looked at her for a moment and then down at his papers.

"Nothing," he answered, shaking his head.

"Nothing? You mean it's gone? All of it? There's nothing left?" she asked, growing more upset with every passing second.

"Not a dime," Henry answered, still looking down at his papers. When he raised his eyes he saw her running to the door and leaving.

"Natasha!" he cried out as the door slammed behind her.

Natasha rushed from the office building and handed the parking valet her stub. She waited impatiently until the valet brought the car up, her mind a jumble of wild thoughts and recriminations. She had only been trying to help Marcellus. Henry must have decided to let him fail, she considered. No, Henry was their friend. She tossed a five dollar bill at the car hop and jumped into the Mercedes. Squealing out of the garage, she headed for her new apartment.

It was a short drive to the luxury building on Doheny. She left the car in front and dashed into the lobby. She would talk this over with Geneva. She knew Marcellus and she certainly knew men. Maybe she could make sense out of all this.

Natasha walked out of the elevator and quickly entered the apartment. Geneva was lying on the couch, talking to a friend on the telephone.

"Hi, honey, guess who I'm talking to," Geneva giggled. Natasha ignored her and walked straight into the bedroom. She pulled out a suitcase and went to a bureau that held some of Marcellus' clothes. She began to select a shirt and suddenly started crying. Her shoulders shook as the sobs grew louder.

Geneva heard Natasha's cries and hung up the phone.

"You o.k., sugar?" Geneva called out as she walked into the bedroom. Seeing Natasha so upset was a shock for her. Natasha had always been the one who was cool and composed, like a queen. Natasha let Geneva put an arm around her shoulder and lead her to the bed. When Natasha's crying was under control she told the whole story to Geneva.

"Natasha, you'd better tell Marcellus before he gets out," Geneva warned and lit a cigarette.

"I don't know if I can," Natasha said softly, rising to pack some clothes for him.

"Yeah, well if you don't, he's gonna think it was you

that sold him out and not that lawyer,'' Geneva explained. Natasha shook her head sadly and tossed a silk shirt into the suitcase.

"I just can't believe Henry would do that to Marcellus. They were such good friends, and Marcellus trusted him so," Natasha sighed.

"Honey, when it comes to money, ain't no such thing as trust and friendship. And if a lawyer's involved, forget it kid," Geneva scolded. Natasha dabbed at an eye with a handkerchief and added some cologne to the kit she had put in the suitcase.

"How do I tell him, Geneva?" Natasha asked in helpless whisper. "What do I say?"

"You tell him the only thing you can, the truth," Geneva said seriously. She watched Natasha finish packing the small suitcase for Marcellus and start for the door. Geneva got up from the bed and ran to catch Natasha at the front door.

"Take care, girl," Geneva said giving her a peck on the cheek. Natasha forced a smile and a wink for Geneva and turned away quickly. As the door closed Geneva could tell that Natasha was weeping again. She hoped that Marcellus wouldn't be too hard on her.

Two hours later, Natasha pulled into the prison parking lot and took the suitcase to the reception room for visitors. Several other women were there to see their men along with some mothers. Two uniformed guards carrying metal detectors moved about the drab green room. They checked through all the handbags and Natasha's suitcase before allowing the visitors to proceed to the next room where they could see their loved ones. Natasha gave a little smile to the guard that was by the door and his face lit up. She could have smuggled a case of dynamite into this place, she mused.

Once in the visitor's room, Natasha looked across the long table that divided the prisoners from the visitors to find Marcellus. She saw him and sat at the table opposite. He smiled and leaned across the wide table to kiss her. She passed a white packet of cocaine pellets into his mouth with her tongue. Marcellus sat down and after checking to see if the guards were watching, took the packet from his mouth and pocketed it.

"How's it going, baby," Marcellus asked, seeing the pain in her eyes.

"Fine. I brought your clothes for tomorrow. I'll be here to pick you up at nine," she anwered with a hollow cheeriness.

"The sooner the better! How's Henry?" he asked.

"Well, uh, I've been meaning to tell you, Marcellus," she began, not knowing the words.

"Tell me what? Something wrong?" Marcellus pursued. He wanted her to spit it out, but he certainly wasn't concerned.

"Well, you see, I mean . . . Henry, he said there was an investigation into your financial holdings," Natasha said, looking down at her hands. Marcellus was getting impatient. He'd never seen her this tongue tied.

"I don't have any financial holdings," he laughed.

"I know, but he said if they found out about the money in Switzerland, you'd lose your appeal and . . ." Natasha hesitated. There was no turning back now. It was no use to wait until tomorrow.

"And?" Marcellus prompted, drumming his fingers on the thick oak table top.

"He made me draw out all the money and give it to him to invest for you, but the investments didn't go well and . . ." Natasha said and stopped. "And, well, now there's nothing left."

233

Marcellus blinked once to see if this was a dream. What she had just told him sounded fantastic.

"Nothing left? What the hell are you talking about?" he asked sharply, trying to understand what she was telling him.

"Henry made some bad investments and the money's all gone," she stammered, tears beginning to trickle down her high cheek bones. Marcellus leaned toward her, his eyes slits of anger.

"For Christ's sake, Natasha, there was over a million dollars in that account! You mean to tell me that you drew it out and gave it to Henry without telling me first?" He hissed.

"Well, he was your lawyer. I figured you trusted him," Natasha gasped through the tears. Marcellus leaned back in his chair. The expression on his face was a mixture of anger and disbelief. He abruptly stood up and glared down at the sobbing Natasha.

"You stupid little motherfucking bitch!" he shouted. Every head in the room turned to see what the commotion was about. A guard rushed forward and grabbed Marcellus by the arm and led him back into the depths of the prison. Natasha picked up the suitcase she had brought and stood up to leave. The guard by the door smiled and touched his cap as he opened the door for her. She rushed past him and ran out the exit.

Marcellus was escorted by the guard to his cell. He was silent while the guard locked the bars behind him and sat down on his bunk, stunned by Natasha's words. He suddenly jumped off the bunk and slammed his fist into the wall. His knuckles left a bloody patch on the plaster.

"Of all the dumb, motherfucking . . .!" he shouted at the stone walls. He dropped to his knees next to the bunk and reached under the mattress. He found his freebase pipe and took out the packet of cocaine pellets that Natasha had given him. Sitting on the bunk and leaning against the wall, he dropped a pellet into the bowl and fired it with his butane lighter. He inhaled the rich smoke fiercely, taking deep tokes. His eyes closed to better feel the rush that surged through him. When his eyes opened they were filled with supreme rage. He inhaled the rest of the smoke and quickly dropped in another pellet. Again he strained to draw all the smoke into his lungs at once. He could barely feel the beads of sweat break out all over his body or the throbbing veins that stood out on his neck.

He dropped another pellet into the pipe and fired it. He opened his eyes and lowered the pipe. There was a tremendous pressure in his chest and he rubbed his hand over it. The base, he thought feverishly, has the power to obliterate the pain. He brought the pipe to his lips again and drew deeply.

Suddenly the pressure on his chest sharpened. He dropped the pipe and holding his chest, fell to the hard concrete floor.

"Goddamn the pain," he cried hoarsely, his face contorted. His entire body contracted. Marcellus vomited all over the cell floor. He felt the surge of his heartbeat like a sledge hammer battering his chest. Marcellus stretched out an arm toward the bars at the front of his cell and tried to crawl forward.

"Help me! Somebody please," he tried to call, his voice a choked series of whispers. His body spasmed him into a ball and it was as if something had burst inside him. He rolled onto his back, his blood red eyes gradually glazing. His chest heaved one last time. Fists flexed and then relaxed. Marcellus was still.

32

Pharoah was sitting at the bar in his new penthouse suite with Snitch seated next to him. Snitch listened as Pharoah read aloud a small item in the newspaper.

"And Armstrong, who was due to be released the following day, was known to prison officials as a heavy user of cocaine. A freebase pipe was found on the floor next to his body and medical authorities surmise this may have contributed to his cardiac arrest. Toxicology tests revealed large amounts of the drug in his system. Medical authorities cite cardiac arrest as the leading cause of death among cocaine users," Pharoah read. He folded the paper and tossed it onto a nearby table.

"I can't believe that nigger's dead," he said.

"He is," Snitch grinned.

"It could be a trick," Pharoah mused.

"Don't get paranoid, Pharoah. He's dead all right. I checked it out. Dropped dead right there on the floor, just like it said," Snitch chuckled. Pharoah still looked serious and very unconvinced.

"I don't believe it. I just don't believe it," Pharoah stated, shaking his head slowly.

"His funeral is tomorrow. Why not pay your respects. Put your mind to rest," Snitch offered helpfully. Pharoah smiled as an idea came to mind.

"I think I'll do just that! In fact, there's something else I'm gonna do," Pharoah laughed. "Let's go see Squeegee." He had figured out a way to make sure it wasn't a trick and needed some fire power.

Pharoah and Snitch left the expensive penthouse and took Pharoah's new limousine to a shabby pool hall in east Los Angeles. They spotted Squeegee by one of the back tables and pulled him aside. Pharoah explained the job he had in mind, but Squeegee was skeptical.

"I don't know, Pharoah. I'm kinda superstitious about things like that," Squeegee said.

"Hey, look, Squeegee, it ain't gonna take you but a second," Pharoah insisted. Squeegee looked down at his feet.

"Yeah, but something like that? Just don't seem right is all," Squeegee whined.

"You ain't gonna be hurting nobody. Besides, I'll give you a half ounce of blow if you do this for me," Pharoah smiled. Gradually a smile found its way to Squeegee's face.

"Well, I guess that'll keep my nerve up," Squeegee happily agreed. Pharoah slapped his tiny hand.

"On the one, Squeegee. On the one," Pharoah laughed. "Tommorow afternoon. I'll pick you up."

The following day Pharoah's new Seville limousine pulled up behind a hearse in front of the Wilson Funeral Home. Squeegee got out of the car and walked up the sidewalk to the chapel section of the funeral home. He checked both directions of the street for cops before entering the chapel.

Inside the dark chapel, Natasha, Geneva and other members of the Armstrong clan were gathered, listening to the organist playing a sad hymn. Natasha and most of the other girls were weeping quietly. Squeegee saw the high banks of flowers that had been set up around the coffin laying next to the Reverend's podium. He stood at the back for a moment to let his eyes adjust to the dim light of the candles and heavy stained glass windows.

The organ music stopped and the Reverend stood up and walked to the podium.

"I'd like to thank Mrs. Collins for that lovely, inspirational solo," he began. He didn't notice the midget that had come halfway down the center aisle toward him.

"I know the family will appreciate it," the Reverend continued. Squeegee pulled a .45 automatic from his belt and leveled it at the casket. Suddenly the chapel was filled with the thunder of his gunfire as the bullets ripped into the coffin. The Reverend ducked behind the podium and all the guests screamed and hid their heads from the assailant. When Squeegee had completely emptied the cartridges into the coffin, he turned and ran from the chapel.

Pharoah had heard the sound of gunfire and smiled when he saw Squeegee run down the steps of the funeral home to the limousine. Squeegee jumped into the back and the limo sped off down the street. He took a handkerchief from his back pocket and mopped his sweaty brow.

"Man, I ain't never doing that again," he exclaimed.

"Not even for more toot?" Pharoah asked laughing.

"Not for nothing! Hey, where's my blow?" Squeegee asked, now laughing himself. Pharoah took a packet out of his jacket pocket and handed it to him.

"Squeegee earned his blow today, that's for sure," Snitch cackled.

"Yeah. If Marcellus wasn't dead before, he's dead now," Pharoah chuckled.

"May the dead rest in peace," Squeegee said, suddenly serious. The trio roared off to celebrate Marcellus' death.

33

The following weeks saw Pharoah conducting business as usual. It was as if Marcellus Armstrong had never existed. The clients, all wealthy and influential, had better manners than to ask any blunt questions. Pharoah was a bit crude compared to their last dealer but that made the whole business seem more chic to them. A potentially dangerous man made their predictable lives more exciting.

Pharoah was truly living his dream of wealth and influence. It was great satisfaction for him to know that he had finally made as much money as the singing group he had abandoned in his youth. He had made it. Arrived. Climbed the mountain. His sudden wealth made him more generous and Snitch and Squeegee enjoyed more cash and cocaine than they had ever dreamed of. Life was sweet.

One evening, Pharoah was hosting one of his parties and the penthouse was wall to wall with elegant gentleman and their designer clad dates. The funky music from his new ten thousand dollar stereo system had many couples dancing. Waiters scurried about with drinks, snacks, and more cocaine for the greedy guests. In various corners of the penthouse suite attractive people were bent over mirrors, snorting coke.

As Henry had explained it to Pharoah, these parties were great for business. At first, Pharoah didn't like the idea of giving all that coke away for free and wanted to charge the guests two thousand a head to attend. It wouldn't begin to cover the outlay, but it would pay for the catering and the extra help. Henry convinced Pharoah that he would end up with many more customers happy and buying. Pharoah was skeptical until he saw it work. Sure enough, the people that already went through thousands of dollars a week, increased their orders.

Pharoah had excused himself to one of the glassed-in balconies to clean a few of his base pipes while he smoked some base with Henry, Snitch and a few lovely women. Henry checked the time on his watch and started to rise.

"Think I'll head in. I'm due in court at nine," Henry said, smiling at one of the pretty women. "I'll talk to you during the week, Pharoah." Pharoah had just finished pouring ether into a pipe and was shaking it to dislodge the cocaine crystals. After he had swirled the mixture for a moment he poured the ether out onto the mirror topped table. He blinked at the fumes that rose from the table and picked up a fresh base pipe and torch.

"Let's hit the base pipe one last time," Pharoah smiled up at Henry and took a puff from the pipe.

"Naw, I got some in the car if I decide to base later. See you," Henry said as he left the balcony.

"More for us, huh, girls?" Pharoah chuckled and handed the pipe to a beautiful girl that had been eyeing the pipe hungrily since Pharoah had picked it up. While she sucked on the pipe, he picked up another pipe and poured ether into the bowl and swirled it through the stem. Again he poured the contents onto the table, waving at the intense fumes.

Henry had managed to squeeze through the party goers and leave by the service entrance to avoid the crush in the front elevator. He surprised the maintenance man who was expecting to pick up a load of garbage and rode down to the garage in silence. Henry climbed into his Rolls Royce and considered his good fortune. There seemed to be an endless supply of young hungry men who wanted to deal. He had been most lucky in that Pharoah was the most ruthless he had ever encountered.

Henry started the car and drove out to the driveway that circled the luxury apartment building. He pulled over to the edge of the drive and parked. He wanted some more freebase after all. Opening up his glove compartment, Henry took out his base pipe and dropped a pebble in.

On the balcony above the Rolls, Pharoah had continued cleaning his pipes and smoking at the same time. The highly flammable ether fumes were thick over the table. He had been working so fast that the ether had no time to evaporate before he poured more on. He was in a hurry to get it over with so that he could disappear with one of the young girls that reminded him of Shelly. His torch for the fresh pipe had gone out and he took another one out of his leather case. Pharoah had filled the bottom of the pipe with one hundred proof rum to cool and flavor the smoke.

He picked up the torch and turned the gas on. Realizing he didn't have a match to light it he motioned for a light. Snitch, always eager to please, quickly took out his cigarette lighter and held it across the table for the torch. The instant he flicked the flint on his lighter, the fumes from the ether exploded. Pharoah cried out and dropped his fragile base pipe. It shattered, soaking him with rum. His clothes quickly caught fire and he leapt up from the table screaming.

Down in the driveway, Henry had tossed a pellet of base into his pipe and idly looked out of the window to the building. His eyes followed the balconies up the side until he found what he knew was Pharoah's balcony.

Henry lit the base and took a puff before he saw Pharoah's flaming shape against the high window.

Henry shook his head in disgust and inhaled more freebase smoke. He started the engine and the black Rolls Royce glided down the driveway and into the traffic. There'd be others, he knew. There would always be others.

DOPEFIEND
THE STORY OF A BLACK JUNKIE
by DONALD GOINES

Donald Goines is a talented new writer who learned his craft and sharpened his skills in the ghetto slums and federal penitentiaries of America. DOPEFIEND is the shocking first novel by this young man who has seen and lived through everything he writes about. ■ DOPEFIEND exposes the dark, despair-ridden, secret world few outsiders know about—the private hell of the black heroin addict. Trapped in the festering sore of a major American ghetto, a young man and a girl—both handsome, talented, full of promise—are inexorably pulled into the living death of the hard-core junkie. ■ DOPEFIEND is an appalling story because it rings so true. It is also a work of rare power and great compassion. DOPEFIEND will draw you into a nightmare world you will not soon forget.

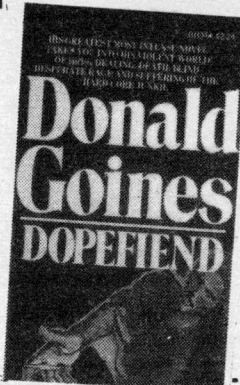

HOLLOWAY HOUSE PUBLISHING CO.
8060 MELROSE AVENUE, LOS ANGELES, CALIFORNIA 90046

Gentlemen: I enclose _____ ☐ cash, ☐ check, ☐ money order, payment in full for books ordered. I understand that if I am not completely satisfied, I may return my order within 10 days for a complete refund. (Add 50c per order to cover postage. California residents add 6% tax. Please allow three weeks for delivery.)

☐ BH044, DOPEFIEND, $2.25

Name_____

Address_____

City_____ State_____ Zip_____

PB101

SUGARMAN

FICTION—The dude known as Sugarman was young, handsome, tough and smart. His well-organized gang was loyal—ready to kill or be killed on Sugarman's orders. He controlled a large stable of beautiful, swift young prostitutes and boosters. Money was rolling in in big bundles. Sugarman's number one lady, the ravishingly beautiful Lola, was dynamite in the sack; so fine that perfume manufacturers could have made money bottling her funk. But none of this was enough for Sugarman. He wanted more. He wanted the kind of wealth and power the crooked white cops and politicians possessed and wielded in the country. He moved to take over the numbers racket launching the bloodiest struggle for power since the days of prohibition. All hell came down! Before it was over, there were countless casualties. And even the survivors had been scarred, maimed or corrupted.

HOLLOWAY HOUSE PUBLISHING CO.
8060 MELROSE AVE., LOS ANGELES, CALIF. 90046

Gentlemen: I enclose _____ ☐ cash, ☐ check, ☐ money order, payment in full for books ordered. I understand that if I am not completely satisfied, I may return my order within 10 days for a complete refund. (Add 50c per order to cover postage. California residents add 15c sales tax. Please allow three weeks for delivery.)

☐ **BH063, SUGARMAN, $2.25**

Name _____

Address _____

City _____ State _____ Zip _____

IVY
BY CLYDE BOLTON

AN EXPLOSIVE SAGA OF COURAGE AND CONVICTION... ONE WOMAN'S BATTLE TO BE A SOMEBODY!

"Out of every great struggle comes a great novel. Clyde Bolton's *Ivy* is simply wonderful... it's a winner in every sense of the word!"

Players Magazine

An extraordinary terse, exciting and vivid novel, *Ivy* is the tale of two struggles, that of a grit poor black girl orphaned as an adolescent in Georgia in the days before the Civil Right movement... and the story of how blacks and their white supporters overcame America's own version of an insidious aparthied, a struggle that turned father against son and tore Ivy Anderson's world to shambles. It is also a story of courage, of Ivy's determination to educate herself against all odds and return to the small Georgia town where she grew up and become the first black teacher at the "white" high school where she once jeered for trying to attend a baseball game. And, finally, *Ivy* is a heroic story of a woman's determination to bring about the downfall of a crooked politician and evil landlord who ignored the law and continued to practice apartheid and a form of slavery nearly a quarter of a century after Civil Rights laws supposedly did away with all that!

HOLLOWAY HOUSE PUBLISHING CO.
8060 MELROSE AVE., LOS ANGELES, CA 90046

Gentlemen: I enclose $_____ ☐ cash, ☐ check, ☐ money order, payment in full for books ordered. I understand that if I am not completely satisfied, I may return my order within 10 days for a complete refund. (Add 75 cents per order to cover postage. California residents add 6½% sales tax. Please allow three weeks for delivery.)

☐ BM832-9 **IVY** $3.95

Name _____

Address _____

City _____ State _____ Zip _____

THE OUTSKIRTS OF HELL
BY CHARLES R. GOODMAN

"Charles R. Goodman certainly knows his way around an adventure tale. His *Bound By Blood* is a wonderful book about the life and adventures of a black Army scout. With *The Outskirts of Hell* he's pulled out all stops. It's a thrilling tale that will keep the pages turning."

Walter Jarrett
Players

The Outskirts of Hell is an epic, a sprawling tale of high adventure, of murder and intrigue. It is the story of a "Buffalo Soldier" named Josh, drummed out of the Army on trumped up charges brought against him by a bigoted officer, who finds his fortune in the gold fields of California. Once again, because of his color, he is cheated and sold into slavery aboard a ship bound for China. There he finds his destiny; more adventure, the love of a beautiful woman and the trust of a very powerful man. As the adopted son of a warlord, Josh is sent back to America to rescue the young son of a proud Chinese family from slavery—and uses the opportunity to wreak a terrible revenge on those who killed his friend, stole his property and sold him. *The Outskirts of Hell* will keep your attention riveted, keep you turning the pages to the explosive end-and make you wish for more! It is one helluva book!

HOLLOWAY HOUSE PUBLISHING CO.
8060 MELROSE AVE., LOS ANGELES, CA 90046

Gentlemen: I enclose $_____ ☐ cash, ☐ check, ☐ money order, payment in full for books ordered. I understand that if I am not completely satisfied, I may return my order within 10 days for a complete refund. (Add 75 cents per order to cover postage. California residents add 6½% sales tax. Please allow three weeks for delivery.)

☐ BH831-0 THE OUTSKIRTS OF HELL $3.25

Name _____

Address _____

City _____ State _____ Zip _____

WHOREDAUGHTER
by CHARLIE AVERY HARRIS
The gripping novel of an incredibly evil, utterly deadly young girl...

Whoredaughter became a professional at the age of twelve. Whoredom was her heritage. Her grandmother had been a whore, her mother was a whore, and she neither knew nor wanted anything else. But it was bitterness and an all-encompassing hatred of men that drove her! ■ Foolishly, men tried to treat her as more than a ho— although disaster waited for all who fell in love with her. Even the rich and powerful white doctor who adopted her became a victim of her cruelty. Only one man could cope with Whoredaughter: Junius, the "Macking Gangster" who saw her for what she was, and forced her to the depths of degradation time after time. ■ Always, she bounced back, to continue blazing her trail of sex, intrigue and murder across the ghetto. Always— except that one last time...

HOLLOWAY HOUSE PUBLISHING CO.
8060 MELROSE AVE., LOS ANGELES, CALIF. 90046

Gentlemen: I enclose _____ ☐ cash, ☐ check, ☐ money order, payment in full for books ordered. I understand that if I am not completely satisfied, I may return my order within 10 days for a complete refund. (Add 50c per order to cover postage. California residents add 6½% sales tax. Please allow three weeks for delivery.)

☐ **BH233, WHOREDAUGHTER, $2.25**

Name _____
Address _____
City _____ State _____ Zip _____

HOT SNAKE NIGHTS

By Romare Duke

"A Compelling Tale of the Mississippi Delta!"

Hot Snake Nights marks the debut of a new writer, one that we feel the world will hear a lot from in the future. Romare Duke's style will be compared to such contemporary American Southern authors as Ernest Gaines and Harry Crews, among others. And while *Hot Snake Nights* is surely to be compared to Alice Walker's *The Color Purple*—at least in mood and a feel for time and place, Romare Duke has his own literary voice. And here, in his first novel, his voice is one that sings the delta blues with all the feelings that, say, a Joe Turner or Bulka White would put into the words. *Hot Snake Nights* is the story of a Mississippi Delta family torn by lust, hate, racism, ignorance and just plain old bad luck—that low down, lonesome blues kind of bad luck where nothing ever seems to go right . . . where the nights are long, the moon is full and somewhere, far across the fields, someone is picking out the blues on a guitar. And then a shot rings out . . . it's that sort of story, one that surprises, one that breaks your heart.

HOLLOWAY HOUSE PUBLISHING CO.
8060 MELROSE AVE., LOS ANGELES, CA 90046

Gentlemen: I enclose $_____ ☐ cash. ☐ check. ☐ money order. payment in full for books ordered. I understand that if I am not completely satisfied, I may return my order within 10 days for a complete refund. (Add 75 cents per order to cover postage. California residents add 6½% sales tax. Please allow three weeks for delivery.)

☐ **BH830-2 HOT SNAKE NIGHTS** $3.50

Name_____

Address_____

City_____ State_____ Zip_____

THE FIRE
By Genia Fogelson

The passionate saga of love and intrigue in a big city hospital!

CHARITY MEMORIAL HOSPITAL

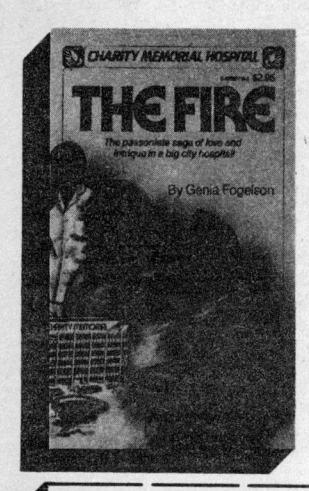

If you like *General Hospital*, *Dynasty*, and *Trapper John, M.D.*, you're going to love *Charity Memorial Hospital: The Fire*, where love—and lust—bloom while both a murderer and an arsonist stalk the hallways! This, the first in a new line of Black Experience books from Holloway House, is filled with people you'll love—and those you'll love to hate!

HOLLOWAY HOUSE PUBLISHING CO.
8060 MELROSE AVE., LOS ANGELES, CA 90046

Gentlemen: I enclose $_____ ☐ cash. ☐ check. ☐ money order, payment in full for books ordered. I understand that if I am not completely satisfied, I may return my order within 10 days for a complete refund. (Add 75 cents per order to cover postage. California residents add 6½% sales tax. Please allow three weeks for delivery.) ☐ BH716-0 **THE FIRE** $2.95

Name _____

Address _____

City _____ State _____ Zip _____

MIDNIGHT'S DAUGHTER

By Jesse Jones

The scorching, Shocking Story of a Woman of the Streets and Her Search for Happiness in a Hostile, Confusing and Bruising World of Drugs, Prostitution, and Violence.

FICTION—Enter the world of Midnight's Daughter, Nellie Pruitt. Her earliest memory was of her father being lynched by a gang of redneck whites. As a teenager she was forced into marriage with an older black clergyman. That union produced her only son, who was soon to be denied her when she fled her marriage convinced she had murdered her husband. Her life took a new and curious twist when she arrived in the Northern city of Detroit and became a prostitute, ultimately winding up in prison for a long term after killing a man in revenge for the death of her pimp. Despite the curves life threw her, Nellie's one overriding goal in life was to find her long lost son. When she finally did, fate played its last trick on her.

HOLLOWAY HOUSE PUBLISHING CO.
8060 MELROSE AVE., LOS ANGELES, CA 90046

Gentlemen: I enclose $_____ ☐ cash, ☐ check, ☐ money order, payment in full for books ordered. I understand that if I am not completely satisfied, I may return my order within 10 days for a complete refund. (Add 75 cents per order to cover postage. California residents add 6½% sales tax. Please allow three weeks for delivery.)

☐ BH722-5 **MIDNIGHT'S DAUGHTER** $2.95

Name _____
Address _____
City _____ State _____ Zip _____

CRY REVENGE!

BY DONALD GOINES

Crap games and smack pits the blacks and the Chicanos against each other in a bloodbath of vengeance!

■ Young, Black Curtis Carson doesn't mean to rip off the Chicanos in his back yard crap games. He just rolls the dice better. But the Chicanos don't see it that way, and when one of their brothers is brutally slaughtered in a barroom shootout, and all because of Curtis's dealings with heroin pusher Fat George, the Mexicans cry revenge on Curtis, leaving his brother with a wrecked body that will forever prevent him from being the basketball star he'd always dreamed of being.

■ Curtis swears vengeance of his own, as the ghetto streets run red with the blood of Black-Chicano warfare!

■ Author Donald Goines, whose established Black Experience best-sellers like STREET PLAYERS, DOPEFIEND, WHITE MAN'S JUSTICE: BLACK MAN'S GRIEF and BLACK GANGSTER, have ripped apart the curtain camouflaging Black life myth and fact, now reveals the bloody, gut-level truth of Black-Chicano hatred!

HOLLOWAY HOUSE PUBLISHING CO.
8060 MELROSE AVE., LOS ANGELES, CALIFORNIA 90046

Gentlemen: I enclose $_____ [ ] cash, [ ] check, [ ] money order, payment in full for books ordered. I understand that if I am not completely satisfied, I may return my order within 10 days for a complete refund. (Add 50¢ per order to cover postage and handling. California residents add 6% sales tax. Please allow three weeks for delivery.)

[ ] BH069, CRY REVENGE!, $2.25

Name_____

Address_____

City_____ State_____ Zip_____

Celluloid Trick

FICTION—Young, black and beautiful Gloria's dream for four long years was to follow in the footsteps of her older sister Marion and to escape from her miserable existence in the swamplands of Alabama where she lived with her ailing mother and her sadistic, alcoholic father. When the big day finally arrived and Gloria found herself in Hollywood, where she believed her sister was a highly paid model, her dreams were abruptly shattered. Marion, her sister, was a caricature of her former self because of her addiction to heroin. And she had an illegitimate baby boy, ill-fed, uncared for. Innocent and naive in the ways of the world, Gloria was coerced into entering the world of pornography in order to support her sister and nephew. The torments she suffered before finally freeing herself from the sordid world of "celluloid tricks" could be the story of any young girl lured into the seamy underworld of Hollywood porn.

HOLLOWAY HOUSE PUBLISHING CO.
8060 MELROSE AVE., LOS ANGELES, CALIF. 90046

Gentlemen: I enclose _____ ☐ cash, ☐ check, ☐ money order, payment in full for books ordered. I understand that if I am not completely satisfied, I may return my order within 10 days for a complete refund. (Add 50¢ per order to cover postage. California residents add 15¢ sales tax. Please allow three weeks for delivery.)

☐ **BH056, CELLULOID TRICK, $2.25**

Name _____

Address _____

City _____ State _____ Zip _____

THE LIFE

By Dennis Wepman,
Ronald B. Newman &
Murray B. Binderman

The Lore and Folk Poetry of the Black Hustler

FOLK POETRY / On the streets of the inner city, in bars and "shooting galleries," poolrooms and prison yards, lively verses about the hustler are recited and learned. Here is an authentic collection of these folk poems that speak for the subculture known as "sporting life" or more recently as simply "the Life." Typically, they deal with those activities that characterize the Life: pimping and prostitution, the sale and use of narcotics, and a wide variety of confidence games.

Known as toasts, they are like jokes; no one knows who creates them, and everyone has his own version. Like all orally transmitted folk material, they are spread over a large area and may last a long time, and their form and content may change with each telling until they take on something of a communal character. But toasts, like any other stylized form of expression, follow certain poetic conventions of their own. Most, for example, are rhymed and composed of four-stressed lines:

You forget the quote that the Christians wrote about honesty and fair play. For you can't live sweet not knowing how to cheat; The Game don't play that way.

HOLLOWAY HOUSE PUBLISHING CO.
8060 MELROSE AVE., LOS ANGELES, CA 90046

Gentlemen: I enclose $_____ ☐ cash, ☐ check, ☐ money order, payment in full for books ordered. I understand that if I am not completely satisfied, I may return my order within 10 days for a complete refund. (Add 75 cents per order to cover postage. California residents add 6½% sales tax. Please allow three weeks for delivery.)

☐ BH275-4 **THE LIFE** $2.50

Name _____
Address _____
City _____ State _____ Zip _____

TRICK BABY

By Iceberg Slim

THE STORY OF A WHITE NEGRO

Author Robert Beck, better known by his ghetto pseudonym, "Iceberg Slim," tells the story of a blue-eyed, light-haired, white-skinned negro called "White Folks," the most incredible con man the ghetto ever spawned! Beck knew him well, knew where he was coming from. Folks was tormetned by the hateful name, "Trick Baby," but he chose to stay in the black ghetto of southside Chicago because that's where he could turn the tables and exact his revenge! The petty triumphs of the white world weren't for him, but through the con game struggle between the spider and the fly he could overcome his deballing shame, lure his victims into traps and become a deadly predator in the inner city jungle! Beck tells his story in the gut level language of the con artist, with the bitterness and despair of the trick baby!

HOLLOWAY HOUSE PUBLISHING CO.
8060 MELROSE AVE., LOS ANGELES, CA 90046

Gentlemen: I enclose $_____ ☐ cash, ☐ check, ☐ money order, payment in full for books ordered. I understand that if I am not completely satisfied, I may return my order within 10 days for a complete refund. (Add 75 cents per order to cover postage. California residents add 6½% sales tax. Please allow three weeks for delivery.)

☐ BH827-2 **TRICK BABY** $3.25

Name _____
Address _____
City _____ State _____ Zip _____

BLACK GANGSTER

HIS BRUTAL AND POWERFUL NOVEL ABOUT BLACK ORGANIZED CRIME—STORY OF A TEENAGER WHO BECOMES A DETROIT MOBSTER.

FICTION but it's based on personal experience! A large part of Donald Goines' 39 years was spent being a successful pimp with a new Cadillac, a thief, an operator of corn liquor houses, an armed robber and a small time heroin dealer. He lived the life of the streets and made it pay. And out of that experience he created Prince, the hero of BLACK GANGSTER! It's the story of the shocking, uncharted world of black organized crime and the rise of Prince, a fledgling black "godfather"; who goes from teenage ganglord to powerful Detroit mobster. Like the gangsters of the Twenties, he begins with bootlegging and branches out into dope, prostitution and protection rackets!

DONALD GOINES, savagely gunned down at the age of 39, was the undisputed master of the Black Experience novel. He lived by the code of the streets and exposed in each of his 16 books (some written under the pseudonym Al C. Clark) the rage, frustration and torment spinning through the inner city maze. Each of his stories, classics in the Black Experience genre, were drawn from reality as Donald Goines poured out the anger, guilt and pain of a black man in America!

HOLLOWAY HOUSE PUBLISHING CO.
8060 MELROSE AVE., LOS ANGELES, CA 90046

Gentlemen: I enclose $_____ ☐ cash, ☐ check, ☐ money order, payment in full for books ordered. I understand that if I am not completely satisfied, I may return my order within 10 days for a complete refund. (Add 75 cents per order to cover postage. California residents add 6½% sales tax. Please allow three weeks for delivery.)

☐ BH263-0 **BLACK GANGSTER** $2.45

Name _____
Address _____
City _____ State _____ Zip _____

THE BLACK EXPERIENCE FROM HOLLOWAY HOUSE

★ ICEBERG SLIM

AIRTIGHT WILLIE & ME (BH269-X)	$2.50
NAKED SOUL OF ICEBERG SLIM (BH713-6)	2.95
PIMP: THE STORY OF MY LIFE (BH850-7)	3.25
LONG WHITE CON (BH030-1)	2.25
DEATH WISH (BH824-8)	2.95
TRICK BABY (BH827-2)	3.25
MAMA BLACK WIDOW (BH828-0)	3.25

★ DONALD GOINES

BLACK GIRL LOST (BH042-5)	$2.25
DADDY COOL (BH041-7)	2.25
ELDORADO RED (BH067-0)	2.25
STREET PLAYERS (BH034-4)	2.25
INNER CITY HOODLUM (BH033-6)	2.25
BLACK GANGSTER (BH263-0)	2.45
CRIME PARTNERS (BH029-8)	2.25
SWAMP MAN (BH026-3)	2.25
NEVER DIE ALONE (BH018-2)	2.25
WHITE MAN'S JUSTICE BLACK MAN'S GRIEF (BH027-1)	2.25
KENYATTA'S LAST HIT (BH024-7)	2.25
KENYATTA'S ESCAPE (BH071-9)	2.25
CRY REVENGE (BH069-7)	2.25
DEATH LIST (BH070-0)	2.25
WHORESON (BH046-8)	2.25
DOPEFIEND (BH044-1)	2.25
DONALD WRITES NO MORE (BH017-4)	2.25

(A Biography of Donald Goines by Eddie Stone)

**AVAILABLE AT ALL BOOKSTORES OR ORDER FROM:
HOLLOWAY HOUSE, P.O. BOX 69804, LOS ANGELES, CA 90069
(NOTE: ENCLOSED 50¢ PER BOOK TO COVER POSTAGE.
CALIFORNIA RESIDENTS ADD 6% SALES TAX.)**